The Institute

We began with spoons, scooping dirt out one spoonful at a time. It was a lunch hour prank. Our team, which was Sylvia, Grant, and me, Terry, represented the creative side. The suits had Naomi, Penelope, and Ralph. The spoons were plastic. We got them from the institute's cafeteria. Sylvia commented that we shouldn't be taking the only edible items from the only eating establishment on campus, but insanity prevailed, as it were, and we took a box of them.

We found two good sites near the physical resources building. It was shady, which was good, this being an Arizona summer, and the ground felt kind of springy. Unusual for desert ground, but we didn't argue.

"Now what exactly are we trying to do?" asked Ralph. He looked directly at Sylvia. He was in love with Sylvia. Everyone knew it except Sylvia. She thought he was short, bald, fat, and boring. All of this was more or less true, but it didn't stop him from thinking she was tall, dark, lovely, and fascinating. Which was also more or less true.

"Ask Terry," said Sylvia. "It was his idea."

They all turned to me. Me, I gave up on love a long time ago. There is very little in the world more cruel than love. Poor Ralph's infatuation was ample evidence of that. If the world had been made with people's feelings in mind, such a man would never fall in love with such a woman. Nothing good could come of it.

Not that I was such a man. The institute hired me for my flair with intuition. I could usually tell what was going to happen in the next few minutes. A modest gift, but enough to snag me $100K per annum for basically sitting around thinking up crazy scenarios for the future of the planet. It's tough work, and really, no one has to do it but that doesn't stop us.

"Competition, my fellow cogitator's," I said. "We spend the hour scooping up dirt with these spoons. At the end of the hour we compare piles of dirt. The bigger pile wins."

"Not the smaller?" asked Penelope. She thought that was a clever idea. She's in the accounting department.

Grant laughed. He liked to laugh at the suits. "Having a blonde moment?" he said.

Penelope was blonde, but so was Grant, so you could look on it as a self-deprecating comment. Which is the way Penelope saw it. "You should know," she said.

"I offer only accolades for my esteemed colleague," said Grant. He liked to talk like that. "But I have to agree with the doubters in the group. What is the point of this?"

"Games don't need points," I said. "They are fun."

Naomi looked down at the dirt. "This doesn't look like fun," she said.

"Jobs aren't supposed to be fun," said Sylvia.

"I get crazy ideas," I said. "The least the rest of you could do is help me follow through on their execution and see where they lead."

The spoons was one of those ideas. I wondered how many spoonfuls of dirt there was in the earth. Why would I wonder that? No reason. Except the institute paid me to think of such things. Their motto was that valuable information could come from anywhere at any time. It was up to them to create an environment in which the value could flourish. Where, in effect, I could flourish.

Some employees of the institute lived at the institute. There were no rooms or apartments on campus. You would find them sleeping on chairs in lounge areas, or rolling out a sleeping bag in their cubicle. If they had a cubicle. A lot of people just kind of wandered around from place to place. They stopped and chatted with you for a few minutes, finding out what you were up to, or just gossiping about other employees, or even just asking if you saw the ball game last night. Then they wandered on. We called them the browsers.

Others, and Grant fell into this group, remained in their sanctuaries and worked on a specific problem for hours on end, for days straight. They neglected to eat. They became removed from society and even from the human race to a certain extent. Nothing could get them out into the world except something crazy.

The spoons and the dirt. I went to Grant with the proposal. He was skeptical at first, pointing to a pile of papers on his desk. He read several of them a day. He understood most of what he read. I found this awesome and frightening. I had looked though some of them in the past. It was like looking at a very foreign language. I don't try any subterfuge with Grant. He was way too smart to be fooled and I was way too stupid to try to make it work.

"You need to get out. You need to put your hands in dirt and feel the planet touch you. You need this. Trust me."

Ralph did trust me, occasionally. It was because of this that I tried not to use his trust too often. I didn't want to break that connection. Ralph was probably the smartest of all of us. And he would be the first one to agree with you if you mentioned it. He was also methodical, dedicated, and tireless. All ingredients for insanity soup if you let it fester.

Naomi, on the other hand, came to the institute as an administrator. She was not driven or haunted by her talent. Her job was to make sure everyone was happy. To that end she had the authority to procure whatever anyone needed for their little projects. In the past this has included giant steel drums, thousands of live mice, airplanes, and hunks of gold. She got most of it cheap. She had a skill which we all admired. Without people like Naomi such places as our little institute would not function.

I took a spoon out of the box. I held it up like it was an Olympic torch. Now here is where things got kind of odd because now everyone else held up their spoons. I knew that was going to happen. I had this vision in my head of it happening. Not like a dream, or anything. Just a small picture of everyone holding up their little plastic spoons. This is what happens. It is my talent.

But. This time I had some trouble attempting to correlate it with them. The people in my little vision were not the people I had convinced to dig in the dirt. They had different faces. I was slightly alarmed by this, but did not let it bother me.

We set to work. The suits took a few steps away. They kneeled down and stuck their spoons into the dirt. Two of them broke. Observing this, we turned our spoons around so the spiky side was away from our hands and stuck them into the earth methodically, softening up the ground. Then we took the bowl part and scraped them across the loosened earth. We pushed away a lot of material this way.

The suits, seeing our method, adopted a similar one. Penelope and Naomi used their spike heels to soften up the ground. Sylvia immediately protested.

"Aren't we supposed to be using only the spoons to dig?" she said.

Naomi stopped pounding the earth with her heel. Ralph listened intently to Sylvia. "We're not digging," said Naomi. "We're preparing the site."

Everyone turned to me for adjudication. They knew I would be fair.

"No heels," I said. "Only spoons. Those were the original terms."

Naomi and Penelope abandoned their heels.

We all returned to digging and scraping with our plastic spoons. I saw us doing this for a long time. After a few minutes Sylvia spoke again.

"I didn't mean to make a big deal out of the heels."

"It was no big deal," said Ralph. "You were perfectly within your rights to question the execution of the competition."

Grant and I exchanged a brief glance. Ralph would support Sylvia in anything she did short of committing overtly criminal acts, and even then he might make an exception for some criminal acts that he might consider unworthy of being criminal.

"It was just a question," said Penelope. "It's not like Sylvia was bravely resisting an oppressive regime."

"I didn't say that," said Ralph.

"Teammates," said Naomi. "Let's not get into a squabble over nothing."

"No squabbling," said Penelope. "It's just that Ralph needs to get a reality check every now and then."

"I'm not enjoying this lark as much as I thought I would," said Grant.

"You want to quit?" said Sylvia.

"No. I've committed to at least an hour. I'll put in my hour."

"Should we be looking for fossils or something?" said Penelope.

"If we find any, we could save them," I said. "But this isn't an archaeological dig. We're doing this as an exercise."

"An exercise in what?" Penelope.

These sorts of things are usually my idea. I have a reputation for them. Once I had us stack toothpicks as high as they could reasonably go. We got to several meters before the project was abandoned. I look for simple things with little or no consequence. That's what people at the institute need.

In the outside world, the world that doesn't even know the institute exists, no one wants to do simple things for the sake of doing them. It is always about eating. They use spoons for transferring food from plates and bowls into their mouths. Nothing wrong with that, except that such uses will not rewire your brain.

I was looking for ways to rewire brains. Today, spoons were it.

But then the questions come. Questions like Penelope's. There is a kind of way of being which rejects answers and questions. The people at the institute, me included, find themselves in the cause and effect mode so pervasively that we end up not knowing any other way. This spoon business is like lateral thinking for the body. It makes you look at the world and your place in it in a completely different light. It is a good way to create yourself anew.

"Maybe it's hard to remember," I said, "back when you were a child. Think about yourself being two or three years old. You probably played in the dirt. It's one of the defining practices of a certain brand of childhood and should probably be part of every child's life. There was no reason for it. We just liked to put your hands in the earth and spread it on our bodies and faces. Just liked being in it."

"So we're supposed to be like children?" said Penelope.

"Something like that."

"I'm a grown woman."

Grant appeared to be absorbed by the dry and dusty dirt coming up in clouds under his scraping spoon, but he was taking in the conversation.

"You might be over-thinking it," he said to Penelope. "There's a principle of meditation that allows for the absurdity of certain actions. You don't have to have a good reason for everything you do. Digging with plastic spoons might just fall into that category. We are made whole by engaging in such activities."

Penelope looked doubtful. "Sounds like crazy nonsense to me."

"Crazy nonsense is the best kind of nonsense," said Grant.

"I'm kind of enjoying it," said Naomi. She had a pretty good pile of dirt next to her. We were going to have a hard time catching up to her.

"Okay," said Sylvia. "We don't care about fossils that much. How about creatures? If we find live thingies in the dirt, do we save them? Are we going to keep them for some experiment?"

I shook my head, noting that Sylvia also had a pretty good volume of dirt going. "It's not a purpose-driven exercise. That's the point we should try to remember, except not in a deliberate way. It's a kind of awareness of the activity. We don't have a goal."

"Well," said Ralph. "This was presented to us as a competition, remember?"

I remembered. The team that had the smallest pile was required to buy the members of the other team a dinner at a nice restaurant to be determined later.

"That was just the McGuffin," I said. "What I really wanted was all of us to get out here and experience the joy of doing something for no good reason to be doing it."

My spoon broke as I dug and scraped. The bowl went flying off the handle and landed next to Ralph. He stopped his scraping and picked up the piece from my spoon. He examined it like it was an important biological discover.

"I like the scratches in the plastic," he said. "It's resembles a miniature rock drawing. And the way the dust from the dirt lodges in the lines. I do believe you have created a work of art of sorts here, Terry."

Ralph held the bowl even closer.

"Hey," said Penelope. "Look at it on your own time. There's a dinner at stake here."

"Oh, right," said Ralph. He tossed the bowl aside and kept digging. I went to the box of spoons and took out a fresh one. I saw that there were only about five left.

"I don't think we brought enough spoons," I said.

"We could make a new rule," said Naomi. "We work until all the spoons are broken."

"Wouldn't that mean it would be to a team's advantage to purposely break spoons if they were ahead in the digging?" said Naomi.

"What's wrong with that?" said Penelope.

"It changes the nature of the competition," said Grant. "Which we could do if we were all in favor of it. Although I'm guessing none of us would be."

He looked around at every face. We were a mess. Dirt on our knees, hair unkempt, sweat on our brows, and foreheads. We had all ruined clothes. For some of us that didn't matter since our clothes were rather shabby to begin with. I'm thinking of my team, mostly. We were creative types, after all, used to wearing funky clothes and thrift store bargains.

The suits team, on the other hand, they were dressed much more expensively. I was sure that they didn't want to do this in their nice clothes, but the idea only came to me this morning. Naomi, as administrator, has always recommended that the suits go along with whatever the creatives come up with. Barring, of course, overt criminal or antisocial acts which might get the institute into trouble. Her philosophy was that the institute exists to make the creatives happy, and everyone should do whatever it takes to make the creatives happy. After all, our thoughts and ideas are the product of the institute.

"Grant's right," said Naomi. "We don't want to change things in the middle of it."

"Oh Naomi," said Ralph. "You would accept the moon being made of cat brains if Grant said it."

Naomi put down her spoon. "Excuse me," she said.

"I'm just saying," said Ralph. "You know it and I know it. We all know that whatever the slobs say, you will go along with it."

"Slobs?" said Sylvia. "We're slobs?"

Ralph turned red. You could actually see his face melt into panic. "Not you," he said quickly. "I didn't mean you."

Naomi laughed. "And what if Sylvia said the moon was made of cat brains?"

Ralph turned redder. An uncomfortable silence descended on the scene. It didn't look like anyone was about to rescue Ralph. I thought about it, but then decided the entertainment value that would be lost was not worth it. Ralph finally came to a semblance of dignity, bent his head, and began scooping out dirt from the hole.

Grant had an amused look on his face. Naomi and Sylvia looked frustrated and ready to toss in their spoons. I wouldn't have blamed them. I was ready to do the same. This was not turning out to be one of my more inspired ideas.

We all worked quietly for a few minutes. Eventually a pleasant blending of scraping noises filled the air. Grant cleared his throat. "I looked into the history of spoons just before we began this," he said.

No one answered.

"I discovered a few things." He left the statement hanging in the air like bait. None of us wanted to get hooked on that particular line.

"I could tell you about them, if you wanted to hear them."

Naomi coughed.

"Okay," said Grant. "I thought you'd never ask. I found out that they have been made of all kinds of things. Wood, originally. In fact the word is actually old English meaning chip or splinter of wood from a larger piece. But they have been made of shell, ivory, flint, slate, bronze, silver, horn, brass, pewter, and latten."

"What's latten?" said Penelope.

"It's an alloy of zinc and copper."

"You forgot plastic," said Penelope.

"Of course," said Grant. "Plastic. Wooden spoons were considered so useless after other material came in that Cambridge professors used to award wooden spoons to those students who got the lowest grades."

"Oh," said Sylvia. "That's just cruel."

Grant nodded. "Silver spoons were a mark of prosperity. They became very important for a while. Almost a measure of your wealth."

"Don't forget spooning," said Penelope. "I love spooning."

"Right," said Grant. "The term is used for all kinds of things."

"Greasy spoon," I said.

"There's playing spoons," said Naomi. "I heard someone play the spoons once, they were incredible. I never knew it could be such a beautiful instrument."

"People like to put spoons on their noses," said Grant. "It makes them feel silly in a good way."

Ralph stopped digging and looked at his spoon. He wiped off the dirt and applied it to his nose. It hung there for a split second, then dropped to the ground.

"Try breathing on it," said Sylvia.

Ralph picked up the spoon, and held it front of his mouth and slowly expelled a puff of air on it. He put the spoon back on his nose. This time it held.

Everyone clapped politely. Then we all wiped off our spoons, breathed on them and put them on our noses. We looked at each other, grinning.

"Why is this so much fun?" said Penelope.

"Don't ask why," I said. "It doesn't matter."

"Everything matters," said Naomi. "Everything."

The spoons began dropping from our noses. We picked them up and returned to our digging. A kind of seriousness seemed to descend on our group. The grins were gone. The good feelings were evaporating, as though the spoons on the noses interlude used up all of our humor. Grant glanced at me with an expression that seemed to ask *What happened?* I didn't know what happened.

"I like to spoon jam out of a jar," I said. "Standing at the fridge, with the door open. Just spoon up a big helping and swallow it down."

No one followed up on that. I sighed.

"Ever notice how a word loses its meaning after you say it a lot?" said Sylvia. "Spoon spoon spoon spoon. It's just a noise to me now. I can hardly make it mean what it's supposed to mean. My brain won't do the work."

"Spoon spoon spoon spoon," I said. "Huh."

Penelope repeated spoon several times. "Yeah," she said. "It's like your brain gets tired."

Ralph threw down his spoon. "I'll tell you what's getting tired," he said. "This. This is stupid. I'm done."

"No," said Naomi. "You can't quit now. We're winning."

I looked at the holes and the piles of dirt. She was right. The suits were winning. "If Ralph wants to quit," I said. "It's his right. We shouldn't make him stay against his will."

"Easy for you to say," said Naomi, "your team is putting in a poor showing. If we went down to only two diggers, you'd probably start winning."

Ralph was sprawled out on the ground, with his pile of dirt next to him.

"Hey Ralph," said Grant. "Can I have our spoon?"

Ralph waved his hand dismissively. "Go ahead," he said, and tossed it towards Grant.

"What a minute," said Naomi. "That's our spoon. You can't have it."

"Ralph gave it to me," said Grant.

"But Ralph is on our team. He can't just give away our team's equipment."

"Nope," said Grant. "Ralph isn't on anyone's team. He quit. Therefore he is a free agent, as is his spoon."

"No way," said Penelope. "Naomi is right. The spoon belongs to our team and the other team can't have it."

"This is ridiculous," said Grant. He reached for the spoon on the ground and picked it up. "I've got it. Possession is nine tenths of the law."

"I've always wondered what that meant," said Sylvia. "Surely it can't mean that if you have something in your possession, there is a ninety percent probability that you own it."

"Actually," I said, "that's probably about right. I suspect that only about ten percent of objects are ever in a state of being stolen at any one time."

"You have no basis for that statement," said Ralph, languidly, from his base on the ground.

"Just a gut feeling," I said.

"Gut feelings are not arguments."

"But I'm often right about these things."

"Everyone is right about their gut feelings some of the time, but you don't use them as a basis for reliable predictions of reality."

"Bring it back to the present, boys," said Penelope. "The spoon. We should retain the spoon."

"I think we should distribute the remaining spoons evenly between the two teams," said Grant. "That's the fair way."

"An excellent idea," I said. "Does everyone agree?"

"What about Ralph's spoon?" said Naomi.

"We'll deal with that after we have distributed the remaining spoons."

Naomi seemed doubtful but murmurs of assent arose from everyone else, including Ralph, who, it seemed, was beginning to revive his interest some. He tilted his head up for a better view of everyone and held it there with his hands interlaced at the base of his skull.

Naomi got the box and counted. "There are eight here," she said. "Four each." She handed four to me and kept four for herself.

"There," I said. "Now that each team has their own spoons, there is incentive to take care of them and try to keep them from breaking."

"Hear hear," said Ralph. "Possession is nine tenths of responsibility."

"Wait," said Penelope. "There's still the question of Ralph's spoon."

"Uh uh uh," said Grant. "I believe you are referring to my spoon."

"That has not been determined," said Penelope. "It's still an open question, although we have the greater claim."

"Not to me," said Grant. "Possession, remember?"

"I always thought that saying about nine tenths had more to do with the number of laws," said Ralph.

We turned to him. "Do tell," I said.

"Yeah," said Ralph. "I bet if you categorized all the laws in the world by what they addressed, like ownership, assault, killing, buying, selling, contracts, wills, speeding, and so on, I think you'd find that ninety percent of them would have to do with the ins and outs of possession. Stuff. Who owns what, under what circumstances, and for how long and so on."

Grant nodded. "The man makes a good point. I bet almost all law *is* about possession."

"Enough with the abstract theorizing," said Penelope. "That spoon is ours. Hand it over."

"Let's be fair about this," said Grant. "I claim the right to possess this object. You claim the right to possess this object." He took the spoon between his fingers, held it up for all to see plainly, and coolly snapped it in two.

Sylvia laughed. Ralph clapped his hands. Penelope and Naomi shook their heads. I didn't know what to say. My team member had done a completely unsportsmanlike thing.

"Grant," I said. "I expected better from you."

"My rebel streak," said Grant. "It comes out at odd times."

"You wouldn't have broken it like that if you thought you had a legitimate claim to it," said Naomi.

"Rebels do crazy things," said Grant.

Naomi wanted to press her point. "Just admit it," she said. "You destroyed it because you couldn't own it. At least not legally. Thieves are much less likely to care about objects they steal than the people they stole it from."

Ralph held up his hand. "I would have broken it," he said.

"Ralph," said Naomi, "you're not helping. And you're not on this team anymore."

"I can still have an opinion," said Ralph. He had apparently grown tired of supporting his head, since his hands were now at his sides and his head rested on the ground so he appeared to be talking to the sky.

Penelope had returned to digging, as had Sylvia. They were both industriously piling up dirt and making their holes bigger by the second while the rest of us were waylaid on this side issue.

"No matter what Ralph says," said Naomi, "we have a legitimate claim to that broken spoon."

"It's all yours," said Grant. "I'll even let you have our half, just to show you there are no hard feelings."

"An *intact* spoon," said Naomi. "You need to hand over one of your good spoons."

"Now wait a second," I said. "No one has established anything yet, much less a claim to one of our intact and unused spoons."

"We can consider it a punishment for destroying property," said Naomi. "Grant needs to pay some kind of restitution for purposely destroying a spoon which did not belong to him."

"The question of possession is still undetermined," I said.

"Not to me it isn't."

"You know why I came to this?" said Ralph.

We looked at him. "No," said Naomi. Irritation dripped from her voice.

"I thought Sylvia and I could work in close proximity and I could ask her out."

Sylvia, who had been scraping along patiently and industriously, stopped for a second without looking up. The absence of sound was unnerving. We were all embarrassed for her and for Ralph. Then she resumed her scraping.

I glanced at Grant. His eyes were wide, but he said nothing. Did that mean it was up to me to guide the discussion back to things that didn't matter, like the spoons?

"Be that as it may," I said, "the issue at hand is who is entitled to our spoon? Our *good* spoon. Not the one that Ralph had been using and scraping up and turning into something second hand."

"Oh stop it," said Naomi. "A used spoon works just as well in this enterprise as a new spoon. They are completely equivalent."

"Are they?" said Grant. "A used spoon is likely to have a weakened shaft and be more likely to break."

"Not that much," said Naomi.

"There's no way to be sure," I said, "but I think Grant has a point."

"He's on your team," said Penelope. "Of course you think he has a point."

We had, by that time, been outside for close to an hour. No one seemed to be getting ready to go back inside. We all had responsibilities at the institute. We should probably have been thinking about getting back inside and fulfilling them.

"Here's what's been bothering me lately," said Grant. "Here's why I broke the spoon. It had nothing to do with who owned it. It had to do with this problem I've been working no. A guy from the government brought it to me. It's kind of interesting, but also kind of depressing. If it was within their power to thin the world's population by fifty percent, who should they eliminate?"

As a conversation stopper, this beat Ralph's confession of being attracted to Sylvia.

"I mean," said Grant, continuing in a blandly thoughtful voice, like he was narrating a boring documentary, "what criteria would one use?"

"Such questions are outside the parameters of what we research," said Naomi.

"Oh, yeah, I know that," said Grant. "I should have told him to fuck off, but I didn't. I said I would consider the question and get back to him with an answer."

Naomi took a deep breath and exhaled slowly. "Grant," she said, "we don't have a lot of rules at the institute so you all can feel free to do as you please, more or less, but the few rules we do have are therefore doubly important. You should have reported this guy immediately."

"I know," said Grant. "But I didn't do it."

"Why not?" I said.

"He made the problem sound too interesting."

"I had a question like that once," said Sylvia. "A rep from some multi-national wanted to find out how to target his company's products's deaths."

"What?" said Ralph.

"I remember something about this," said Naomi.

"Yeah," said Sylvia. "She told me her research department had determined a certain percentage of users died from their product. However, they were concerned that some of those deaths were losing them loyal customers. She wanted to know how to shift the percentage so that only occasional users of their products died."

We had all dealt with the realties of the marketplace. Most of us had come to the institute to do pure research, thinking for the sake of thinking, or, at the very least, thinking for the good of humanity blah blah blah. But we also got a kick out of being asked things by prominent people in business and government. It was how we measured our status.

"Maybe they should have asked you to make their products so they wouldn't kill anyone," said Penelope.

"Can't be done," said Grant.

Sylvia nodded. "You can optimize that result, but given a sufficient sample size, you will never get zero fatalities. Fletcher proved that in a paper in *Proceedings of the American Statistical Foundation* a few years ago. It was a pretty impressive—and devastating—result."

"Yup," said Grant. "That was the paper that changed everything. It smashed the holy grail of perfection into little shards."

"Well, actually," I said, "I think Gödel did that about a hundred years ago with his incompleteness theorem."

"Well sure," said Grant. "But that only referred to mathematical sets. It never had any real application to real world problems."

"Grant's right," said Sylvia. " Gödel's result has been way over-applied to all kinds of fields where it didn't belong."

"Just goes to show what I've always said," said Ralph. "Math is not necessary. Just a game with symbols."

"Excuse me," said Penelope, "but without math you wouldn't have a paycheck. Money would be just pieces of paper."

I could see the discussion lining up along math lovers and math haters. It could be interesting. My own view was that math was an approximation of the world as we might know it, but it was in no way an accurate picture of the world. More of an elaborate metaphor. Naomi put a stop to it before it could get started.

"This is all very interesting," she said, "and I'm glad you have such strong opinions, but I'm trying to make a point here." We became as attentive as a dog who has just been reprimanded by its owner. "I want you all, when confronted with this situation, to do as Sylvia did at that time. She proceeded according to the rules. She reported the incident to us and we took action."

"What kind of action?" said Ralph. "I didn't hear about this."

"We told the rep that her question was not welcome here. We also suggested it amounted to conspiracy to commit murder and reported her to the police."

"I'm sure that went far," I said.

"It didn't go anywhere. They thought we were crazy, but that is not the point. We have to keep the reputation of the institute as pristine as possible. Everything depends on our image. We can't be seen as possibly working as death merchants."

Ralph put up his hand. He was still staring at the sky. "Yes, Ralph," I said in a school teacher drone.

"The rep from the company, she wasn't suggesting they increase their kill rate, was she?"

"No," said Sylvia.

"So how can it be conspiracy to commit murder?"

"They were acknowledging that their product killed people inadvertently. What they were trying to do was have their product kill people other than the ones it was killing by accident. It was targeted killing. They were purposely trying to kill other people."

"That's a harsh way of putting it," said Ralph. "And the authorities did not agree with you."

"Not this time," said Naomi. "But even if legally it wasn't a crime, it still stunk to high heaven and we were right to have nothing to do with them."

"So what about my dilemma?" said Grant. "Anyone want to help me out, purely as an academic exercise?"

"While we're at it," said Penelope, "let's review the experiments of Dr. Mengele and see if we can't come up with some better methods than he employed. Purely as an academic exercise."

"Touché," said Grant.

"Touché, indeed," I said. "Penelope, I didn't know you had it in you."

"Well why do you all look so surprised," she said. "Do you think I'm an airhead or something just because I'm in accounting?"

"I know I always did," said Ralph. "Not anymore."

Penelope grabbed some dirt and threw it at Ralph.

"Oops," said Ralph. "I just switched back to my original opinion."

Penelope threw more dirt on him.

"Hey," said Ralph, sitting up. "Some of that got in my eyes."

"Good," said Penelope.

"Children," I said. "Let's focus. No more squabbling. Especially petty squabbling."

"That's the best kind," said Ralph.

"Well," said Grant. "What are the parameter here? Do we decline anything we feel uncomfortable about? I told the guy I would think about it and get back to him."

"Wrong," said Naomi. "That is not the procedure."

"I know," said Grant. "Let's just indulge me for the moment."

"I think," said Ralph, "that I would do some kind of lottery thing. Divide the world into people with an odd number of letters in their names and those with an even number of letters in their names. Flip a coin. Heads are even, tails are odd. Whichever comes up, the corresponding people are earmarked for extermination. Simple."

"We are not having this discussion," said Naomi.

"I agree," I said. "Let's keep digging. Wasn't it fun to just sit out here and dig?"

"Look," said Ralph, "I don't know why you're all so squeamish about this. We deal with death all the time. It's just a thought experiment."

Naomi threw a spoon at Ralph. It landed on his chest. "Dig," she said.

Ralph picked up the spoon. He looked as though he was going to throw it back, then sat up and began digging.

"All I'm saying," he said, "is that a lot of our questions are about death. Death and money. The EPA sets standards for certain contaminants. The standards don't tell us the level at which there will be *no* deaths. It sets a level of *acceptable* deaths. No deaths would be too expensive. A few deaths, well, that's the cost of doing business."

"That's a terrible way of looking at it," said Penelope.

"It's the truth. It's what happens. To eliminate those last few deaths would be astronomically expensive, so we don't do it. The economy could not take it."

We scraped the dirt for a while. No one wanted to say anything. We were tired, cranky, and thirsty. The sound of plastic spoons in the dirt seemed a soundtrack for a coarsened existence. Suddenly none of us felt good about being part of the institute.

"I could dig up this dirt for the rest of my life," I said.

"So you wouldn't have to think about what we do?" said Ralph.

"Something like that."

"We do good work," said Naomi. "I'm not ashamed of any of it."

"There was a teacher I had in high school," said Grant. "He was a brilliant guy. Had a doctorate in economics. He was just a little too delicate for the rough and tumble of corporate and government life. So he went into teaching. Always struck me as odd, the man and his circumstances. But he was a good teacher. Way over qualified, but then that's the kind of teacher you really want. They know stuff and they want to help you learn how to know stuff. He once told me that human behavior, for all its supposed complexity and richness, comes down to the three Fs. Feeding, fighting, and fucking."

"I would have loved to have had such a cynical teacher," said Ralph.

"I don't think he was being cynical," said Grant. "He was just telling me what he had learned in life. I appreciated it very much."

"Well," I said. "I could stand some feeding right now. I'm kind of hungry."

"I'll fight you for it," said Sylvia.

"I'll fuck you for it," said Ralph.

We all turned to him.

"What?" he said. "I thought we were doing a bit."

"Honestly," said Naomi. "Sometimes you're kind of a dolt."

"Ah," said Ralph. "That would be the fighting part. But you don't want to get into it with *me*. I'd take you down in a second."

"Just try it," said Naomi. "I'd squash you like a bug."

"Getting squashed by you would be an honor," said Ralph, with a grin on his face.

Naomi rolled her eyes. "Anyone else want some food? I was thinking of getting a pizza."

Sylvia and Grant nodded their heads vigorously. "Pizza sounds great," said Sylvia.

"All right," said Naomi. "I'll go get it, but your team has to send someone with me or you'll have an unfair advantage over our team."

"Are we still doing the stupid competition?" said Ralph. "I'll go with you."

"Yes we are doing the stupid competition," said Naomi, "and you can't go with me, you dimwit. You're on my team."

Ralph slapped his forehead and dropped his mouth open into a wide O.

"I'll tag along," said Grant. He stood up, dusted off his pants, and joined Naomi heading to the parking lot on the other side of the campus.

I took the opportunity to survey our work so far. We had dug maybe half a foot into the ground. We had piles of dirt next to the holes. The competition was not nearly as fun or interesting as I had suspected. Yet there was something compelling about it. I knew none of us wanted to quit.

"I'm ready to quit," said Penelope.

"We can take a rest," said Ralph.

"No rest, just quit."

"I kind of thought we were all enjoying this," I said.

"Maybe you are," said Penelope, "but I was going along with it because Naomi said we should. We always try to keep you creative types happy happy happy."

"You seemed to like it before," I said. "Did the discussion upset you?"

"No one ever told me we were deciding who dies and who doesn't," she said.

"We don't decide that," said Sylvia. "We just do thought experiments. That's all they are."

"But then people, other people, use our thought experiments for things."

"That's true," I said. "We can't help that. It doesn't mean we don't do valuable things here."

"Maybe," said Penelope. "But Grant's question. It was just creepy and gross beyond words. There's no reason to be thinking up things like that."

"Governments do it all the time," said Ralph. "There are all kinds of contingency plans about mass deaths and what to do about them. It would make your hair curl."

"All of us can decide we don't want to do anything we don't want to do," said Sylvia. "I have no problem with the questions we tackle or the subjects we investigate. If there is anything that bothers us, we are free not to pursue them. It's that simple."

"Hear hear," said Ralph. "The woman makes sense. We are free agents, allowed to choose our destiny."

"I just sometimes think I should be working for some other organization," said Penelope. "Like some animal rights group, maybe, or a children's hospital."

"All perfectly noble institutions," said Ralph.

"But then, we wouldn't do things like this, I'm sure. You people are all crazy, at least a little bit. It makes it interesting."

"Well," said Ralph. "Terry and Sylvia and maybe you are stark raving bonkers, I will agree. But I myself am perfectly sane."

I had fallen back into scraping dirt and letting my mind wander to nothing in particular. It was a way of avoiding much of the issues that we were talking about. I had had many crises of conscience about my stint at the institute. There was the opportunity cost of being here. My talents might be better used in some other endeavor. Who was missing out on what I might be doing?

The question haunted me like a ghost that pops nails out of the frames of houses. Eventually the house collapses. But in the meantime it's kind of fun to think about ghosts in your house. They lend an air of exotic appeal to your life. If I really thought about it, I would have to admit that nothing I did at the institute really changed anyone's life for the better. Once you get onto that track, there's nothing for you but a slow spiral into depression, and who wanted that?

So I avoided it by coming up with these ridiculous exercises, which, in a strange way, was welcomed by the others. Did they all feel the same way as me? Were they all here so they could avoid facing the hard decision to leave or stay? Were they trying to cleanse themselves with some physical activity? All good questions that I wasn't sure I wanted to have answered.

"You still with us?" said Ralph.

I looked up. "Nothing we do really matters," I said. "You ever think about that?"

"Never mind," said Ralph. "You aren't still with us, so that's okay. Go back to your home planet."

"In the end nothing matters. Not what anyone does."

"The hundred year rule," said Sylvia.

"What's that?" said Penelope.

"It's a question you ask yourself when you get overly stressed about something. 'Will this matter in a hundred years?' Usually the answer is no."

"So then, based on that, you suddenly destress?" said Penelope.

"Exactly," said Sylvia.

"Does it work?"

"I don't know, I've never been stressed."

That stopped everyone.

"*Never?*" said Ralph. "That's hard to believe."

"Oh, I've had some bad days and I've been on edge and so on. But never stressed so that I thought things wouldn't work out. Never so that I couldn't sleep."

"You must not keep up on what's going on in the world," said Ralph.

"Ignorance is bliss?" said Sylvia.

"Something like that."

"I'm fully aware that the planet is in trouble, that nations can't seem to get along, and there isn't anything we can do about it. But, you know, in a hundred years, it won't matter."

"Well," I said, "I guess it's fine that you find comfort in that, but a hundred years? There are people alive now who will still be alive in a hundred years. Certainly most of our children will still be around then. And our grandchildren. It's not really a useful measuring stick of what matters. Everything we do matters to someone. Even if it matters for a few minutes, even a few seconds, we should still be aware of it and know that we need to do things right."

"Yeah," said Ralph. "Like if I asked you—Sylvia—to go to bed with me, your answer wouldn't mean much in a hundred years. But it would mean a lot for the next hundred hours. At least to me."

"It wouldn't mean anything to me for even a hundred seconds," said Sylvia.

"But that's the point, isn't it?" said Penelope. "We don't live in long chunks of time. We live in the moment. And moments are important to us."

"I had an inquiry from a woman once," I said. "She was suicidal, at least she said she was. She wanted to kill herself, even told me how she planned to do it. She was going to have a great meal at her favorite restaurant, then she was going to walk out without paying the bill because she always wanted to do that, and then she was going to stroll over to the highest bridge in town and jump into the river. She said she heard we were ranked the smartest think tank in the country, so she wanted to know from me why she shouldn't do that. I wasn't sure if it was a prank or not, and I had no idea how she found my number, but I guess it probably wouldn't be that hard, and I was scared shitless because I didn't know what to tell her. I asked for her number to call her back but she said no way. She didn't want me calling 911 or a psychologist or anything that would come to her house and talk her out of it. She wanted a rational reason not to jump off a bridge. I wanted to get her a counselor, a crisis interventionist. Something. She told me she was at a pay phone. She would call me back in two days and hear my answer."

Penelope had her hand in a fist up to her mouth. Ralph looked half way interested. Sylvia stared at the ground.

"Did you report it to Naomi?" said Ralph.

"No," I said.

"Well you should have."

"What happened?" said Sylvia.

"I don't know. She never called back."

"Never?"

"I came early the day she was supposed to call and I stayed very late. Nothing."

"Did you have an answer for her?" said Ralph.

"I had researched a lot of historical writing on the meaning of life. I had theories and I had things that people did for themselves to make themselves feel better."

"She wasn't wanting to feel better," said Ralph sharply. "She had a specific question for you. Did you answer her question?"

"Well of course she wanted to feel better," said Penelope. "That's why she called Terry."

Ralph shook his head. "She didn't call Terry, specifically. She called the institution. We're supposed to be about life. If we can't even come up with a good reason not to give up your life, what good are we? Terry, you should have opened up the question to all of us. You should have let us all have a crack at the answer."

"Yeah," I said. "I did a few things wrong. I thought I could save her all by myself and it became kind of an ego thing. I didn't really have a good answer for her. I mean, I've thought about suicide. Hasn't everyone?"

"Of course," said Ralph. "So what? Fleeting thoughts with no consequence aren't important in the long run or the short run. They're just random nerve firings."

"I think it's awful that you never heard from her again," said Penelope.

"I still think about her," I said. "I wanted to talk to her. I was prepared to talk to her for days if that's what it took. Someone was asking me the most profound question imaginable and I could not come up with anything. It was very humbling. For the next few days I read the paper more carefully than I ever had before, looking for any report of someone jumping off any of the bridges in town."

"And?" Sylvia.

"Nothing."

"Maybe it was a prank," said Penelope.

"Didn't sound like a prank. Or feel like one. It seemed very real."

"I'm not sure how I feel about you telling us this," said Sylvia. "Now I'm going to worry about this woman who I've never met and know nothing about."

Ralph's cell phone rang. He pulled it out of his pocket and tapped it. "Hello," he said. He was silent for a second. Then his face turned white. "What?" He looked stunned.

"What is it?" said Sylvia.

My heart was going like crazy. Penelope looked scared.

"Did you call 911?" said Ralph. Pause. "Where are you?"

We heard a siren in the distance, slowly getting closer.

"What is going on?" said Sylvia.

Ralph put his phone on speaker and placed it on the ground. Naomi's voice sounded from it. She was stressed and scared.

"The fucker side-swiped us," she said. "I didn't see him coming. Neither did Grant. Oh, fuck, Grant. He bled so much. I'm sure he's dead. Oh, fuck fuck. I'm just hanging here, upside down. Oh, I hear them. The ambulance. Thank god. Fuck. My leg hurts. Are you there, Ralph?"

"We're all here," I said. "Is anyone helping you?"

"The car's turned over. I can't reach the seat belt. Grant. Oh fuck. Grant. I think he's dead. I can't reach him. There's someone ripping off the car door."

We heard a clattering, like Naomi's phone fell from her hand.

"Naomi," said Sylvia. "Naomi?"

We heard voices, not Naomi's. They were calm and measured. The paramedics.

"Where are you going to take them?" said Ralph loudly into his phone. "What hospital?"

We heard a voice saying "Who's that?"

Another voice telling Naomi they were going to get her out of there. Then some scuffling and the phone went dead. Ralph redialed several times. Each time the message said the call could not be completed.

"I think something happened to her phone," said Ralph.

"Maybe one of the paramedics stepped on it."

"We have to go there," said Sylvia.

"We don't know where they are."

Penelope stood up and put her hand to her forehead and scanned the horizon. "We just follow the sound of the sirens," she said. "They can't be far. They just left a few minutes ago." She pointed across campus. "There. Let's go."

We all got to our feet. I felt dizzy from the blood draining out of my head. We stood beside our piles of dirt, still holding our plastic spoons. We dropped them into the holes, and began walking briskly in the direction Penelope had indicated. Naomi was hurt and Grant was dead. Maybe. It felt unreal.

We were supposed to be part of one of the smartest places on the planet, but when a friend was in trouble, or possibly dead, we had no resources other than wanting to be there for them. Wanting to be there just to be close to them. It couldn't help anyone, really, it was just important. We all had work to do. We could be doing it. None of that mattered. We could even have continued to dig our holes. None of that mattered either. We fixed our view on the horizon and just kept on walking.

We walked and walked. We became nothing but walking machines, the kind you might see in an industrial movie about how to make robots. Or about how robots are taking over the world doing things that people don't want to do. All of those things came to my mind. I wanted to find a way to help Naomi, but she was probably being helped in a competent way by people who would never get into the institute because they weren't smart enough. Yet they had the knowledge to actually help someone. And they weren't going to be at the scene anymore. They had surely removed Grant and Naomi by now. Taken them to a hospital. Was Grant really dead? The thought kept getting in the way of my thinking. It was almost all I could think about.

"Has anyone else noticed that the horizon is receding?" said Ralph.

"Now that you mention it," said Sylvia.

It was true. The horizon looked much farther away than it did when we had started walking and we had been walking for about five minutes. Penelope shook here head. "You people are three kinds of crazy," she said, "which is about two and half kinds too many."

"You don't see it?" said Sylvia.

"Of course I see," said Penelope. "So what? Don't dwell on it. Just walk."

Ralph stopped. I bumped into him. Sylvia stopped too. "There's no point," said Ralph, "if we can't make any ground."

Penelope kept walking. We watched her get smaller and smaller.

"She's determined," I said.

"She doesn't want to do nothing," said Ralph. "It's an admirable trait, to want to help."

"This is all so crazy," said Sylvia. "We can't be here just talking like everything is fine when we just heard that Grant is dead and Naomi is hurt."

We were stopped at a road. Across two lanes there was a median strip. Penelope had walked over it and continued on. We couldn't see her anymore. The horizon was still a long long way off and the site of the wreck was no where any of us could see.

"Maybe it was a joke," said Ralph.

"Naomi doesn't joke like that," said Sylvia.

She was right. Naomi was too serious. "But Grant would," I said.

"It wasn't Grant on the phone."

"He might have talked Naomi into it."

"No," said Ralph. "That's just not something she would do. It isn't."

"Besides," said Sylvia, "she just sounded too scared. If you're not an actress you can't make that kind of thing sound as convincing as she did."

"Yeah," I said. "You're right. I was just hoping."

I noticed we were all breathing harder than we should. Desk jockeys getting even a little exercise is often not a pretty sight.

"Thing is," said Ralph. "I was ready for that pizza. Think it's still there?"

"What," I said, "in the car?"

"They probably didn't even get it yet," said Sylvia. "They were still on their way. They weren't gone even five minutes."

"Yeah," said Ralph. "I think you're right. I wonder if they phoned ahead to order it. Then it might be ready just about now. We could go pick it up. I'm really really hungry."

I was about to tell Ralph that he was possibly the most insensitive person I had ever met, with the possible exception of my dog, except she wasn't a person, when I realized that I was really hungry too.

"You know," said Sylvia, "I should shake you out of yourself for once in your life but I'm pretty hungry too."

"See?" said Ralph. "You all think I'm a jerk, but I'm just responding to my biological programming. It's not anything I can change."

"Or want to change?" said Sylvia.

"Hey, you just said you are as hungry as me."

"I just wish," I said, "that we knew where they were going. What hospital."

"Or what morgue," said Ralph.

"Jesus," said Sylvia.

"There's no point in not facing the truth," said Ralph. "Naomi did say she thought Grant was dead."

"Naomi doesn't know. She was also hysterical."

"She said Grant was bleeding."

"She still doesn't know." Sylvia was insistent. Ralph wanted to insist right back at her, but backed off. I had the fleeting thought it was because he still entertained hopes of getting in her pants and didn't want to get her upset.

"True," said Ralph. "She doesn't know."

"I'm worried about Penelope," I said.

"Sure," said Ralph, "but I'm also worried that we are just standing here doing nothing, while the world slides away from us."

We all tracked our eyes across the horizon. I wanted to run as fast as I could, but I saw that the horizon was impossibly far away. There was a wide expanse of green grass between us and the edge of the world. We could easily fit several civilizations, a few moons, some stars, and maybe a galaxy or two in that space.

"You're the smart one," I said to Sylvia. "What's going on here?"

"We're all traumatized by the news," said Sylvia. "We're so emotional that we're bending reality into something different."

"That's the best you can come up with?" said Ralph a little too quickly. He looked like he regretted saying it even before he finished the sentence.

"You have a better idea?" said Sylvia.

"I'm not the idea man," said Ralph. "I'm just support for you brains."

"Then why criticize what you don't know about?"

"It's my right as a human being and sentient creature to criticize."

"I've never heard that before," I said.

"It's in the constitution," said Ralph.

"He's being ridiculous," said Sylvia.

"I'm hungry," said Ralph.

"And in the meantime," I said, "we've lost three people. Just gone. Where did they go?"

The question wafted from my mouth, rose up on currents of air, and spread across the sky like smoke dissipating from a chimney. We watched the words with fascination.

"How'd you do that?" said Ralph. We watched his words escape his lips and float up into the air as well. They took longer to dissipate.

"Um," I said. "I didn't. It just happened." We were fascinated by the smokiness of them. All three of us watched the clouds of them slip away into the sky.

"Let's sing," said Sylvia. The words drifted up from her mouth as well.

"What song?"

"Did Grant have a favorite song?"

"What an odd question," said Ralph.

"Not really," said Sylvia. "I want to remember him."

"I thought you didn't think he was dead."

"I just said there was the possibility," said Sylvia. "That's all."

I watched Sylvia and Ralph's words pepper the air between them. How was it that I had never noticed this before? When people spoke, their words were printed on the air in colored smoke. I realized that this had been happening for centuries. Don't ask me how I knew that part, it just felt exactly like old knowledge, the way you know a mountain has been there for centuries without anyone having to tell you anything about geology or deep time. You can tell just by looking at it.

The smoke words were the same way. The other thing I saw was that as the horizon receded, all the stuff between us and the horizon was melting into a uniform color and texture, something like a carpet of moss.

"Hey," I said. "What's happening to everything? It's all going away."

Ralph and Sylvia ignored me and began singing a song. I didn't recognize the tune but assumed I would after a time. Then I realized that it was not an existing song. Sylvia and Ralph were making it up as they went along. They hummed and sang notes. The smoke from their mouths filled the space between and around them and mingled into a rainbow concoction of powdery air.

But the music. They harmonized and played off of each other's phrasing. I had no idea either of them had the ability or the inclination. They seemed to be enjoying themselves as well. They motioned for me to join them, but I declined with a quick shake of my head. They were way out of my league as far as music went. They were doing things I didn't know it was even possible to do.

The billows of smoke rose high above them. They seemed to float higher than the sky, if that was possible. We all three looked up and watched the smoke fill the yawning expanse above us. Then they stopped. Everything stopped.

"You sing beautifully," said Sylvia. "You have a beautiful voice."

"As do you," said Ralph.

"Hear hear," I said. "Why did you stop?"

"I sensed that Grant had heard it all and was not listening anymore."

"Oh," I said. "Of course."

"Don't make like we're crazy," said Ralph. "That's why I stopped too."

"Because Grant was done listening? Grant isn't even here."

"Grant has moved on," said Sylvia. "That happens. He wanted to stay, but he couldn't."

"We're supposed to be the smart ones," I said to Sylvia. "The rational ones, remember? We're supposed to have brains in our heads." I regretted that last sentence. I turned to Ralph. "No slight intended to you," I said.

"None taken," said Ralph. He had a big grin on his face.

"The rational view doesn't know everything," said Sylvia. "At best, it can sometimes eliminate certain things, but it will never have all the answers because rationality is a world view that does not encompass the randomness of life. And I came up with that with my very own brains."

Now it appeared I had insulted them both, but I could not understand how. "I was only thinking about Penelope and Naomi and Grant," I said. "We won't find them by singing songs and making colored smoke."

"How do you know?" said Sylvia.

I tilted my head in acknowledgment. "I don't know. I can't know. No one can know. I'm just saying that most likely our best course of action is to try a little rationality."

"Well," said Ralph, "the ground appears to be stretching, our sound is getting turned into colored smoke. Care to bring a little rationality to that situation and explain it to our satisfaction?"

As Ralph talked I couldn't help noticing the smoke from his mouth was changing color, becoming more dense, and twisting into recognizable shapes.

It was like the animals that clowns make from balloons, except the smoke was doing the twisting on its own. I watched it writhe and form. Before long there were sculptures of animals stuck to Ralph's head. I saw snakes, birds, horses, and penguins.

"You could work the carnivals with that talent," I said to Ralph.

"Yeah," said Sylvia. She reached out and took one of the penguin models. As she held it in her hand it shrunk to a tiny replica of the larger original. Ralph and I stared at it in her palm. As it shrunk it gained more detail. It was no longer a featureless smoke thing, it had color, texture, and weight.

Then it moved. Ralph and I were startled. We stepped back. "Whoa," said Ralph.

Sylvia didn't flinch. She held her hand very steady. The model had been resting on its back. Now, animated, it got to its feet and waddled over to the base of Sylvia's thumb. Sylvia laughed. "It tickles," she said.

I reached toward it with an extended finger. "Careful," said Ralph. His voice was rapturously quiet.

I held my finger steady. The penguin moved toward it and seemed to sniff at it. It was momentarily fascinated by it, then squatted down on Sylvia's palm and appeared to want to go to sleep. It leaned over on its side, took a deep breath, and got very still.

"Now what?" said Sylvia.

"Looks like you have a friend," said Ralph.

"I should put it back on your head."

Ralph shrugged. Sylvia looked in my direction.

"Don't ask me," I said. "I didn't give it shelter and the false promise of a home."

"Very funny," she said. "I didn't know this was going to happen."

A crow suddenly flew into our circle, black wings flapping, sending smoke trails off the ends of the feathers. Ralph jumped back. "What the fuck," he said.

The crow paused at Sylvia's hand, snatched up the penguin, and flew away in a burst of black. Sylvia's hand was shaking. Her face indicated nothing less than shock.

"Well," said Ralph, "looks like your problem got taken care of."

Sylvia looked up at him.

"Oh," said Ralph. "Sorry. That was insensitive of me, wasn't it?"

"Where did that crow come from?" she said.

"There are crows all around here," I said.

"None of them has ever swooped down and snatched something from my hand."

"I bet you never had a juicy miniature penguin before," said Ralph.

We both looked at him.

"Well, what do you want me to say? We're in a strange place. I don't know what's causing it. Look around."

We scanned the horizon again. None of the features that were familiar to us were still there. The buildings and roads had disappeared. We saw only a green expanse, extending not only as far as we could see, but as far as we could imagine.

"We need to stick together," I said. "As soon as we split up, we disappear."

"Agreed," said Ralph. He now had his hand around Sylvia's shoulder. Sylvia leaned into him. The color had returned to her face.

"I think we never should have started digging those stupid holes," she said.

"The holes have nothing to do with this," I said automatically, my back instantly up and my defenses instantly aroused.

"She's not saying you're evil or anything," said Ralph. "It was just a strange thing to be doing and it may have done something to reality."

"Ridiculous," I said. "Crazy. Nuts. There's no basis for such a conclusion."

"You ever read *Alice in Wonderland*?" said Sylvia.

"An it-was-all-a-dream story," said Ralph. "Didn't care for it. Same reason I didn't like *Wizard of Oz*. Lazy storytelling."

"Well, those are only two of the classics of world literature, but never mind," said Sylvia. "*You* know what's good storytelling, unlike millions of others who have loved both stories."

"Boy," said Ralph, "I just can't seem to say anything right today, can I?"

"Go on," I said to Sylvia, ignoring Ralph. "What were you about to say?"

Sylvia gave Ralph a withering look, although Ralph did not wither under it. Instead he shrugged and looked like a goofy school kid.

"What I was going to say," said Sylvia, "was that in the Alice book things happened that made no sense. And yet, Alice was cared for the whole time and she survived all the crazy things that happened to her. It was like she had guardian angels looking after her. Or the universe decided it would make sure she was safe. She had friends, is what I'm getting at. They were invisible, but they were there, keeping her safe. I feel like we may be in a similar situation."

"But," I said slowly, "that was a book. This is real life."

"There goes that rationality thing again," said Sylvia. "You really use it as a crutch. You need to let it go."

"Well," said Ralph. "I need to register a point of agreement with our Terry here. We can hardly say we are under the protection of benign creatures when Naomi gets injured in an accident and Grant bleeds to death in the same accident."

"That happened before the weirdness began."

Ralph pondered this for a second. "I would argue that it was the beginning of the weirdness, and therefore sets the tone for what has happened to us."

Sylvia seemed to think this made a certain amount of sense. "And what *has* happened to us?" she said.

"No idea," said Ralph. "It appears we are on a featureless landscape where once there was a civilization. It may be a test."

"Who's testing us?" I said.

"Scientists?" said Ralph.

"In white lab coats, no doubt," said Sylvia.

"Well, you have a better idea?"

"I keep going back to the digging," said Sylvia.

We waited for her to elaborate. We had all three stopped walking. The expanse around us seemed to have flattened out even more than it had been.

"I bet," said Ralph, "that if we could walk for a long time, we'd get to the edge of the planet. I think our globe has become a pancake. Hah!"

"There's no evidence for that."

"Oh, isn't there. Look at the horizon."

I looked. So did Sylvia.

"Do you see a sharp edge where it meets the sky?"

I did not. It got fuzzy and smoky, like there was no end to it.

"I see what you're getting at," said Sylvia. "If it was still a globe, then, being featureless, it should drop away from your line of vision with a clean break, only that isn't what has happened. The horizon fuzzes out. It's like it's still there, but so far away that we can't quite make out its features."

"Exactly," said Ralph. He was so proud of himself.

"So where did Penelope go?" I said.

"Still walking, I imagine." said Ralph.

"Nothing like this should be happening," I said. "None of this makes sense."

"Whoa there," said Ralph. "No time for a melt down. We all need our wits about us."

I *was* starting to get a little panicky. Where was that coming from? I usually took things in stride.

"Anyone thought about food and water? What are we going to eat? How are we going to survive?"

"We should keep walking," said Sylvia. "There's nothing here. There has to be something further on."

"Has to be?" I said.

"We can hope there is. How's that? Hope is a good thing, isn't it?"

"Hope is all we have," said Ralph.

I shook my head, more to get myself on track than to contradict Ralph. He saw what I was doing. I put my hand through my hair and smoothed it out as best I could, trying to give myself some semblance of dignity.

Ralph turned to Sylvia. "So which way should we be going?"

Sylvia looked up at the sky. The sun was low on the horizon, but appeared to be hanging there motionless.

"I would like to have as much daylight as possible. Agreed?"

"Agreed," said Ralph. I hadn't thought about that up to now. It was going to get dark. Would it be cold? Too cold for us? Where would we find shelter?

"Terry?" said Ralph.

"What?"

"Sylvia wants to walk toward the sun. You with us?"

"Sure," I said.

We started walking. The air was pleasant, the ground was not too difficult. In fact, it was really quite nice to be with them on this hike. I could almost forget the predicament we were in and how truly strange this whole day had become. I put my hand in my pocket and found a spoon there. I did not remember putting it there. I held it up for Ralph and Sylvia to see.

"Very good," said Ralph.

"No," I said. "This spoon could be the reason for all of this."

"Oh," said Ralph, unease in his voice, as though he thought I was crazy, or would soon become crazy.

"He has a point," said Sylvia.

Ralph stopped walking. "Which is?" he said.

Sylvia and I stopped walking as well. Ralph and I looked at her and waited.

"If the spoon digging somehow brought this on, then the spoon must have some kind of power. It could be the disruption in the fabric of reality that we are now experiencing."

"Coulda woulda shoulda," said Ralph. "This is all wild speculation. It's a plastic spoon. It has no magical power."

Sylvia rolled her eyes. Ralph was not buying any of it. I didn't know what to think. Did spoon digging have some kind of power I did not know about?

"I'll bet," said Sylvia, "that no one has ever had a spoon digging competition before."

Ralph frowned. "Maybe," he said. "There's no way of knowing for sure. But maybe."

"All right, then," said Sylvia. "If it's true, that means we did something that has *never been done before.*"

"Okay,"

"We created something new. In response, the universe became something new to accommodate it."

"Interesting theory," said Ralph. "Impossible to prove, and I have a few problems with it. People are doing new things all the time all over the world. We don't see the universe becoming crazy different all the time. It just doesn't happen."

"How do you know?"

"I go to bed at night. The universe is one way. I wake up in the morning. The universe is the same way."

Sylvia said nothing in answer.

"Compelling argument," I said.

"There's all kinds of things we don't know about," said Sylvia. "It could be that our memories are changed at the same time that everything else is changed."

"We can concoct fantasy scenarios for the rest of our lives," said Ralph. "But it doesn't prove anything. It doesn't bring us any closer to anything we can understand."

"I think I have the answer," I said.

They turned to me.

"It isn't a test and it isn't some weird universe things. What we are undergoing is a dream. We're living in a dream."

"Yawn," said Ralph.

Sylvia shook her head and gave me a pitying look. "Ralph's right," she said. "That's boring."

"What does it matter if it's boring?" I said. "We're trying to find out what's true."

"Here's something," said Ralph. "Maybe the planet is not exactly being flattened, maybe it's becoming inverted and this flattened state is just a phase on the way to becoming re-sphered again, only the sphere is going to curve in the opposite direction. We're going to be inside the earth."

"Hollow Earth?" said Sylvia. "To quote you: yawn."

"If that was true," I said, "then the sun would be in the center of the earth?"

"Yeah," said Ralph.

"So it wouldn't set."

"Nope."

I looked at the position of the sun again. It had not moved, just hung there above the horizon, like it was a Christmas ornament hung on a Christmas tree. "Fits the facts," I said.

Sylvia was not buying it. "Facts?" she said. "It fits one fact. One. That's not enough to say anything at all conclusive about our situation."

"It's the best we've got," I said.

"I disagree," said Sylvia. "What forces made this happen? Who would want it to happen? How is it being powered? How would the earth invert itself? Or if that's not what's happening, how would some outside force invert the earth?"

"All reasonable questions that may or may not be answered in time," I said, "but for now it's all we have."

Sylvia pointed at the sun. "It's not overhead. If this was a hollow sphere and we were stuck on the inside then wherever we were the sun would appear to be overhead."

"That's assuming," said Ralph, "that the sun was in the exact center of the sphere. It appears that it may be off center. To us it appears closer to the horizon."

"And that's another thing," said Sylvia. "What horizon? There is no horizon if we are inside a sphere."

"Or," I said, "more properly we would speak of the horizon being everywhere around us all at once."

"That's not a horizon," said Ralph.

"We need to expand our definition of what a horizon is," I said.

"We can call it something else if we want, but it is not a horizon under any definition," said Sylvia.

"Actually," said Ralph, "I was speaking metaphorically."

"Then say so," said Sylvia.

"When you speak in metaphors you don't have to say so," said Ralph. "That's the point. Reality is bent through the lens of your metaphor. It is understood that it is somewhat different from normal ways of speaking."

"It wasn't understood to me," said Sylvia. "I'm afraid that we are veering away from doing anything about our situation because we are enamored by the exoticness of it."

"Don't worry," said Ralph, "we are all fully aware of our situation."

"Is Penelope? We don't even know where she is. What about Grant and Naomi?"

I was only half listening to them by this time. I still had the plastic spoon in my hand. I bent down on one knee and stuck the spoon into the mossy surface we were walking on. It went in easily and I was able to pull up a clump of dirt. I tossed it onto the moss and stuck in the spoon and gently pulled up another clump.

The ground under the moss was glowing red. It was warm. Squirmy things writhed within it. I looked at them and my stomach churned, knowing that I might have to survive by eating them. Sylvia and Ralph stopped talking. They looked at what I was doing. "Not this again," said Sylvia.

"If digging unmade the world, then maybe I can remake it by digging again."

"Totally ludicrous thinking," said Ralph. "You'll only plunge us deeper into the morass."

"Shut up and help me," I said. I felt the spoon bend under my hand and I was afraid it would break. That felt like it would be disastrous. There was nothing else to dig with.

Ralph pulled his wallet out of his pocket, removed two credit cards from it, and handed one to Sylvia. She took it wordlessly and descended to the ground and began scoring the moss with a corner of the card, then used the edge to pull up piles of red warm earth. Ralph did likewise. I saw that Ralph had more credit cards in his wallet, so if the spoon should actually break, I had options. Bolstered by that fact, I dug with more energy, increasing the pace until I was pulling up clumps every second or so.

Before long Sylvia's hole merged with mine and soon after that Ralph's excavation got close enough to ours that the wall between them collapsed. We now had a hole about half a meter wide and maybe 50 centimeters deep. The red glow was mesmerizing. We wanted only to be in the hole, digging through the earth for years. Maybe forever.

Sylvia stopped. Ralph stopped a few seconds later. I continued until I realized they were staring in my direction in a kind of stupor. I didn't want to stop. "Keep digging," I said.

They were both staring past me, as if I didn't matter. Suddenly I felt a *presence* I had not felt before. I stopped digging. The sound of my own breath filled my ears. I slowly turned my head to see what Sylvia and Ralph were looking at.

Naomi stood behind me. Her hands were on her hips and she had a scolding expression on her face. What was this about?

"Where is Grant?" I said.

"He's with Penelope." She laughed.

"Ok," I said. "Where's Penelope?"

"With Grant," said Naomi. "She grinned as wide as she could. She opened her mouth and laughed. Her teeth were all red, the same shade as the dirt we were pulling up.

"What's going on?" I said. "Do you know anything? We only have guesses."

Naomi didn't say anything. She put her finger to her chin and made noises like gears churning.

"You ask too many questions," she said.

"Naomi," said Sylvia. "Do you remember me?"

"You?" said Naomi. "Sure. You're the smart one. The one who isn't afraid to use her brains."

"But do you *remember* me? Do you remember where we worked and what we did?"

Again the hand on the chin. "We killed people, didn't we? For the greater good or something? There are people that need killing so we did what had to be done."

"No," said Sylvia. "You're thinking of the armed services. Or the mafia or something. We weren't either of those. We worked at a place that invented things. Came up with ideas."

"With ideas for killing people," said Naomi. "It's always about that. Feeding fighting and fucking. We left the feeding and fucking to others. We handled the fighting, which meant, more or less, the killing of things. Animals, civilizations, people, and so on."

Ralph was supposed to be the cynic in the group, now here was Naomi acting as strange as I had ever seen her.

"Hey," said Ralph, "speaking of feeding, where's that pizza you promised us?"

Naomi turned to Ralph and displayed her red teeth. Ralph winced. "What are you afraid of?" said Naomi.

"Not afraid," said Ralph. "Hungry. I want food."

I remembered the squirmy things in the earth. Naomi reached down to the ground, grasped dirt, and pulled up a clump of it like a crane pulling up a mound of earth. She shook it through her fingers. The dirt slipped through. The squirmy things remained in her hand. She displayed them to Ralph, who cringed.

"You have got to be kidding me," he said.

Naomi popped them in her mouth and chewed them with gusto. "They really wiggle around in your mouth until you chomp down on them and their juices squirt out. They have a complex taste, kind of like garlic wrapped in fennel with a hint of sweetness like honey. You should try some." She grinned. "It's also how I got my red teeth. You like?"

Ralph covered his eyes with one hand and held out his other, as if stopping traffic. I wanted to be amused, but I figured I would have to eat the things eventually myself and I felt my stomach clench.

"We're trying to figure out what's going on," said Sylvia. "Do you know anything at all?"

"One thing I know is if you keep digging you'll come to the bottom of the earth. You probably don't really want to do that, but it's okay to go down a little ways, just to get some food."

I felt my face flush. Sylvia and Ralph looked at me like I had pulled the pin on the grenade and let it slip out of my fingers and bounce along the floor out of reach. "It's not my fault," I said. "The digging. I just thought it was a harmless prank."

"One thing I figured out," said Naomi, "is that this has been going on for a while. I've seen some people who have been here for a long time. They're all green. Mossy skin like you've never seen in your life. They don't say much, but if you talk to them and really insist, they'll tell you a little. Like that there isn't anything to do about this. And that no one, *no one*, really knows anything."

"I can't accept that," said Sylvia. "Where are these people?"

"You don't find them. They kind of run into you."

"Like that accident," said Ralph. "Did that car run into you like that? Was that one of them?"

"No," said Naomi. "That was in the old world."

"So Grant is really dead?"

"I thought so then."

"What do you think now?"

"He was going to die. He was on track to die. But something happened. I followed him and we ended up here."

"How did you follow him?" I said.

"How does anything happen?" said Naomi. "I didn't know what I was doing. We were trapped in the car. He couldn't move. Neither could I. I heard the sirens, knew help was coming, but also knew they wouldn't be in time. There was just so much blood. So I—moved. I stepped out of myself and went over to Grant, floated, kind of, and held him while he died. While the blood drained away. It was a terrible cut. So awful. I wanted to save his life. It was that simple. Not one of the three, I guess. But there it was. I looked back at myself, hanging upside down in the driver's seat.

"I looked dead. Or at least unconscious. Not in this world. Not *of* this world. Or that world, back then. You know what I mean. So I wrapped myself around Grant and stopped the bleeding somehow. Don't really know how exactly. Instinct. Grant died. I didn't get to him in time. And then he didn't die. He flipped into this world. He was still hurt, but he was still alive."

We listened carefully, not fully comprehending, but not doubting her in any way. I could tell even Ralph, the eternal cynic and doubter, was persuaded by her story.

"Where is Grant now?"

"Hard to say," said Naomi. "Once he recovered, he said goodbye to me and started walking."

"To the horizon," said Ralph.

Naomi blinked. "Yes, the horizon. Where else?"

"Everyone seems to want to walk to the horizon," said Ralph.

"Grant said something about that, I think."

"Are we ghosts?" I said. "Are we all dead?"

"Not sure about that," said Naomi. "I sure don't feel dead. But I do feel *different.*"

"What about Penelope?" said Sylvia. "She went looking for you."

"Never saw her," said Naomi.

"She was heading in the direction of the crash when all the weirdness starting happening. We thought for sure her walk had flipped things into anarchy."

"Nope," said Naomi. "Never got to us. At least not that I could see. Nearest I can tell, she was caught in the flip, just like we all were."

"Well," I said, "we have to find her."

"That might be hard," said Naomi. "If not impossible."

"Didn't we have a motto at the institute along those lines?" I said.

Naomi sighed. "Yes," she said. "I remember. 'There's no such thing as impossible.'"

"So inspiring," said Ralph.

"Inspiring or not, it's what we lived by. We shouldn't stop now."

"It may be what you lived by," said Ralph. "I just wanted a paycheck."

I glared at him, annoyance obvious on my face. He shrugged.

"And what about Grant?" said Sylvia. "What about Penelope and Grant? We should have everyone together. We shouldn't be split up like this."

Naomi took a breath and let it out slowly. "I don't know where you're getting those ideas, honey. We're here and we do what we have to do, or what we are compelled to do. There is nothing else."

"You called it the flip," I said.

"You have a better name?" said Naomi.

"I'm just thinking what we need to do is flip it back. Maybe we should do the reverse of what we did."

"What exactly would that be?" said Ralph.

"We need to find that original excavation and put the dirt back in the holes we were digging."

"To find it we need to know where it is. Any idea how we could do that?"

"Not yet," I said.

"And even if we did find it, how do we know putting the dirt back will do anything?"

"We've got to try something," I said. "We can't just be here, existing."

Naomi laughed. Then she turned around and started walking away. We stared at her, dumbfounded.

"Where you going?" said Ralph.

She indicated the horizon with a wave of her hand.

"We need you back here," I said.

She kept walking.

"Come on," I said to Sylvia and Ralph, "let's go after her."

We began following Naomi. She kept getting farther away from us. We hurried our pace, but she continued to accelerate away from us. She did not increase her pace, but somehow her strides covered more and more ground with each step. It was clear that she was never going to be within reach. I stopped walking. Sylvia went on a few more steps. Ralph a few more beyond her, as if on automatic, but it was clear that Naomi was not going to be part of us. She was as distant as the sun, still hanging stubbornly a few degrees above the edge of the green. The light from it was dimming. We all three noticed it.

"What's going on?" said Sylvia.

"Night?" said Ralph.

The sun was getting dimmer more rapidly. It would soon be completely dark. We stared at each other, our features getting muddy and indistinct. I felt the world drop out from under me. Without light we had nothing left but ourselves and we weren't feeling very good about that. Instinctively we moved closer to each other. It immediately felt better to feel their warmth.

"This ground probably doesn't hold much heat," I said. "We're going to get cold pretty soon."

"I'm not worried about it," said Ralph. "This place is weird, but it isn't nasty. It will provide for us."

The air went very still. I had not noticed it before, but there had been a breeze blowing all the while we had been in the flip. I was already calling our new existence "the flip" in my mind. It seemed very natural and Naomi's use of it gave me comfort in an odd way. Whenever I used it I felt comfortable as well. The smoke came out of our mouths again. I put my hand in Ralph's words. It felt warm. "All we have to do," I said, "is keep talking. The smoke will keep us warm."

Sylvia put her hand out and immersed it in Ralph's words as well. "I'll be damned," she said. "You're right."

We settled down on the ground and stretched out, huddled around an imaginary fire like we were kids on a camping trip.

"I'm still hungry," said Ralph.

"Forget about food," I said.

"*I* can forget it," said Ralph, "but my stomach can't."

"Sylvia," I said, "tell us a story."

She cleared her throat. "I'm not much for stories," she said.

"Tell us about your life. We need to fill the air to keep warm." I was starting to feel a little chilled. We needed to talk.

"My life," said Sylvia. "Okay. I was born in Tucson. Lived on a ranch outside of town. My parents owned horses and stabled other people's horses. We gave rides in the desert to tourists. I was in girl heaven. Horses all the time. I rode them whenever I could, and loved taking care of them. No brothers or sisters. Just me, my parents, and the horses. Got sunburned a lot. My mother didn't like that, tried to keep me indoors during the hottest parts of the day, but I just wanted to be outside all the time. Grew up. Started getting noticed by boys. Didn't notice it at first, then kind of liked it. Realized there was more to life than horses, I guess, but I'm not about to tell either of you the details."

"Darn," said Ralph.

"Took off to Europe just before my senior year. Was shocked at how ignorant I was. Art, history, all kinds of people, different food, land, customs. It was a big case of culture shock. No one ever told me any of that. Or, if they did, I didn't listen. Came back and everything here seemed so small. Insignificant. Had a couple of teachers who said I was brilliant. Worst thing ever. Now I was self-conscious. I wanted to learn more about the world. Started reading as much as I could. Fell into science. Loved the way the scientific mind figured stuff out. Majored in chemistry and physics. Top of my class, although that didn't matter to me. I was just absorbing it all. Starting to see deep connections in everything. Isn't that what we're supposed to be learning? What we're supposed to be trying to do?"

"Yep," I said.

"Well, anyway, I was sought by everyone. Multi-nationals, chemical companies, weapons builders, the whole military-industrial complex. They wanted me bad. But I opted for a small start up making sustainable energy systems for home use. It was a good system. I still think something like it will go gangbusters at some point, but we were too early for the market. No one wanted it. The company went bust, I lost my job, tainted goods on the job market. Kicked around for a few months, saw an ad for the institute. Applied and here I am. Still single but okay with that."

I could see nothing in front of me. Sylvia's voice was there and I assumed Ralph was still where he had sat down, but Sylvia's smoke was everywhere. The chill was out of my bones, for which I was happy. Now if the wind didn't kick up we would be okay, but I wasn't sure that the wind would stay down. And how long was night time going to be? Was the sun going to come back, ever? Too many questions.

"Ralph?" I said. "Your turn."

"Aaah, yes. My life story. You really want to hear that?"

"Not that much," I said. "But we need to fill the air. Keep warm. Go."

"Oh, all right. Let me see. My parents tell me I was a real crier when I was a kid. No one knew why. Gave myself a hernia. They had to do surgery. I kept the neighborhood up at night. Finally settled down after a while and grew up not saying much at all. From noisy all the time to near silence. They were equally perplexed by that. In school I was the classic nerd, right down to the glasses holder in the shirt pocket. White shirt. Everything was about computers and science and stuff like that. Then I got a girlfriend, and she was not that much interested in technical stuff, so I kind of abandoned it myself. Took to art and music to impress her, but she moved on and I found I kind of liked the artsy stuff better than the techy stuff. I grew my hair long, wore sandals, wrote poetry. I was embarrassing, but didn't know it. My family traveled a lot. We took trips at the drop of a hat. Road trips, train trips, backpacking trips, it didn't matter as long as we were moving. Criss-crossed the whole country and parts of the world too. My father was—is—an accountant. I took accounting courses to have a career to fall back on. Discovered management. Oh boy. Suddenly I knew what I wanted to do. Coordinate talented and skilled people to get jobs done. Figured the institute was a good place to find talented and skilled people. Found the people in charge and talked them into hiring me. They didn't want to. Didn't see the need. But my innate ability to bullshit worked in my favor. Here I am."

His words felt thicker than Sylvia's. Kind of overwhelming, almost. Like he was going to choke us. I didn't exactly have a problem breathing, but I was on the edge of having a problem breathing.

"Your turn," said Sylvia.

"You mean me?" I said.

"Well, yeah," she said.

"I think we've said enough," I said. "The smoke is getting a little too thick."

I heard Sylvia and Ralph both wave their hands. The smoke thinned a little.

"Oh," I said. "Very good."

"This stuff is amazing," said Ralph. "Anyone know what it's made of?"

"Ether," said Sylvia.

"Our thoughts," I said.

"Very funny," said Ralph. "Really, though. You two are supposed to be the brainiacs here. What is it?"

"We can come to that later," said Sylvia. "I want to hear Terry's life story."

"Right," said Ralph. "I want to hear Terry's life story too. I've been aching to hear it for years."

"Don't be mean," said Sylvia. "Terry?"

"Don't remember much about my childhood. People tell me that's weird, but I have very few memories of anything before about age ten or eleven. Born in small mining town in Ontario. My father was a miner. He hated it, but he was from the old country and had few skills. Didn't even know the language. I think in later years he came to accept his lot, but when I was a teenager he had this rage about his life that came out as resentment towards me. I was some kind of music prodigy. Played the piano like a great musician at three. Composed symphonies at four. Gave concerts. But my parents were uncomfortable with it. Didn't understand it, so they yanked me from that life and had me playing with the other kids. Baseball, hockey, that sort of thing. I was reasonably good at it. Don't remember anything about the music. Don't have the urge anymore. Probably a childhood thing. In school discovered math. Jumped into it like it was mother's milk. Could not get enough of numbers and their relationships. Only thing, I wasn't all that good at it. Never even in the top thirty percent of my class. Majored in math in college. Really struggled to keep up my grades. A calculus professor told me I had too much of an imagination to be good at math. I didn't know what he meant then, but he wasn't being mean or anything. He was very kind to let me know my limitations in a very gentle way. I kept at it, plugging away doggedly. It took me hours to see things that more talented students saw in a couple of seconds. It was just all so beautiful, though. I wanted to be a part of that beauty, that lovely description of nature. I did get a degree, finally, but my grades were barely good enough to qualify. I was not what most employers were looking for. There were all sorts of stars out there in my graduating class. I tried my hand at writing fiction. Got pretty good at it, but there was no way to make a living. At least I never found a way.

Naomi saw some of my more futurist pieces in a few magazines. She got a hold of me and offered me a job. Said she liked my imagination and needed some of my kind of crazy ways of thinking at the institute. That was two years ago."

"And now here we are," said Ralph.

"Everyone cozy?" I said.

"It's kind of nice," said Sylvia. Her voice sounded sleepy.

"Sounds like we're all drifting off to sleep," said Ralph. "Is that really what we should be doing now? Won't everything just slip away from us while we're asleep?"

"We don't have anything near us," I said. "There's nothing to slip away from us."

"I mean Naomi. She seemed to know something about what was going on and now she's completely gone. We'll never find her again."

"I wouldn't worry about that," said Sylvia. "She'll find us."

Their voices were distant sounds buried in the fog of their previous words. I was a little amazed that the fog was still blanketing us, and I was still thinking about the other necessities, like water and food. What if one of us got hurt? We had nothing, not even the most rudimentary of first aid kids. We were like one of those test subjects that get put out into the wilderness with nothing but a knife and told to survive for a few days. Except we didn't even have a knife. Only plastic spoons. Worse than that, we didn't even have a wilderness stocked with provisions like animals, plants, rivers, and such. We had only a featureless plane that none of us understood.

"And when she does," I said. "What then? How will she get us back to where we were?"

"There is no back," said Ralph. "I think we're stuck here for good."

"There's no way to know that," said Sylvia, still sleepy.

"I know," said Ralph. "Just an opinion. You're certainly free to ignore it."

Another silence, the kind that passes between people when they have nothing to say but want to keep talking anyway.

"You really played symphonies when you were a kid?" said Ralph.

"I have the pictures to prove it. Not to mention a big scrap book of newspaper stories and all kinds of trophies from music competitions."

"What I don't get is how anyone could forget something like that," said Ralph. "That would have to be a big part of your past. How can it just disappear?"

"My parents were scared by it. Said I wasn't old enough to be involved in that world. They were probably right. They said I could take it up again when I was older. Never did though. Somehow the continuity was lost. They got rid of my piano. Tossed out all my music books. A connection was severed and I never had the urge to reconnect."

"But if you were doing that kind of thing when you could barely talk, it must have been innate in you. It must have been a core thing in you. I still don't get how it would just disappear."

I had been asked the question before. No one could really believe that I was no longer interested in music. The thing is, I was probably never really *interested* in it, it was just something I was good at. But being good at something and wanting to do that something are completely different things. No one ever understood that and I didn't think Ralph would, so I didn't try to belabor the point. "It's a mystery," I said.

"When I was growing up," said Sylvia, "people said I should be a dancer."

"Oh?" said Ralph.

"But I didn't want to be a dancer."

"Horses, right?" said Ralph.

"Exactly. I just liked to ride. So what if I was good at dancing, which I was, but didn't really like it. I went to classes that my parents paid for. They loved seeing me in recitals and performances. But it was all so—I don't know—pedestrian, I guess. It was just me. I wanted to be with the horses, riding. It was as simple as that. I could see that if I pursued the dancing I might get really good at it. Maybe even have been in a dance company and made a living. I don't know. But I still never would have liked it. Makes perfect sense to me."

Ralph let out a deep sigh. "Either of you ever think that maybe you were destined for things other than what made you feel good?"

I couldn't see Sylvia or Ralph's faces through the fog. It made it difficult to know how to gauge some of their remarks. Was Ralph being serious or was he teasing us? Impossible to tell from his flat and muffled voice.

I put my head down on the moss and stretched out on my back. I wanted to see stars above me, but there were none. Only the fog, which I had asked us to create to keep warm. I wondered now what was on the other side of the fog. Maybe this world came to life after dark and we shouldn't be concealing it. It would be easy to walk out of the fog, but I wasn't sure we could then walk back in.

"Sylvia," I said. "You want to tackle that one?"

"The conversation is getting too heavy for just before sleep," said Sylvia.

"I agree," I said.

"No," said Ralph. "It's just one simple question. It won't take long to answer. Do either of you think there is a higher purpose that we should yield to?"

"Do you?" I said.

"Well, yeah. My career is all about that. I don't do things for myself, I help other people do things for the betterment of society as a whole."

"Oh my," said Sylvia. I could detect a mocking tone in her voice.

"Sure, laugh all you want," said Ralph, "but it's true. There are bigger things than me. There have to be. Anyone who says different is just fooling themselves."

"Even if you're right," said Sylvia, "and I'm not saying you're wrong, just going along with the premise, who is to say that we have to pay attention to it? It's just a higher power that's all. Insects are smaller and weaker than people. We can crush them without even thinking about it. But they don't care. They go about their lives in blissful ignorance of the high powers among them, walking around stomping on things all time."

"So we're like insects, then?" said Ralph.

"Kind of, if you accept your higher power premise."

"No, it's not like that. It's more that the higher power is an idea we have in us. It's something we create just by being human beings."

"So we create our creator?" I said.

"I didn't say anything about creator, I just said higher power. There's a difference."

"Not to most of the world. They're pretty much considered synonymous."

"I know," said Ralph, "but most of the world is wrong about that. There is no reason to put the two together. Just as there is no reason to put creation and morality together. The good has nothing to do with making anything, be it animal, vegetable, or mineral."

"Oh my head," said Sylvia. "We should be having this discussion at a small table in a cafe, while sipping espressos."

"Yeah," said Ralph, "with some pastries."

"Oh no," I said. "Let's not get started on food. We'll just torture each other."

"Terry's right," said Sylvia. "No food talk. I'll go crazy."

"Seems to me, we're already crazy," said Ralph.

"I also can't tell where you guys are," said Sylvia.

I blinked. "I haven't moved," I said.

"Me neither," said Ralph.

"Put out your hands," said Sylvia. I waved my hand around, trying to make contact, but I touched nothing. I pushed aside some of the smoke. I felt Ralph's hand waving in the air as well. "I can't find you," said Sylvia.

"Snap your fingers," I said. An instant later I heard muffled snapping sounds. It sounded so small in the smoke, like a voice lost in radio static. I reached for the sound. I was sure Ralph was reaching too.

"Can't find you," he said.

"I'm here," said Sylvia, but her voice was smaller, thinner. I felt adrenaline rise up in me. I was instantly afraid that we were going to lose her as we had lost everyone else.

"Ralph," I said.

"What?" Ralph's voice, but different. Smaller, like Sylvia's. Really, just about to disappear, it seemed. "Terry?"

"I'm here, but you are both fading rapidly."

"Is it this damn smoke we made?" said Ralph.

"No. It's this place. The world. We should try standing up."

I stood. I heard very faint shuffling noises, like they were standing too. The smoke was still enveloping me so I couldn't see more than a few inches. It was warm, but it was confining. I told myself not to make that mistake again if I could help it. We would just have to endure a little cold in the future. If there even *was* a future for us.

Sylvia's rate of finger snapping was slowing down. It picked up speed momentarily, as though she had a last oomph of energy for it, then it began slowing down again.

"I can't keep doing this," she said.

"Clap your hands," I said.

I heard the smallest clapping sound. I began running toward it. I couldn't see the ground, so the going was a little strange at first, then I got into the rhythm of it.

"What's going on?" said Ralph.

"I'm running toward Sylvia. Follow my voice." I began singing a song I remembered from my childhood.

"Are you sleeping,
are you sleeping,
brother john?
brother john?
Morning bells are ringing
morning bells are ringing
ding dang dong
ding dang dong."

"I can barely hear you," said Ralph. I could barely hear him. I sang the song again as I ran. Louder and louder, I sang it over and over. But it was no use. Eventually I could not hear Sylvia or Ralph. I called their names. No answer. I stopped. Only the sound of my own breathing filled my ears.

I called their names. The smoke lifted or cleared away, I wasn't sure which. There was no warmth from it anymore. The sky was black. No stars. Maybe Ralph had been right about us being inside the earth. But where did the sun go? Why did it just wink out, and was it going to come back? I had no answers, only questions, and they were beginning to irritate me. I had managed to lose everyone within less than a day. I had no provisions and I did not know how to escape this world.

I felt the ground under me with my hand. It appeared to be dry and free of vermin. I sat down on it with my arms wrapped around my legs and my chin on my knee. Sleep would not come now. I would just wait for the morning. If there was going to be a morning. My breathing became less strong and mellowed into a steady in and out. A gentle rocking.

After a while I became aware of a weight on my forehead, as if something was hanging from it. I put my hand up to it, expecting some kind of injury and maybe a little bit of blood, but instead my fingers encountered a smooth and cool surface, like a piece of marble. It was heavy and solid.

My heart rate increased and my spine tensed with a puckering frisson running from my neck to my buttocks. A *growth* was anchored at the center of my forehead. I felt around the base. It appeared to be about an inch in diameter. I followed it's length away from my forehead. It extended a foot or so out and tapered to a sharp point. It had ridges, like a compressed helix.

I was a unicorn.

Wildly, I felt around my feet to see if I now had hooves. Negative. Still standard issue human legs and feet. I was happy for that. Another quick check revealed I also had no tail. It appeared it was just the horn. Right there above my eyes and below my hairline. I lifted my head. The weight felt wrong, like it was something else from somewhere else. And now that I was a unicorn, what was I to do with this horn?

No answer came. The night was as dark as ever. If I had a horn, then probably Sylvia and Ralph had one as well. Not to mention Naomi, Penelope, and Grant. We had probably all shape-shifted into creatures that did not even exist, except in imagination and myth. And what exactly did that mean, anyway? Was I now a unicorn with unicorn thoughts? Or was I still a human with merely a unicorn horn?

It would probably have been a good thing to try to pursue these questions, but I was getting tired of the weirdness that was now my life. I looked up at the sky. The horn on my forehead was beginning to feel natural, like it had been there forever. I found that I *wanted* hooves on the ends of my legs. It would have felt right, while this just felt wrong. I stood up and called out to the emptiness.

No one answered.

Then someone answered.

"Hello," came a voice I had not heard before. It was as faint as Sylvia's and Ralph's had been.

"Hello," I answered back.

"Sing that song again," it said. A male voice. Music lover? I sang "Are You

Sleeping" several times. As I sang I heard footsteps come closer, then I felt the presence of someone very close. I stepped back. "Careful," I said. "I have a horn on my forehead. Don't want to hurt you."

The voice laughed. "Warning accepted. I'll take a step back."

I strained my eyes to see something, anything. But the darkness was so complete I could not even make out an outline, or a flash of anything, much less a full figured human being. If the voice was a human being's.

"I'm Fletcher," said the voice.

"Terry," I said, then remembered the name. Fletcher. "You wrote that paper," I said.

"Worst thing I ever did."

"The one that said no sufficiently large enterprise can guarantee zero fatalities if the danger index is above a certain threshold."

"Yup. Wish I could turn back the clock and eliminate it from the world. Too many people took it to heart. Especially people in your line of work."

"You mean the thinkers?"

"Yup. The mullers of the world, sitting on cushy chairs in ghastly offices. I like to call you people the cubicle zombies."

I suppose I shouldn't have taken offense, but I did. "That's a harsh characterization," I said. Fletcher was a pretty irritating fellow already and I had barely met him. We were maybe the last two people on this world, and he was picking a fight. I took a deep breath.

"Oh," said Fletcher. "Sorry. Didn't mean to offend. I actually got the term from one of your colleagues. Or at least she was a colleague, once. Got out of the game after—"

"After reading your paper?"

A pause. I imagined him grinning. "Well," he said. "Actually, yes. She found me and told me all about it. Said reading my paper was the most life-changing thing that ever happened to her. Said I made everything so clear that she had to chuck her career and take some time off and really reevaluate what she was going to do with her life. Can you imagine?"

"I think so."

"It was so much responsibility to put on me. I never asked her to give up her livelihood and become some kind of bohemian."

"Quite," I said, sarcasm dripping from my voice.

"I say," said Fletcher, "have I offended you in some way?"

I hated that he was perceptive enough to notice. It's much easier to mock people who don't know what's going on.

"No," I lied. "I'm just so upset by this crazy horn I now have."

"May I?" he said. I felt his hand hovering in the darkness. I reached for it and guided it to the base of the horn. He ran his hand over its length. "Remarkable," he said.

"Yeah," I said. "But it's still annoying."

"Kind of like my situation with your colleague, who's name I now do not recall. I had written an academic paper for an obscure journal of mathematics and suddenly I was some kind of guru. Reluctant, to be sure, but a guru nonetheless. She was the one who said she could not bear being a cubicle zombie any longer. I rather liked the phrase and have used it ever since."

"A lot of important work gets done in cubicles." Even as I said it, it sounded so ridiculous and weak I winced at myself.

"Yes," said Fletcher. "I'm sure. Listen, I don't mean to be forward or rude or anything, but do you happen to have any food?"

"Damn," I said. "I was going to ask you the same thing."

"Ah, well. Just as I thought."

"There's worms in the ground. I saw someone eat them."

"Oh yes," said Fletcher. "I know about those. I think I shall have to be a little more hungry before munching down on those."

"Yes," I said. "My thoughts exactly. What's a little more critical, I think, is water. Have you found any?"

"No," said Fletcher.

I sighed. "Prospects do not look good for us. Like in your paper, some are doomed to expire."

"Not my fault," said Fletcher. He had a light and optimistic disposition that would have been amusing in most circumstances, but just seemed blind to the facts in our present predicament.

"How did you get here?" I asked.

"I was to meet a Naomi at her institute. I believe she wanted to offer me a job."

Our Naomi? "She wanted to make you a cubicle zombie?" I said.

He laughed. "Something like that. I think she wanted to have me on staff as a trophy associate."

Naomi never mentioned this to me or anyone else I knew. Not that she had to tell us what she was planning to do or who she was wooing for the institute. Still, such things usually do get around. "Were you seriously considering such an offer?" I said.

"There's nothing wrong with getting the best price one can command," said Fletcher. "And there is a seductive attraction in being able to pursue any path one chooses, with no strings attached."

"We zombies generally have that freedom," I said. "We kind of like it."

"Touché," said Fletcher. I felt his grin in the air.

"So you were meeting Naomi?" I said.

"I came early to walk the campus and get a feel for the place. I saw a group of people, six of them, in a corner digging in the ground. I wanted to see what they were doing, so I approached them."

"That was us," I said. "Me and some of my colleagues."

"Ah yes," said Fletcher. "And what was the digging about? You appeared to be using spoons."

"One of the crazy things we cubicle zombies get into."

A long pause. "Indeed?"

"You had to be there. It sounded like a fun idea at the time."

"If you say so," said Fletcher. "As I approached from some distance, two of your party departed."

Naomi and Grant, I thought, going to get the pizza.

"I thought," continued Fletcher, "that they were like rats leaving a burning building. They had that aura of fear and desperation."

"I think maybe they were just hungry and tired and you misinterpreted that as fear."

"Certainly possible," said Fletcher. "In the event, I hesitated. I wondered what you all were doing. But then began walking toward you again. Then, inexplicably, the campus melted around me into this featureless and seemingly endless plane. Can you explain that?"

"No," I said. "We were discussing it just a few moments ago, trying to come up with something coherent."

"We?"

"Ralph and Sylvia. Two of the diggers you saw. We had filled the air with this warm smoke, to keep the cold away. Then they kind of drifted away. And then you showed up."

"I have been walking since I got here," said Fletcher. "I must say, nothing in my experience up to now remotely resembles this."

I didn't want to tell him that we probably caused it, the spoon digging brigade. "We think that one of the people who left has died," I said.

"Oh no."

"Yes. His name was Grant. He and Naomi were going to get us a pizza. A short time later we got a cell phone call from Naomi. She was in a car wreck and Grant was bleeding badly. She thought he was dead. Then everything changed, as you saw."

"Why, that's ghastly. I'm so sorry to hear that."

"Have you seen anyone on your walk?" I said.

"No, you're the first. And I haven't actually *seen* you yet, if we want to be quite accurate about the situation."

"Accuracy is important."

"Yes," said Fletcher. "Do you have any idea what we should be doing now? What I mean to say is, where do we go from here?"

"We need to find water," I said. "Without it, we're sunk. Aren't you feeling thirsty?"

"Very."

"My friend Ralph says this place will take care of us. I'm not at all convinced of that."

"Your friend sounds like a very trusting soul."

I thought about that. Ralph was a cynic at heart, but he was a softie when it came right down to it. He thought he despised the human race, but he would lay down his life for any of us, I was sure of it.

"Ralph pretends to cynicism," I said. "But he's a sensitive soul."

"Many cynics are," said Fletcher.

That sounded like the opening to a long discussion. Fletcher, I was sure, would be a good person to discuss most anything with, but all of that seemed wildly beside the point at the moment. If we did not find a good supply of water soon, everything would be moot.

"Have you investigated the possibility that there is ground water under here?" said Fletcher.

"We dug a little," I said. "But all we found was dirt and worms."

"May I suggest that we need to dig deeper?"

I wanted to think that there was, perhaps, a lake or river somewhere and all we had to do was keep walking. But that possibility was as unlikely as Fletcher's groundwater theory. Neither seemed possible.

"I have an idea," I said.

"Splendid," said Fletcher. "Let's hear it."

"One of us should dig, while the other should look for a ground level source of water."

"I see," said Fletcher. "It would double our chances of finding water."

"Exactly," I said. "Then, when and if one of us is successful, we find the other."

"I must point out that in situations such as this it is usually advisable not to split up."

"Yes," I said. "Usually I would not suggest it, but I believe we are in a dire situation."

"Quite right," said Fletcher. "I agree completely. However, we have both walked quite a bit and not found water. If we both dig we can proceed more quickly. We could find water much faster."

"But if there is no ground water," I said, "or if it is hundreds of feet deep, we will surely perish."

"If there is no ground water," said Fletcher, "then there will be no surface water."

He was making sense. And I did not like the idea of splitting up either. "Have you had some experience in such things that I don't know about?"

"I had some survival training," said Fletcher. "When I was in the war."

"The war?"

"You want to know which one?"

"There are so many," I said.

"No," said Fletcher. "I think you are mistaken on that point. There are many incarnations, but only one war."

Another statement meant to lead to a much larger discussion?

"You speak in enigmas," I said.

"I don't mean to," said Fletcher. "I try to state what I know to be true. Isn't that the best anyone can try for?"

"It doesn't bother you at all that our situation appears to make everything in our lives up to now irrelevant and perhaps even ridiculous?"

"As I say," said Fletcher. "I have been in the war for a long time. I have come to understand my own death as not particularly frightening. Soldiers develop a philosophical attitude to such things."

I did not know how to take some of Fletcher's remarks. Could he be at all serious about this war nonsense?

"Do you prefer being a soldier to being a cubicle zombie?"

"What an interesting question," he said. "I must think about it for a time. In the meanwhile, won't you join me in digging?"

I wanted to. I told Fletcher I was ready. I went down on my knees and prepared to pull up clumps of dirt. And yet, when it came right down to it, I could not. It seemed futile. I dug for a few more seconds, but there was no enthusiasm in me. I could not summon it. I rose, lifting my horn-laden head slowly and with some measure of pain, and turned from Fletcher and began walking.

"I say," said Fletcher. "Where are you going?"

I didn't answer him.

"Terry!" he said. "You can't leave me now. We had an agreement to dig for water. Terry!"

Fletcher's voice grew quiet. I just continued walking. My friends were out here somewhere and I needed to find them. I could no longer bear to just remain in one place and dig.

I noticed a small sliver of light curving ahead of me. Was that the start of a new day? The sun rising or whatever a sun does when it is inside the earth?

The light from the sliver illuminated my hand. I was relieved to see it was my regular hand. Nothing strange about it. My feet hurt. I suddenly noticed that. It was as though my shoes no longer fit me. Above my head the stars were not there. Where were my friends? I wanted to find them. I was hoping they wanted to find me.

Fletcher was right there behind me. He was persistent, I had to give him that.

"Terry," he said. "It's terribly bad form for you to just leave me in the lurch like that. We had agreed to dig together. Why did you just decide to break our agreement for no reason? We need to find water. You said so yourself."

"I didn't want to dig anymore," I said. "Digging got us into this mess."

"That's wild speculation on your part. People have been digging in the earth for centuries. It has never caused the world to change so drastically as this."

"How do you know?"

"Please, Terry. You are becoming delusional. Probably from lack of food and water. We must use our last strength to find water. Won't you stop and dig with me now?"

I did stop. I looked at him. The morning light showed his features. He was kind of an ordinary looking man. Nothing special about him. Nothing to indicate he had authored a revolutionary paper that would change the way people thought about processes forever.

But then I didn't know what a person like that *should* look like. Why should a person look like anything? Did I look like what I was, a cubicle zombie?

"I don't like the way you call people cubicle zombies."

"Fair enough," he said. "I'll stop doing that."

"We're not zombies," I said.

"Agreed. It was an insensitive and wholly inappropriate way to speak of someone. I will no longer do it."

The tip of my horn was an indistinct blur at the center of my vision. It floated around in front of me like a blind spot in my field of view. Was I going to have to get used to this?

"I hate that I have a horn in my forehead," I said.

"I would hate such a thing as well," said Fletcher. "I see that having the horn will cause you to behave in certain ways that may not be in your best interest."

"I didn't stop digging because of the horn."

"Agreed. I was not implying that you did. Rather, I was making the case for anomalies as the basis for erratic behavior."

"You have too many answers," I said.

"I would like to see you behave in your best interest."

"You are too kind," I said, trying to make sarcasm drip from the words. Instead I just sounded childish.

"I want you to behave in my best interest as well," Said Fletcher.

That made me laugh. "Good for you," I said. "I like that kind of honesty. But you see, I don't need to act in your best interest. I don't know you. I know my friends and I want to find them. Why won't you let me?"

"Water," said Fletcher. "Have you forgotten about our need for water?"

I had not. I was feeling woozy and dizzy. "Walking expends less energy than digging," I said. "We could dig ourselves to death in a fraction of the time we could be spending walking and searching."

Fletcher sighed. "You are determined," he said.

"I have determined," I said. "I have determined that it would be quick suicide to dig."

"You prefer the slow suicide of walking?" said Fletcher.

He spoke rapidly and without inflection. He was stating facts and asking questions in a monotone which I did not find irritating, strangely enough. Instead it was soothing. It was as though he was trying to make me feel good by admitting that I had something on the ball while he was lacking in—something.

"How long were you in the war?" I asked.

"You don't want to hear about that," he said.

"No, I do." I stepped away from him and began walking. He kept pace with me.

"Do we talk?" he said. "Or do we just walk? Should we be doing the two activities concurrently?"

"You have a strange way of expressing things," I said.

"In the war, we learned many languages and many idioms and ways of speaking. It was our chief survival tool. I would tell you more about it, but I am concerned that talking on top of walking would expend more energy than I have to spare."

The sliver of light had expanded to a thick arc. Soon the sun was going to peak over the horizon. Maybe. Nothing could be taken for granted on this world.

"Did you engage in battle?"

"Of course. It was a war."

"Did you kill innocents?"

"Not on purpose."

"It's never on purpose, is it?"

"That's too broad a statement," said Fletcher. "It is well known that during the war many innocents have been targeted for torture, recreational violence, rape, and so on, as well as death."

"Did *you* do any of these things?"

"No. But I have killed soldiers, allied and enemy, who did. Out of a sense of rage that I could not control."

I mulled that over for a while. "Did you believe in the objectives of the war?" I said.

"There were no objectives."

"Really? You mean none that you knew of, or none that were officially sanctioned?"

"The war was an exercise, as they has always been. It was meant to demonstrate the extent of our power to others of the species."

"Well," I said. "That's an objective, isn't it?"

"Not a conscious one. It's biological instinct. The leaders that send us into battle have tactical and strategic objectives in mind, but these are little more than excuses. The ones who fight the war might believe in such things at first, but as soon as we are in the fray it is all about survival. Idealism withers in a heartbeat."

"Did your work on the paper come from your experience in the war?"

"It informed it, but it did not directly lead to it."

"At the institute we debate the morality of supporting war efforts."

"I can well imagine," said Fletcher.

"Usually we have no conclusion to the debates. They go on and on. It's actually kind of boring, if you want to know the truth."

"War is more or less boring most of the time. Your debates are not a series of discreet events. They are really one long, unending debate, just as the war is one long unending war, though it is perceived by history as a series of discreet conflicts. Now tell me more about why the six of you were digging in the ground with plastic spoons."

"No," I said. "I don't think so."

"I told you about my war experiences."

"To a limited extent," I said. "You have described some aspects of it in very limited terms, but I don't have a picture of you in the field, doing your soldier thing."

"You don't need to," said Fletcher. "All you have to do is look at yourself right here and right now. I told you soldiering was about pure survival. That's what you are engaged in at the moment."

I looked around the landscape we were traversing. No change from the previous day. It suddenly seemed too depressing to go on. I stopped. Fletcher stopped with me.

"We aren't going to find any water, are we?" I said.

"It appears unlikely," said Fletcher. "The environment is featureless. Without hills and valleys and such, it is difficult to see how a lake could collect or a stream could flow."

"I see your point," I said. I was very thirsty. My mouth and throat were dry. My stomach felt flattened against my spine. I had known hunger pangs in the past, but nothing like this. My body craved sustenance and there did not appear to be any forthcoming.

"Then we dig," I said.

Fletcher grinned widely and clapped me on the back. "Now you're talking," he said. "We dig! Yes, we dig!"

He dropped to the ground and began scraping it with his hands. I dropped beside him and did likewise. As inadequate as the plastic spoons were, I wished we had them now. The ground was hard and dense. My fingers would not last long. Neither would Fletcher's, subjected to this kind of abuse. He didn't seem to worry about it, though. He got in there with enthusiasm.

Periodically he rose to his feet, kicked at the hole to loosen up some of the dirt, then dropped down again to scoop it out with his hands. The worms writhed on the edges and in the piles we displaced.

"So many of these," said Fletcher. "Have you eaten one yet?"

"No," I said, gritting my teeth against the thought.

"You said one of your colleagues did?"

"She seemed to like them. I am not at the point where I want to try them yet."

"They might give us some moisture," said Fletcher.

"I'm afraid I would vomit, which would drain me of even more fluids."

"Oh, yes," said Fletcher. "That would not be good."

"No," I said, actually a little amused by his understatement. I stood up and kicked at the hole as he had done. My shoes were not exactly made for this kind of work, but the soles were tough and dug into the ground with a satisfying power.

I went back down on my knees to pull up what I had loosened. We soon fell into a rhythm. Stand and loosen with shoes, bend and scoop with hands. Repeat. Then we took turns. Fletcher would loosen with his shoes while I scooped out with my hands. We would do this for a few minutes. Then I would stand and loosen while he scooped. We did this for what seemed like hours. We eventually had a hole about waist deep.

"Feel any moisture?" I said.

"None," said Fletcher.

"Should we by now?"

"It really all depends," he said. "Some places will have damp ground very near the top, others will not."

"Are we just working ourselves to death?"

"It may be," said Fletcher. "But I would rather perish trying to do something than just wait for death."

"Is that a soldier's perspective?"

"I would think a human being's point of view, soldier or not."

"I feel so inadequate, like I never learned anything in life. What's the point of any knowledge if you can't use it to save yourself when you need to?"

"Is this the latest installment of your debate?" said Fletcher.

Was it? I was no longer able to decide. The academic issues that we debated at the institute seemed completely irrelevant now. We had to live. That was all that mattered. Which meant, according to Fletcher's code, that I was as much soldier as he was. "How many people did you kill?" I said.

"What makes you think I would answer such a question?" said Fletcher.

"Aren't we talking here? Aren't we having a bonding experience in which we share aspects of our lives?"

"You speak in a strange way," said Fletcher. "You did not want to tell me about your spoon digging."

"Okay," I said. "Here's the truth. At the institute we have competitions. The brain power against the management power. This one was my idea. I suggested we use plastic spoons to dig into the ground. Whichever team pulled up the most dirt within an hour would win. I convinced enough of my colleagues that this would be entertaining that they came out and engaged in the activity."

"I see. What other activities has this spirit of competition led to?"

"In the past we have made art from post-it notes, we have built structures using toothpicks, and we have made replicas of Stonehenge using various materials."

"If you don't mind me saying," said Fletcher, "these all sound like astoundingly trivial activities."

"Yes," I said. "Well, that's the point, you see. We engage in these terribly complex ideas in our work, but when we are not working we like to do things that are, as you say, trivial."

"A kind of relaxation by play?"

"Yes," I said. "Exactly."

"Huh."

"You sound as though you think it ridiculous."

"It just seems to me that your time could be spent more productively, while also being relaxing. You could exercise. Perhaps have running competitions. There's nothing to clear the mind like a good run."

His attitude was rather irritating. Why did he need to criticize how we do things? "Are you some kind of spy?" I said. "Have you been sent to check up on us?"

Fletcher laughed so hard I thought he was going to pass out. His face turned red and he struggled to catch his breath.

"It wasn't that funny," I said.

"Oh, yes it was," said Fletcher. "Me, a spy. That is rich. Truly amusing."

"What then?" I said. "Why are you so interested in our leisure activities?"

"Well, it's just curiosity is all. I would expect such a trait to be part of your make up. All of you."

"Sure, but you seem to be focusing on the spoon digging."

"It's what I saw. I didn't actually get into the building, recall. And besides, you said yourself it could be the genesis of this odd situation in which we seem to have found ourselves."

"I'm very curious about something. I wonder what you would taste like."

Fletcher's eyes went wide and his mouth dropped open. "Indeed?" he said.

"Haven't you? About me, I mean. Oh, everyone says people taste like chicken, but most of them have never tasted a person, never eaten human flesh as it were. One of us will die before the other. I was wondering if you died first, would I have the guts to survive by eating you. And what would you taste like. Curiosity, you see. Just wondering, is all."

"A perfectly horrid line of thought," said Fletcher.

"The thing is, I would have to do it quickly. If I wait too long, then you would go bad. Rot, as it were. So I would have to consume as much of you as I can, seeing as how we lack refrigeration or any other kind of preservation method. The ideal thing would be for you to remain alive while I hacked off pieces of you over a few days or weeks. That way I could survive for a long time on your energy. That would be cruel, though, wouldn't it? Unless you were in a coma and didn't know what was going on. That would be ideal for me. And all this goes for you as well. I mean, should I expire first, all these considerations fall upon you. The moral issues are mind-boggling."

"Now you're just baiting me," said Fletcher. "You're just *trying* to get me to feel offended."

"It's not academic. I estimate we're less than a day away from death."

Fletcher's face grew very dark, as though he had stepped into shadow. His whole demeanor suddenly grew sinister and I was afraid of him. If I had had a weapon I might have used it on him. As it was, I had only my body, clothed in office attire, which was getting ragged and torn from all the digging. I did have my shoes, but they were likely of limited use against Fletcher, who looked more fit than me, and, in any case, had shoes as well. I expect that he had also been trained in self defense. As well as self offense, if it came to that.

But my skin was electric. I was trembling with anticipation. It was as though everything had suddenly turned to menace me. Not just Fletcher, but the entire world. All of existence. Then I remembered the horn on my forehead. In an instant I felt stronger than anything in my immediate environment. Fletcher did not have a sharp horn on his head. Fletcher was not as lethal as I was. I was filled with energy, and this surprised me, considering the depleted state of my body. How could I feel so strong, when I had had almost no energy input in the last day?

"You would contemplate consuming me, but are squeamish about eating worms?" said Fletcher. Attempting to deflect the conflict to something more benign? Was he afraid of me? Afraid of my horn, more like it.

I took a step back. Why wait for Fletcher to expire? Why not dispatch him right here and now and use his flesh to continue my own existence? Why not, indeed. I lowered my head. Now Fletcher stepped back. He raised his hands in a gesture at once threatening and protective. A stance from some variety of martial art, no doubt. But I had the sharpest object withing miles. I didn't need martial art.

"We can work together," he said. "Together we have hope. Alone, we are lost."

"We could be lost anyway," I said.

"We don't know that yet."

"I'm so hungry. And thirsty."

Fletcher said nothing.

I said nothing.

The sun was over us. It was not particularly hot, but it gave off a strong illumination, as though we were in a spotlight. Shadows around us were sharp and distinct. I never wanted to be in such a position. I had always assumed myself to be the sort of person that needed to be away from the fray of the world. I imagined my horn impaling Fletcher, red blood staining its whiteness. This was a vision as uncomfortable to me as anything I could have imagined.

Within a second, all my surging animosity and adrenalin subsided to nothing. I felt completely exhausted and not in the mood for any kind of fight, mental or physical. My legs trembled and my hands shook. I held my arms, trying to quell the tremors. "I'm sorry," I said. "I feel so ridiculous. If I could holster my horn, I would."

I raised my head and tried to smile. My mouth wouldn't go that way.

Fletcher was still wary, but seemed to accept my change of heart, at least tentatively. "I'll chalk up your threatening behavior to exhaustion and delirium brought on by hunger and thirst," he said. "But I warn you that if it should happen again, I will not be as kind."

"Fine," I said.

He bent down and fished a few worms from the pile. "We need to do something to bond us again," he said.

I had a good idea what that was. "I told you," I said, "it'll make me sick."

"Don't chew them," he said. "Just drop them in the back of your mouth and swallow." He tilted his head back and let one of the writhing things fall into his mouth. He closed his mouth and swallowed hard, without chewing. He looked at me. "There," he said, "nothing to it."

I felt the corners of my mouth pull down. I tried to pull them back up, but I could not make them do it. "Do you feel them?" I said. "In your stomach, I mean."

Fletcher looked up at the sky, considering the question. "No," he said. "Once they're down there, I can't tell they're any different from a sandwich."

I looked doubtful.

"Well," he said, "okay, maybe a little different. But it's a very subtle thing. It's not unpleasant at all. They feel like butterflies in your stomach. A kind of anticipation. Very refreshing in an odd sort of way." He pulled up a particularly large specimen, tilted his head back, and let it slip down his throat.

I looked down at our pathetic little pits. It would take ages to reach water, if there even was any. I did the calculation in my head over and over again, hoping for a different result which did not come, would not come, ever. I sighed long and hard and surrendered myself to the inevitable. I gingerly reached into the pile of dirt and carefully extracted a writhing worm. It did not feel slimy, as I had feared. It was more leathery, smooth and dry. It surprised me with how pleasing it felt in my hand. I held it between the tips of my thumb and index finger.

"That's it," said Fletcher. "You've got the idea."

I tilted my head back, as Fletcher had done, but the motion made me instantly dizzy. "Whoa," I said and returned my head to the upright position. I gritted my teeth, waiting for my head to return to a stable state. "I think I'll just put it back there instead of dropping it in," I said. I had noticed that Fletcher had not removed all of the dirt before consuming his worm. "Didn't the dirt scrape your throat on the way down?" I said.

"You're over-thinking this," said Fletcher. "Put it in your mouth and swallow. There's nothing to it."

I was ready to run. Had all my systems primed to flee this scene, but Fletcher's disapproving look affected me in an odd way. How could his look make me do anything? I was frozen. Could not move a muscle. He tried to change his expression to encouragement, but it did not work. He was truly disgusted with me. I didn't like that, and wondered why it mattered to me.

"I don't know if I can remain buddied up with someone who refuses to take the simplest action in order to survive," said Fletcher. He took a handful of the worms and stuffed them into his mouth. This time he chewed.

I felt a pressure on my head, as though I was getting cooked in the sun. Like my skull was expanding. Would I explode? What was happening to me? Nothing. Nothing was happening.

I put the worm on the back of my tongue. It was sweet. The surge of sensation obliterated all other considerations for the moment. I actually enjoyed the feeling of it on my tongue. There was no gag reflex whatsoever. I swallowed. It was as though I was merely helping it along the path it had chosen.

I immediately sought another one. Found it, and swallowed it. The few grains of dirt that it took with it were not unpleasant in any way. They were like a crunchy seasoning. The next few I tentatively chewed. As Naomi had suggested, they were like little packets of honey, or honey-soaked bread.

Fletcher and I spent the next few minutes consuming the worms with gusto. Where only a few moments ago he was ready to dismiss me from his life, now, suddenly, we were comrades in the grand struggle for survival. *Feeding, fighting, and fucking.*

"Sure hope there's nothing poisonous in them," I said. "Otherwise we are sunk."

"How much water do you think each one has?" said Fletcher.

"Not enough, really. Even if they were all water, we would have to eat hundreds of them, probably, to hydrate ourselves properly."

"Well, we don't have much else to do," said Fletcher.

"I would still like to find my friends," I said.

"That, my survival buddy, is a fool's errand."

"I know," I said. "But as you say, what else is there to do here?"

"I see your point," said Fletcher. He looked down at the hole we had dug. "Do we continue this exercise?"

"You were very keen on it," I said.

"That was before I tired myself out on the effort."

"It is exhausting work, I'll give you that," I said.

"I say we chuck it."

"But if we don't dig and we don't search for friends, what exactly are we to do all day?"

"I'm all for sleeping," said Fletcher. "I'm tired. Aren't you tired?"

"I slept," I said.

"All this food I just ate. It's making me drowsy." He dropped to the moss, curled up like a baby, tucked his hands under his head, and closed his eyes. "Watch over me," he mumbled. "I don't want to get killed in my sleep."

And then he was asleep. I stood over him, feeling as absurd as, probably, it was possible to feel. I hated the horn on my forehead. I was not a unicorn. Had never been a unicorn, and had never aspired to the state of unicornness. So what was I doing with a unicorn horn? If Ralph was right, then this was part of this world's master plan of benign intentions. It was there to protect me. Protect me from what, was the question. There were no predators here. There was nothing. Nothing.

I felt a rumble under my feet. Earthquake? Possibly. The rumble shook the ground. My teeth chattered. I needed to piss. I walked away from Fletcher, who was snoring happily on the ground. There was no cover. I felt absurdly vulnerable as I unzipped and pulled out my penis. I was halfway through before I realized the significance of the fact that I was pissing. I had taken in enough moisture that my body was letting some of it go.

The urine was dark yellow, almost brown. That was not a good sign, I knew. The darker the urine, the closer to dehydration, and possible death, one was. The puddle didn't stay long on the surface. The ground absorbed it in no time at all. I tucked everything back in, zipped up and turned around.

Fletcher was gone. I let out a groan. I did not want to be alone again. It was not safe to be alone here. When people were alone, they turned into things like unicorns. Madness was everywhere when I was alone. My heart was beating a mile a minute. My face felt hot. The blood in my arms almost burned through my flesh, it felt so hot. I knew that was adrenaline. I was scared. Give myself a minute. Fletcher was probably right here. I just got turned around on this featureless landscape.

The ground shook again. An aftershock? Very likely. So this was a geologically active world. I turned around slowly and surveyed my surroundings. No obvious damage to the landscape. No crevices opened up in the ground. And no Fletcher. Okay. Don't panic. Look for the pile of dirt we had unearthed. He had been near there, and couldn't have gone very far in just a few minutes. That dirt had to be around here somewhere.

Then I remembered that the landscape here stretched. That was the first odd thing we noticed about this world, or alternate reality, or whatever it was. The land stretched. Each location multiplied itself. That was why we were on a mossy landscape. The moss had stretched so much it was all that we could see. If we had been standing on a sidewalk when the flip happened, there would have been nothing but a gray hard surface for miles and miles. Then we would surely have died. No way to dig under concrete with just hands and shoes. So it must still be going on, the stretch. Fletcher had been taken from me by the stretching of the landscape. So had the hole we dug. It was exactly the way Ralph and Sylvia had disappeared. So Ralph's idea that we were inside a hollow sphere was wrong. We were still on the regular globe, but it was stretching. Perhaps growing immensely. All because of our spoon digging? It did not seem possible. In any case, I was not learning how to reverse the situation. How did I get the globe to reassert its original size?

More rumbling. It must still be proceeding, the stretching. For all I knew it would go on forever. Eventually everyone would be completely isolated, unable to remain close enough to anyone else unless they were touching. Unless their feet were so close to each other that the ground had no room to stretch between them. The embrace of another was the only way to defeat the ultimate isolationism.

Feeding. Fighting. Fucking.

That phrase of Grant's kept coming back to me. To reduce human existence—all existence, for that matter—to three basic items. It seemed too cynical to be true. It seemed like an absurdist's diatribe. And yet, what was this landscape I was in now if not the most absurd thing imaginable?

Another shaking of the ground. This time worse than before. Worse than I would have thought possible. The ground went up and down quickly, a vibration like a washing machine with an unbalanced load. Then it shook sideways, knocking me to the ground. My head struck the moss. My neck hurt from the weight of the horn. I waited for the rumbling to stop.

After what seemed longer than possible, it did stop. With my ear to the ground, I heard things. The worms were rustling around down there, probably as spooked by shifting ground as I was, but there was more than that. Farther down, way past the worms, I heard something else. It was a kind whistling. No, not whistling, exactly. A wind. A rush of air. I pushed my ear into the ground, as though I could dig a hole with my lobe. I plugged up my opposite ear with my finger.

Now the rushing sound was so strong it felt as though it was going right through me. I wanted to dig to that sound, but remembered that I had been digging for some time with no real result of any consequence. I thought that perhaps Fletcher was curled up on the ground like this, similar to my own position here, so he could listen to the rushing air as well. And maybe it had put him to sleep, like a lullaby might put him to sleep.

Was this the sea that we hear in seashells? Was there an ocean under the surface of this world? Then why do we not find it? We dig and we dig. We find only the worms. Are they carrying the ocean within them? The moss against my cheek felt like the softest of blankets. I did not want to rise from it and I did not want to leave it. It even felt good to have my horn resting on the moss. It took some of the pressure away from my head and neck. My neck was developing a good solid pain that did not seem to want to go away.

And my head ached from the weight. I did not think I could keep this horn. I had to find a way to get rid of it. I grasped the horn in my hand and tested its strength by bending it. It seemed not to yield at all. What I wanted to do was score it around the base. Enough so that it would have a weak point, from which I could snap it off.

However, as with everything else here, I had nothing to score it with. Hold on. That wasn't exactly true. I had my set of keys. I reached into my pocket and pulled them out. Keys on a ring. There was my house key, car key, garage key, office key. Just four. Four keys for my life.

Now which was the sturdiest? Which offered the most jagged edge? I ran my thumb along all of the them. The house and garage key were worn pretty smooth. Not much cutting power there. The office key was sturdier and the teeth were more edged. They had not been worn down as much. I held it as firmly as I could between my thumb and forefinger, exactly as I had held the worm before swallowing it.

I began a sawing motion on the horn, just above the point where it met the skin of my forehead. I sawed for at least five minutes, or so it seemed to me. When my arm and fingers began to feel fatigued, I switched the key to the other hand and kept sawing. After a while I ran my finger along the base of the horn.

The progress was disheartening. Just the tiniest scratch after all that work. But it was not completely futile. It was a start. I determined that if I kept going, I should be able to have the horn off in less than an hour. At that moment, in my state of despair, it seemed the best thing I could do. It was at least some productive activity. I kept sawing.

My fingers began to hurt from being in a cramped position. It was a completely unnatural position to be in. My arms were getting tired as well. Pain shot up and down my arm. I stopped and let myself rest a little. I put my ear back to the moss. The rushing sound was still as strong as ever. I ran my thumb along the base of the horn. There was a satisfying depth to the groove. Not very deep, but definitely there. I was wary of trying to snap off the thing before I had a proper weak point. I did not know how far into my skull the base went. For all I knew it was embedded in my brain and trying to break it off too deeply might cause serious damage to my thinking process. Yet I did not want the thing there. It was doing me no good at all.

I felt weak, but thought I could summon the strength to do at least this one task. Was it possible? I pulled on the horn, testing it. I felt a definite tug on my forehead. I felt pressure all the way to my temple. This alarmed me and I stopped trying to bend the horn. I felt fluid oozing where I had sawed. This was more alarming than anything I had experienced in the last two days. It sent a shot of adrenaline all through me. I shook with fear.

The horn was not inert material, as I had thought. I had guessed that it was like an elaborate fingernail. Instead, it appeared it was more like bone or teeth with a living, or at least dynamic, center. And yet, there was no pain. The fluid dripped out. I dabbed at it with my finger and held the finger close so I could see it. It was pinkish, like diluted blood. More adrenaline, although this time it did not alarm me. I was able to observe the effect almost as though it was happening to someone else.

Could one get inured to the effect of adrenaline? Perhaps so. I had a decision to make. Do I continue with the operation or do I leave the horn as is, perhaps to heal itself? Neither option sounded particularly appealing. And there was the sound underlying the world. It was still there. Still rushing like an eternal river, or the ocean slopping up on a shore. The waves going to and fro.

I recalled years ago being told the salt in the ocean was the salt in our blood. We carry the ocean in us. I always thought this an absurd notion. Still did. The salt in our bodies may have come from when we were sea creatures, but it is not accurate to then say we carry an ocean in our veins and arteries.

I wanted to debate the issue with others. They would not. They were so enamored of the romantic idea of pumping the sea through their hearts that they did not understand how ridiculous the very thought of it was.

The fluid was dripping, now. It flowed over my forehead, down to my temple, where it hung and dripped onto the moss. My blood was leaving me, slowly but inexorably. What I needed now was a way to staunch the flow. I decided that snapping off the horn was out of the question. If I did so, it might open the spigot on my blood and I would surely die. Not that that seemed like such a bad thing in my present situation. It might even be better to die quickly of blood loss than to expire from thirst and starvation.

Nevertheless, there was still hope that I *might* survive. If the world had flipped like this with no rhyme or reason, then it could as easily flip back with no rhyme or reason.

I took my key and held it against my sleeve at the shoulder. I sawed through the material until I created a tear and then ripped it off the rest of the way. I took the sleeve, thus severed, and wrapped it around the base of the horn, tying the two ends together in a tight knot. The pressure felt good and I hoped it would stop the flow. I stood and surveyed my immediate surroundings again.

It was more than depressing to be in this featureless landscape. It was discouraging and demoralizing. I could see that I was falling into despair. I shook my head and told myself to snap out of it. Walk, I said. Just walk. Do something.

I began taking steps. The motion of my arms and feet pumping blood and moving muscles was a tonic of sorts. I felt as though I was alive again after being more than dead for a long time. And yet, the odd thing was, it had only been a day or two since the flip happened. Could one fall so far so quickly?

I was more thirsty than I had ever thought it possible to be. I was working hard and I was not sweating. That wasn't good. It meant I had no moisture left in me, nothing to excrete. I expected to start hallucinating, and braced myself for it. Only, in this environment, how could I tell if I was hallucinating or not?

I needed water. I stopped walking and plunged my hand into the moss. I pulled up hunks of it and kicked at the earth beneath it. The worms were there. That wasn't an hallucination. I hoped. I ate some of them. Then I dug some more and ate more, uncovering writhing heaps of them.

I wondered what they lived on. They must have access to water, somewhere. Ah, but they were my access to water. They found water and stored it for me. I ate as many as I could. They filled my belly and I felt very pleased indeed.

I laid down on the moss and stretched my hands and legs as far as they would go. That felt much better than walking. The moss was at least inviting. I believe I remained there for several years.

I got up and walked for several more. The sun went around and around the sky in a rapid dance, then in a blur, etching its path against the blue dome. The darkness of night and the light of day flickered rapidly, like a strobe light. This went on for many many years.

Eventually the rate of flickering increased to the point where there was no flicker anymore. I was in a perpetual twilight gray. I felt myself age. I was getting wrinkly and weak. The shirt sleeve at the base of my horn had grown crusty, then withered away to threads. Somehow the cut I had made had healed over, horn material smoothing over the crevice.

But the horn was softer. It had attracted some kind of parasite, I supposed, that burrowed into it. It left grooves on the outside. I had never seen or felt the bugs or whatever they were, but they must have done their work quickly and gone away. I felt no older, but I must have been months or years older than I was. I kept walking in the twilight. I tried to think of ways to determine if this was an hallucination or if it was really happening to me. Was a dream the same as experience? Were thoughts the same as reality? It was a debate I would have loved to get into in the air-conditioned confines of our plush offices at the institute. It would have had a simultaneous air of frivolity and seriousness. I could imagine Grant and maybe Naomi getting in on it, trying to tease out the metaphysics of existence and reality.

We might have stayed late, maybe into the night, discussing it. We would have had pizzas delivered and we would have devoured them with gusto. Maybe some wine after. The institute did not frown on drinking on premises. The policy was to make us happy, within reason.

But all that seemed completely beside the point now. Discerning reality from fantasy was no longer an academic exercise and it was not in any way entertaining. It had now become crucial to my survival, and I saw that I had no real skills in it, nothing to guide me. Descartes had the answer, or so he thought. He doubted everything that he could possibly doubt and in the end realized there was only one thing that he could not doubt, and that was that he was doubting.

Circles within circles, but it meant a lot to him. "I think therefore I am." The act of doubting proved he had to be there to do the doubting. How marvelous for him that he found comfort in that. I imagined it must have come after a night of drinking. Only someone under the influence of a substance that would alter their consciousness could find comfort in such a thing. In his ultimate quest to understand and prove the existence of God, though, it was a dead end. He could not take the notion of his existence any further and his philosophy foundered on his attempts to do so.

In the end the comfort he found was false, though there is some question as to whether he knew it or not. He may have been comforted by his own ignorance, which, in the end, is probably better than nothing. I found no comfort in anything. Mere existence is not comfortable.

The streak of the sun's path hung around me like a floating ring, a bleached rainbow etched into the sky. This flip was the most peculiar thing imaginable. How could anything cause such an occurrence? That was the question. But in the end who cared? I just wanted to get out of it. I kept walking. The horn was getting so soft that it drooped in front of me. I considered the horn. Glad I was able to repair it after my ill-advised attempt to sever it. But perhaps the repair never really worked. Maybe it was drooping now because of what I had attempted before. Who knew?

Owning a unicorn's horn on my forehead was a completely new thing to me. Not something I could possibly understand yet.

I considered my teeth and fingernails.

They were still in their normal state, so there was no general softening going on. I was not deteriorating into a puddle or anything like that.

It sounded absurd to even think such a thing, but the flip had made the absurd not only possible but probable.

As I walked, the years went by. Each step felt like I was covering dozens of miles. I also noticed that I was making footprints in the moss. Deep ones that went down several inches. This was new. I was not sure if this was an alarming development or something trivial. I had no guidelines for such things.

I stopped.

The moss stopped with me. I felt like I was at the top of an enormous sphere and by moving I moved the sphere so that I always remained on top of it. It was a feeling of great power to be able manipulate this giant globe. It was as though the globe was my own personal toy. Was such a thing even possible? Everything was possible now. My hallucinations were as real as Descartes's ridiculous musings. My concepts were reality, my thoughts were made manifest.

As I stood, I saw that I was sinking. Slowly, but definitely sinking into the moss. And I went past the moss. I was up to my ankles. I pulled out one foot, then the other. I kept walking. Each step left a deep footprint. I was terrified of stopping. If I stopped, I was sure I would sink into the dirt and be suffocated. I wondered if the same effect would occur if I stretched out on the moss. I didn't wonder enough to actually undertake the exercise necessary to find out. I was now determined that I would not stop. I walked and walked and walked.

There is a comfort that comes from doing the same thing over and over. It is the comfort of eternity, the feeling that everything happens for a reason and that reason is unknown and unknowable to you.

And so I walked. Heels balanced and balancing on the world. But nothing stays the same, ever. My footsteps sunk even further with each step. At first I did not notice, then I saw that my feet left deeper and deeper impressions with each step. The holes were so deep that worms began to fill them. They oozed out of the sides and filled the depression.

Okay, I thought, I was making little bowls of food with my feet. But it was getting harder and harder to walk. There was an enormous effort in pulling my feet out of each hole as I walked. I tried increasing my pace, but with little effect. It was just too hard.

I looked up, wildly, searching for something other than this ground. My pace was getting so slow that I did not think I could go on. I had to stop. I pulled out one leg and plunked it down in front of me. Then the other. It was like wading through three feet of snow. There was no way to continue this.

I wanted to grab the sun band. I reached for it, crazily, as though it would be there for me to hang from. Nothing. My hands grasped only air. I was sinking to my waist. Nothing for it now. I could not pull myself out. I stretched out my hands to attempt to keep myself on the surface. I felt worms at my legs. And then my feet in empty air. I had fallen through the earth. I sunk even more.

My legs were kicking at air. As far as I could tell, the dirt ended at about my knees. This ground, this surface, was no more than a thin skin of material, perhaps three or four feet deep. Now, should I push myself through to the other side? Or should I attempt to remain on this side?

It appeared that circumstances were pushing me to the other side. I was sinking, after all, and would continue to sink. I remembered Ralph's belief that this world would do nothing to harm us. So far, that was mostly true, except it was not really doing anything to make us prosper, either. And what about the other side of this? Maybe it was a different world and maybe it was not so benign.

The wind was pulling me. The air on the other side was grabbing my feet and legs and thrashing them around. Wait. No it wasn't. I was thrashing myself around, unsure how to find purchase in the strange world on the other side.

On the other side. So odd to use that phrase in my mind like it was familiar to me and like I knew what the other side was. Another flip about to happen?

The moss as at my neck. I looked across an expanse of it. My footprints were little blurs going off to infinity. And now the biggest footprint of all awaited me. I had punched through and was about to fall. I said farewell to all I knew. Green ground, gray sky. The moss was up to my chin.

I pulled my arms in close to my chest, held my breath, and pushed myself down. It was unexpectedly difficult, like swimming through molasses. The ground had its own rate of descent, it appeared, and I could not do much to increase the rate. So I continued to hold my breath. Dirt scraped over my skin. Worms tickled my face and arms. They seemed almost affectionate.

Dimwits, I thought. Your only relationship to me is that I eat you. How can you feel any kind of kinship with me? How can you want to make me feel good?

My lungs started hurting. I really needed to grab some air. Panic was beginning to set in. I moved my attention to the other side. My legs were completely free now. They were kicking at nothing. Air swirled around them. I saw that the rush of wind was not so strong as I had first imagined, although it seemed clear to me that the movement of air was what I was hearing earlier when I had my ear to the ground.

I really needed to breathe. I could not last much longer and was starting to consider the consequences of gulping in mouthfuls of dirt. It would be a strange way to die. To the say the least. Drowning in dirt. But then the world asserted its benign agenda again and I pushed all the way through to the windward side of the flip.

A current of air caught me and pulled me away from the hole through which I had just emerged. The ground on the other side of the moss was a more varied landscape. There were hills, and trees, some rocks. The hole through which I had just come was in a depression, a small valley, it seemed.

Since the other side was completely smooth, it must be that I had stumbled upon a soft spot. And a thin one, which allowed me to go through the membrane to the other side. This side. I was still in air. Flying, as it were. Sort of. I tried to control my direction by tilting the angle of my hands but it didn't do much.

From earthbound to airbound. All in the space of a couple of minutes. The air felt good. Cool and refreshing. This was perhaps going to be another benign world. Or benign incarnation of the flip. I wasn't sure which, but was sure I would find out soon enough.

The landscape was charming. Very beautiful and lush. It was just the sort of place I would like to walk on. It was mostly green, but not the uniform green of the other mossy side. It had shades. There were sections where the trees were thick, others where meadow land reigned and others where there was a pleasant mix.

I was sure there had to be water somewhere down there. How else could trees grow? More to the point, how could I get down there to find out?

The wind had me. I was no more than a leaf floating on the current. It was not unpleasant by any means. In fact, it had a certain luxurious comfort I had not experienced in any other situation. It was as though I was cradled in softness. I was not even panicked by the thought that the wind could throw me down to the landscape below if it so chose. I was convinced it would never chose to do that.

Where was Ralph with his crazy ideas of benign worlds? He would like this. He would revel in this. I must learn to be like Ralph, at least a little. What would Ralph do in a case like this? He would sleep.

I closed my eyes. Time passed. I opened my eyes.

The world was dark. I was still airborne. I waved my arms around in he void, trying to get some purchase on the wind. Why didn't I sprout wings instead of a stupid useless horn on my forehead? No point in getting mad about that.

One thing: it was a bit chilly. Not freezing, but definitely on the cooler side of comfortable. I felt no wind and recalled that balloon riders also felt no wind because they were carried on the current. There was nothing blowing against them. A fair thought. Go with the flow. Fine. I've learned that lesson. I was going with the flow. Could we please go on to something different, now? Something new.

Sylvia had mentioned *Alice in Wonderland* earlier. I never read the book, but I knew enough about it to know she was right. This was very much like that. Fantastic events with me going along for the ride. It turned out that it was all a dream. Is that what was going on here? Was I dreaming? No. I would not allow that to happen. That was just a cheap way out of my dilemma. It allowed me to not do anything. I had to do something. There had to be a way to get down to the ground.

Maybe a sail? I took off my shirt and held it in the air. The wind grabbed at it. Did it change my course? I could not tell in the darkness. I also could not tell if I was going anywhere because I could not see. Where was the ground? Above me? Below me?

"Hey Terry, is that you?"

It took me a while to realize those words were not coming from my own mouth or brain. I mentally swam through a thick fog of jumbled thoughts. I reassembled my life in a few seconds, and everything seemed normal again, for a short time. A very short time. "Penelope?" I said.

"Yeah," said Penelope. She was close by, but I could not tell how close.

"How long have you been here?" I said.

"Not sure," said Penelope. "A few days."

"Where are the others?"

"Don't know."

"You have any idea what's going on?"

"I wish I did," I said. "Did you ever find Grant?"

"No. I was getting close to something and then the world just—I don't know—exploded or something. Everything smoothed out and there was nothing. Except moss and worms."

"Yeah," I said. "And dirt. I ate some of the worms. Now I'm thinking I probably didn't have to."

"I ate the worms too," said Penelope. "Then I fell through into here."

I wondered if this was the way of things in the flip. "When Alice ate the cakes and everything changed," I said.

"Who's Alice?" said Penelope. "Where's cake?"

"It's from the book. *Alice in Wonderland*," I said.

Penelope groaned. "You eggheads are always on about something that doesn't matter. Who cares what happened in some book?"

She had a point. "You have a point," I said.

"What we need to do is get down to the ground. And or find the others."

"Why?" I said.

"Why what?"

"Finding the others won't help us. They are probably just as helpless as we are and just as clued out as to what's going on. And what's so great about the ground? I thought I should get down there too, but why? What are we going to find on the ground?"

"Am I going to have to hit you?" said Penelope. "Use your brain. On the ground we can maybe find food and water. If we find the others we may be able to get back to where we were. It took all of us working together with those stupid spoons to get us here. It may take us all to get back."

"Grant died," I said. "Remember? We can't all get back together."

"We don't know that Grant died. And anyway, even if he did, maybe here he's still alive."

"I need to get some sleep."

I felt an impact of something hard on my chin. It stung pretty good. "Hey," I said.

"What did I get?" said Penelope. "I was trying for your face."

"You hit my jaw," I said. "Left a scrape too, I think. Don't you cut your fingernails?"

"Sorry," said Penelope. She hit me again. This time on the cheek with a good strong force. It must have been her open palm.

"Hey," I said. "Stop that. What are you hitting me for?"

"You need it. How have you tried to direct your course of action here?"

I rubbed my face. It still stung. "I tried using my shirt to catch the wind."

"Not bad. Maybe you're not as lame as I thought."

"It's too dark, though," I said. "There's no way to tell which direction we're going in. No reference for up or down. Or anything."

"Come on," she said. "It's not as dark as you think." She took my arm and turned my head to some place she wanted it to go. "See?" she said.

"What?" I said.

"There's some light down there."

I tried to see what she was talking about.

"It'll take a minute," she said.

I sighed and kept looking. I saw only darkness for a few seconds. Then my eyes adjusted. "Oh," I said. "There's outlines of light. Is that what you're talking about?"

"I think those are lakes," she said. "And the outlines are some kind bioluminescent plant that is visible at the shore."

"Or bioluminescent creatures," I said, "that live at the shore."

"In either case," said Penelope, "they have to be outlines of lakes. And that means they have to be down on the ground. That's were we need to go."

We had a plan. Keep our eyes on the prize—the lakes—and we could get ourselves closer to the ground. "We don't want to end up in one of the lakes, though, do we?" I said.

"Probably not," said Penelope. "But who knows? Maybe that's the way back."

That didn't sound right to me. "We don't want to drown," I said.

"Okay," said Penelope. "Fine. We'll avoid the lakes."

She sounded annoyed with me. "You know," I said, "it wasn't me that got us here. It just happened."

"All I know," she said, "is that you had us digging in the ground *with plastic spoons* no less, and then we flipped or flopped or twisted or spun. Or some damn thing. And here we are."

"Yeah, but I had no idea this would happen. It's not my fault. It's just simply not my fault."

"I'll tell you one thing," said Penelope. "If we ever get out of this and back to normal, the first thing I'm going to do is quite the institute."

"I can understand that," I said.

"That's the *first* thing. Then I'm going to sue you, the administration, and anyone involved in hiring you, and the whole institute. There."

"Why would you sue me? Why would you sue anyone? It's an *accident*. No one expected any of this to happen."

"Maybe not, but there should have been guidelines and precautions in place."

"For a fundamental change in the fabric of reality? Something no one was even working on, let alone thought could be a possibility?"

"Are you insane?" said Penelope. "Of course people were working on it. The institute works on everything. There are people trying to develop telepathy.

There are people figuring out faster than light travel. Don't tell me you don't know about these things. Don't you ever talk to anyone else?"

"No," I said. "I mean, yes, I talk to people. We mostly try to figure out how to get more food and medicine produced and distributed. That sort of thing."

Penelope laughed. "I don't believe this," she said. "I don't believe how you can all be so smart and so stupid at the same time. Find Ralph. He'll tell you. He knows a lot more than you think. The institute is always looking to recruit people who can help us all become super human. That's what the institute is really about. They're trying to create the next step in human evolution."

"Ridiculous," I said.

"Oh? Remember that paper you all read, the one by Fletcher?"

"Sure," I said. I debated momentarily the possibility of telling her Fletcher was here in the flip. I decided another time would be best.

"There was a lot more to it than just the idea that at a certain complexity of endeavor, deaths are inevitable."

"I remember," I said. "He also went into detail about the possibility of death being the first step to something different, but he never really explained that very well. It was the weakest part of the paper."

"Sure, it was weak, but that's not the point. Ralph was recruiting him for the institute. Ralph wanted him to be a part of this big project. The institute was going to announce it to the press in a couple of weeks, if Fletcher decided to join us and there was no reason he wouldn't. At least that's what Ralph thought."

I didn't hear a lot after she said "big project." There was a major initiative at the institute and not only was I not considered as a participant, but I didn't even know about it? So Fletcher wasn't telling me the whole story of why he was visiting the institute. And Ralph was very slick. Keeping it all to himself.

"You're saying Ralph wanted Fletcher. They were going to create trans-humans. Or something."

"Exactly. And they were going to harness the power of the mind or some such crap. I don't know. What I'm saying is that the initiative must have gotten away from them. Something happened and now we're here."

"Wherever here is. You're saying that the institute did something to reality?"

"Yes! What else could have happened?"

"I don't know."

"You don't know. You don't know. Of course you don't know. I know you don't know. What I want you to do is apply that elevated freaking IQ of yours and figure something out."

It was a fair request, but I didn't know if I had the wit to attempt it. Was this a good time to tell her about Fletcher?

"Shouldn't we keep trying to get to the ground?" I said.

She grabbed my hand. Her grip was strong. I impulsively cringed from her, then sensed there was desperation behind the grasp and tightened my grasp in response. I heard a long sigh come from her lungs. "You've got to do something about this," she said. "All of you have to."

"I'm trying to figure it out," I said. "It's not easy."

"I know."

"Maybe we should try to reconstruct the sequence."

"We dug with spoons and the universe upended itself."

"Okay," I said. "We got that. What happened when you started walking? Did you see anything unusual?" I was prepared for another off-the-cuff response, but none came. She appeared to be thinking. A long silence ensued.

"Damnation," she said. "Son of a fucking bitch."

"You remember something?" I asked mildly.

"I passed a strange guy."

"Strange?"

"He was kind of dressed weird. Had too colorful clothes. He was trying to be business-like, but he had just a little too much of the rebel in him to fit in, if you know what I mean."

"I think so," I said. "You ran into him."

"Well, walked by each other. He was eyeing me. Like he wanted to asked me out or something."

I couldn't help letting out a small laugh.

"What's so funny?"

"I don't see how you could tell that in a couple of seconds."

"Never been a woman, have you?"

"Okay okay," I said. "He was interested in you."

"Yeah. And I usually don't respond to that sort of thing. Only gets you in trouble, you know? But as he went by, I turned around and looked at him. He didn't even try to hide the fact that he was looking at me."

"Okay, Pen," I said. "I got that he thought you were attractive."

"No, it wasn't quite that," she said. "It wasn't so much that I was attractive as that he thought there was something more to me. I can't explain it, but he wasn't a normal guy."

"What did he look like?"

"He was tall, thin. Had curly hair. There was an air about him, as if he thought he was impressive."

"I know who that was," I said.

"Who?"

"The guy who wrote the article. Fletcher."

"How do you know?"

"Because I met him after the flip. He was coming to the institute."

"Ha!" said Penelope. "I knew it. He was coming to check us out, wasn't he?"

"He wanted to be part of the institute."

"I think he essentially already was. He was doing mind experiments and the flip is the result."

"That's wild speculation," I said. "No basis in fact."

"Hey," said Penelope. "You have a horn growing out of your forehead."

"Yeah," I said. The darkness was lightening. Or else our eyes were getting used to conditions and we were able to see better in the dimness. I noticed Penelope had some odd looking protuberances at her temples. "Hey," I said. "You've got horns too."

"Yup," said Penelope. "How about that. I think Fletcher has a thing for horns."

"Now you're saying the horns are his doing as well."

"When that paper came out and all you eggheads were poring over it, did any of you think to investigate Fletcher? Try to find out anything at all about him?"

"Well sure," I said.

"What did you discover?"

"He was a typical nerd. Graduated top in his class. Studied esoteric subjects like trans-dimensional math, stuff I couldn't understand if I spent years on it. Also was a pretty good tennis player. Never married. No family to speak of. Wrote popular articles under pen names as well. Did a book on flatlands."

"Flatlands?" said Penelope.

"Imaginary universes with only two dimensions. There's a kind of cult literature on the topic. There have been a few novels on it. He did an anthology of stories by various authors, each one set in a flatland universe."

"Go on."

"There's not much else to it. These were things he did in his spare time, for recreation. He was mostly a theoretical mathematician. He worked for various universities, but hated teaching, so looked for work in industry. He was employed as a government statistician, worked for a few insurance companies, and so one. He either quit, or was fired from them all because he couldn't keep his mind on the task at hand. He was always going off in wild tangents."

"Like that famous paper."

"That paper got him into a lot of hot water. Insurance companies don't want to be told that certain activities inevitably involve deaths. They want to think they can optimize all of that out of existence."

"Sure," said Penelope. "No deaths means no pay outs, means more profits for them."

"Right, so to have one of their own employees write a paper that says their belief system is invalid, well, they aren't going to want to keep him on the payroll."

"So he comes to us."

"We have a reputation for freedom and welcoming alternate points of view."

"Which is what got us into trouble."

The light was all around us now. Morning coming? I looked down at the ground. It was as inviting as ever. Green and cool. The lakes were the bluest blue imaginable. I wanted to be down there. I did not feel comfortable hanging in the air like this. I pushed against the air, trying to swim down to the surface.

"Why are we weightless," said Penelope. "Have you thought about that?"

"We're in the flip," I said. "There is no reason."

"There's always reason," said Penelope. "Figure it out."

I continued to push air. It was as if I was in a very thin soup, like the air was escaping and there was nothing left. I couldn't see that I was making any headway. The land seemed just as far away.

"What's the use of all those brains if you can't use them when you need to?" she said.

"I don't know," I said, still swimming.

"You aren't going anywhere," he said.

"You have a better idea?" I said.

"No," she said. "That's not what they pay me for. You're supposed to have all the ideas."

She had a point, but I didn't know what to do about it. My time at the institute had been fun and kind of crazy. I was supposed to generate ideas for evaluation, but that was never what I was really good at. I liked to lighten things up, get everyone involved in crazy activities. I was the clown of the operation. The trickster? Maybe. Every institution needs someone like that. A pot stirrer. A way to break the complacency that inevitably stagnates everything we do. I thought Penelope understood that, but she didn't. Was it time for me to explain it to her.

"You still thirsty?" I said.

"Of course I'm thirsty," she said.

"I thought about drinking my urine."

"If I had any, I might think about it too."

"The thing is," she said, "even though we are thirsty, I don't feel like I'm shutting down. That's the most important thing I've figured out about this place. It's safe. It won't harm us."

Penelope shook her head. "You're delirious," she said. "It's like you are stuck in some endless loop where you cover the same ground over and over again. Listen up. We are not in a normal situation. We have to understand our—" She stopped. "Oh, oh."

"What?"

"Don't you feel it?" She screamed.

Then I felt it too. A pressure on top of me. It was like a giant hand pushed down on me. I began falling. It was not a gentle falling, either. More like a violent push to the surface below us.

We grabbed air, panic gripping us both. I yelled something incoherent. Can't remember what it was. Just a nonsense syllable, long and drawn out.

It was fine to hang in the air and float around for a while, but this was not right. We could not survive this. Penelope screamed too. A piercing screech brought up from the bottom of her lungs and flung out at the world.

We were both drifting down, although she was further along the path than I was. There was a wind now. The air was kicking up around us. We were no longer drifting on the currents like leaves. We were no longer just what we thought we were. We were bodies. Physical beings with weight and substance, enough substance that it could kill us when we landed. If we landed.

I curled myself up into a ball to fall faster. I yelled at Penelope to spread herself out. She did so. I don't know why I wanted to catch her. I wouldn't be able to help her, or her to help me. It was a comfort thing. If I was going to die, then I wanted to be with someone else, anyone else would do, but it was also nice to have someone who I knew and who was a co-worker. Not to mention she had horns, like I had a horn. That made us more than just friends, I figured. It made us relatives of a kind. It was the universe's way of saying that we were cut from the same cloth. Penelope did as I asked.

"I'm scared," she said.

Our speed was increasing. We were tumbling toward the ground. "I'm scared too," I said. "Don't worry about it. Being scared is not a bad thing. Being scared won't kill you."

"I know that, idiot," said Penelope. "The fall will kill us."

Yup. She knew what was going on. I stretched my hand as far as it would go. We were so close. Inches apart. If I could just get close enough to touch her. That's all I wanted, just to touch her. It would mean so much. Even if it was not my final living act. Even if it *was* my final living act. It would be enough just to grasp her hand in mine.

The wind twisted her. Her hand moved away from me. "Ohhhhhhhh," she said, her voice rising.

Her head swung near my hand. Suddenly, her horn was next to my palm. I closed my hand around it. It was slippery. I let go for an instant, then redoubled my effort and dug my nails into her horn.

That was enough. I was able to pull her close. I reached past her neck to her collar, grabbed it, and pulled her closer. In a second she was right up next to me. She grabbed me. I grabbed her. We were in a full body hug. I understood the need for human contact at that moment as I had never understood it before. Now it almost did not matter that our speed was steadily increasing.

I tried to do a quick calculation in my head. We were probably going about 5 miles per hour. The surface, although difficult to gauge, appeared to be about a mile down. How much speed does one gain in that time? I didn't know. Especially, since I didn't know the force of gravity in the flip. It might be the same as Earth's but it might not. Everything was fluid here.

"Are we going to die?" said Penelope.

"This place is benign," I said. "I still believe that. I think."

"Sorry I called you an idiot."

"Don't worry about it," I said.

"You're not an idiot."

"Thanks."

"Just kind of dimwitted about stuff."

"Oh."

"But that's nothing. Everyone is dimwitted about something. Everyone."

"There's a possibility we might not die on impact" I said. "We could just escape with no injuries at all."

"That would be nice."

"What's more problematic is the middle case. We don't die, but we are severely injured. Are you ready for that?"

She shook her head. "What do you mean."

"Well, suppose one of us breaks a back and the other one doesn't."

"Yeah. So?"

"Will the uninjured person try to save the injured person?"

"Is this one of your crazy scenarios?" she said.

"It's more or less the lifeboat problem."

"Ah. Of course."

"How much do you help another person when your own life is in jeopardy. If the lifeboat is filled to capacity, do you risk pulling up another person from the water who is in trouble, when doing so might put everyone in the lifeboat in danger?"

"So people really pay you to think about this crap?"

"They did," I said. "Before the flip."

We were falling even faster now. The ground was looming up like a carpet one might see as one looks under a couch for some lost item. It had texture and it looked lethal.

"I think it's just a few seconds now," I said.

"I'm not ready for this," said Penelope. "I'm not ready to die. I'm not ready."

I wanted to keep my eyes open. I thought we were probably travelling about twenty or twenty-five miles per hour by this time. More than enough to kill us. I thought maybe it was better this way. The middle ground was just too difficult and messy. The ground rose up. We zipped past a tree top. Penelope grabbed me tighter. We impacted on a slope covered in the softest material imaginable. Fluffy leaves was the only way to describe it.

Penelope let out a long ahhhhh of sound. We separated and began rolling down the leaves. Tree trunks loomed beside us. We were lucky enough not to hit any as we continued to tumble down. *This place is benign.* The slope gradually flattened out. We rolled to a stop.

In another situation, the whole ride would have seemed like the most fun anyone could imagine. Here it was just a relief that we weren't in any way shape or form that I could discern, dead. Trees loomed above us. Forest sounds surrounded us as well: birds, leaves rustling, small feet on tree bark: squirrels or chipmunks I was sure.

"Penelope?" I said.

She laughed. "That was a kick," she said.

"Are you okay?"

"Oh yeah," she said. "How about you?"

"No injuries that I can see."

"Oh," she said. "Not quite all okay. One of my horns broke off."

I sat up and looked toward where her voice was coming from. I crawled through the leaves toward her. "Is there blood?" I said. "Mine has blood on the inside."

"No blood," said Penelope. She had her legs tucked under her and was sitting up. She had some bruises visible on her face. One of her horns was cut cleanly off, a smooth stub showing and the angle of the cut was fashionably off to one side. "How on Earth do you know your horn has blood?" she said.

"I tried cutting it off."

"Why?"

"I hated it. It was heavy and in my way. I thought it might cause injury or neck pain or something."

"But trying to cut it off. Man."

"I know. It was not such a smart thing to do, I think."

She looked at the base of my horn. "I see where it healed or something. What did you use?"

"A key."

"Must have been some work to get through that."

"Yeah," I said. "It healed itself. Somehow. But let's look at you. You must have hit your head on the ground or something."

"I hit a tree trunk as I rolled to a stop," she said.

"Ouch," I said.

Penelope shrugged. "Maybe the horn saved me from injury by absorbing the force of the impact.

"Maybe." I moved closer to her and examined the break more carefully. There was no blood or any other fluid that I could discern. "You sure there's nothing else? No pain anywhere? No broken bones?"

"Nope," said Penelope. "I'm fine. Are you trying to find an excuse to get next to me?"

I didn't let her remark change my demeanor. "Come on, Pen," I said. "This is serious. The horn could have fractured your skull as it broke off."

"Stop worrying about me, will you? I already checked around the base. There's no swelling and nothing feels broken. Gives me half an idea to break off the other one. Anyway, we lived! Who cares about anything else?"

"There's wildlife here," I said.

"Yeah, so?"

"There could be large animals, then. Carnivores. Maybe hungry ones."

"Don't be ridiculous," said Penelope. "They won't want to eat us."

"How do you know?"

"Because we aren't from here. They wouldn't recognize us as food."

That seemed to make sense, but I wasn't sure. Didn't carnivores just go for motion? If it moved like an animal, didn't they have the inclination to eat it? Penelope got up on her feet and began dusting herself off. "Oops," she said. She leaned over to one side.

"What?"

"My foot. I think I sprained it." She could not put her foot onto the ground.

"Let me see." She sat down, took off her shoe and pulled off her sock. I didn't see any swelling. "Can you walk on it?"

"No," she said. "That's why I said 'Oops.'"

"Can you limp on it?"

She laughed. "Think so," she said. "There's a little pain, but nothing terrible."

"It could get worse if you walk on it."

"But we have to escape the hungry tigers and bears, don't we?"

"I know it sounds kind of funny," I said. "But yes, we might have to do that, and sooner rather than later."

"Let's just get to one of the lakes," she said.

"How do we do that?"

"Shhhh," she said. "Just listen."

I held still and did as she asked. She put her cupped hands up to the sides of her head so they curled around her ears and slowly turned around. She stopped. "There," she said.

"What?"

"Make deer ears." I put my hands like she had hers and stood facing the same direction she was facing. "Do you hear it?" she said.

"Sounds like water?"

"A creek or stream. We find that and follow it, we'll get to a lake. Come on."

We waded through the leaves. I was not much of a country boy. She saw it immediately. "You never been in the woods before?" she said.

"We don't have woods like this in Tucson."

"Sure we do. Well, maybe not in Tucson, but up in the mountains there are some. And anyway, you haven't lived in Tucson your whole life. Never been camping? Never walked trails?"

"Not my thing," I said. "Much more of a city boy."

"Well, city boy, you won't find any coffee shops or fancy shopping boutiques here."

"No, I figured that out."

We continued on. The trees around us were tall, much taller than any trees I had ever seen. Or read about. They seemed so tall that they did not even fit into the landscape. It was as though they were from some other place and had been planted here by mistake. Or as a joke.

I reached out to them as we passed by. It felt good to touch their barks, rough and dry. Why would creation come up with such water hogs? I wondered. With these beasts around, there couldn't be much water left for anything else in environments like this.

"They sure do shed a lot of leaves," I said.

"It's what makes the forest so healthy," said Penelope. "Everything uses the leaves. It promotes future growth."

"So we can have even more giant trees."

She glanced behind herself and fixed me a stare. "You got something against trees?" she said.

"They just seem out of place. I've always thought so."

She didn't say anything, but I could feel her contempt for my point of view. We kept going. Periodically she would stop and make her deer ears and adjust our path. Soon we didn't need the deer ears to hear the water. The sound was getting strong. The trees were not so tall, now.

"Trees are not out of place," she said, long after I had indicated that I held a differing opinion. "They provide shade, oxygen, shelter, mulch. And that's only part of it."

"Okay," I said. "You like trees and I don't. It's no big deal."

"It's not a matter of liking or disliking. It's all about what makes for a healthy ecosystem."

"But we aren't in a healthy ecosystem," I said. "We don't even know where we are. For all we know trees are weeds. Giant water sucking weeds."

She snickered. "Trees are not weeds," she said. "Honestly, I don't know where you get your ideas."

She argued differently than when we eggheads got together. We usually deferred to each other's opinions, testing out hypothesis and not dismissing anything out of hand. I was willing to allow her idea to be presented, but she was not willing to allow mine. Now how was that contributing to a consensus or even a lively discussion?

It was more like we were each presenting our stubborn preconceived notions and telling each other that the other one was wrong. I didn't like that. I especially didn't like that I fell into the pattern so readily. Didn't my time at the institute tell me anything about how to steer a conversation or debate? Apparently not. It was as though I had never had a true discussion. I was ready to bicker and name call just like Penelope was.

We kept walking. Penelope was much slower than me. She had found a rhythm that seemed to work for her. Step, hobble, step, hobble. We stopped frequently to rest.

The water sounded like a falls. I imagined it falling over rocks. The trees were almost completely gone now. We were in a meadow. We stopped to look around.

The grass was regular grass, just like I remembered on Earth before the flip. There were insects flying about. I heard crows in the air. We stood on the edge of the meadow, with the forest at our backs, and just took in the ambiance.

"Wow," said Penelope. "This is kind of nice."

"Yeah," I said. "It could convert me to country living."

"Get a cabin in the woods?" said Penelope. "Hunt game and grow your own food?"

"Something like that."

"We may still have to."

"I'll be Adam to your Eve."

"Don't get ahead of yourself," she said.

"Shall we go investigate the creek?" I said.

We crossed the meadow. The creek did indeed flow over many rocks. The water looked clear and clean. The shore looked walkable, at least for a little while. We stood on the bank, just taking in the feel of the water cooling the air and filling the space around us with spray.

"I'm tired," said Penelope.

"Me too," I said.

"You think there's any fish in that water?" she said. "I'm kind of hungry, too."

"If there are fish in there, then we need to be extra careful."

"Oh yeah," she said. "Bears, right?"

"Well, yeah."

"And wolves, and cougars, and coyotes, and so on and so on."

"Why do you make fun of my wish to be safe from predators?"

"I'm not making fun. It's more that I'm— Okay. I *am* making fun. But you make it so easy to make fun."

"Glad to be of service."

She sat down on the ground and stretched out the leg with the injured foot. "This looks like a good place to rest for a while." She put her hand up to her broken horn. It was a gesture that she seemed to instantly regret, as though she was doing something very private. I looked away, not even knowing why. "Can we just stay here for a while?" she said. "Maybe sleep a little."

"Sounds like a good idea," I said.

She put her head down on the ground. "I like to sleep on my side," she said, "but these horns make it difficult. Especially the intact one. Can you break it off for me?"

I recalled my efforts to remove my unicorn horn. I was glad I didn't go through with that. "I don't know, Pen. I'm still afraid I'd do you some damage."

"The tree broke it off and nothing happened to me. What are you so afraid of?"

"We don't even know why we have these horns. It could have something to do with the flip. It could be something that we need to hang on to."

"You tried getting rid of yours."

"Yeah, but I think that was a mistake. When in Rome, you know. The flip gave us horns."

"I could try breaking if off myself," she said.

"Sure," I said carefully, not wanting to make it seem as though I was telling her what to do.

"But you wouldn't recommend it, right?"

I hesitated. Then: "Right."

"And you wouldn't help me do it, either."

"Right."

"You are easy to read, Terry."

"I've never denied it."

"What I had in mind was to knock it against one of the rocks. A good sharp smack should snap it right off."

"Maybe," I said. "You could also miss and smash her head into the rock and give yourself a concussion."

"Buzz kill," she said. "I knew you were going to say something like that. That's why I want *you* to break it off."

"Don't ask me that," I said. "I just don't feel comfortable doing that."

The air was getting dark again. Night falling. This side of the flip had a much more regular feel to it. It was as though we were in normal country. I could easily imagine that we were on an outing just outside of town. It was not only normal, but comforting. I felt myself relaxing, despite my fears about carnivorous beasts. Over that way yonder, I imagined, was the city and the institute. It was all just so darned *normal*. All except for the unfamiliar appendages growing out of our skulls.

"Okay, then," said Penelope. "We'll see about that in the morning, after I've been tossing and turning all night." She adjusted herself against the grass and closed her eyes.

"Right," I said. "I'll take first watch."

"What?" she said.

"I'll take the first shift of watching over us. Then you can take the next shift."

"Are you crazy? This isn't a cowboys and Indians movie. Get some sleep."

I sighed. "It's not cowboys and Indians. It's that we are sitting ducks for predators."

She laughed and shook her head.

"Why do you pooh pooh that idea?"

"Because, even if you saw a bear or cougar or whatever, what exactly would you do about it? We have no weapons. They can outrun us. If they wanted to eat us, they could eat us. We may as well just get some sleep."

She made sense, but it still felt wrong to simply ignore the threat. Also, knowing the threat was there would not help in making sleep a possibility. "I'd feel better if we kept watch."

"Fine," she said. "You keep watch if you want. I plan to sleep, so don't wake me up because I am *not* going to keep watch."

That seemed definitive. She turned away from me and huddled down for some sleep. I didn't argue with her anymore. The truth was, I didn't even think we needed sleep. I could have slept as well, kind of craved it even, but I didn't think it was something we needed for our well being or our general health. I was certain that sleep was simply a habit now. Maybe it had always been that. Maybe people didn't really need sleep at all.

I strolled over to the creek shore. There was no moon in the sky. That meant it had not risen yet, or that there was no moon because this wasn't earth. Just some odd place conjured from the mind of Fletcher, as Penelope seemed to think, or a place meant for amusement. Maybe it was none of those things. It could have been just the place we were all meant to be. The afterlife. Was this heaven? Or hell? No. I didn't believe in either of those things. But just because I didn't believe in them, didn't mean they didn't exist.

I walked along the creek bank. Took small steps to enjoy the time I had there. I glanced back at Penelope. I had this niggling notion that I probably shouldn't leave her alone because then she might disappear. Did that make sense? Everyone else disappeared after they were out of my sight. But perhaps the two weren't connected. It could have been that they were going to disappear anyway and that was why they left my sight. None of this seemed to change the fact that being on the bank here, listening to the water, was the most relaxed I had been in a long time.

I looked across the creek, wanting to see something there. I thought I saw some small motion. The hairs on my back and neck flared. Could the carnivores already be here?

I suppressed an urge to call out. Instead I held very still and kept watching.

There was motion on the other side. No doubt about it. I saw shadows moving along the shore. At least two or three of them. In the darkness it was impossible to tell what shape they were. Indistinct blobs of fuzziness, nothing else.

I tried to gauge the wind, having some vague notion that being upwind from them would probably make me at least a little safer. But the wind didn't seem that strong. It swirled around. Impossible to tell a direction from it, because it seemed to come from *all* directions.

I took small steps back the way I had come, still keeping an eye on the moving shadows. They kept moving as well, but in a steady walk, nothing hesitant about them. I got back to the spot near Penelope. She looked odd on the ground. I put my hand on her shoulder, then instantly pulled it back. She was as soft as a pillow.

Cold dread instantly gripped me. I realized I had been too complacent, thinking this was a perfectly normal section of the flip. There was nothing normal in the flip. I had to get that in my brain and keep it there.

Penelope was sinking into the ground. Was becoming part of the ground. I tried to rouse her. I shook her and whispered her name as loudly as I dared, not wanting to draw attention from whatever was on the other side of the creek.

But Penelope was sinking fast. She was being consumed by the ground here. The ground here was the predator.

"Penelope, Penelope," I said. "Wake up." Nothing. She was out like a light, had about as much consciousness as a rock. This is what comes from wanting to sleep. I vowed not to sleep anymore as long as I was in the flip.

It was dark, but not completely. I saw enough to see that Penelope was already more than half submerged in the ground. I tried pulling on her by lifting an arm. It did not good. Whatever was pulling her down was much stronger than me. I held on as long as I could, but she just went deeper and deeper into the soil.

Before long she was no longer visible. There was nothing but an outline of her body in the grass, and a depression where she had been laying.

So I was alone in the flip again. This was getting to be a habit. I stood and looked around, alert for moving shadows. Across the creek I didn't see them anymore. Should I now wait by Penelope's depression, or should I continue to the lake, as we had thought earlier? If the others were here, then they might congregate at the lake as well. It seemed a natural place to want to be.

"Hey." A familiar voice. "Terry? Is that you?" Sylvia.

I looked across the creek again. Only shadows were visible. "Sylvia?"

"Oh, Terry. Thank goodness. We thought you were dead."

"Sylvia, it's great to hear your voice. Who else is there?"

"Ralph and Naomi."

"Hi," said Ralph. "How long you been here?"

"Not long," I said. "We fell through from the other side, the mossy side."

"Who's we?" said Sylvia. "Have you seen Grant?"

"No," I said. "I thought maybe you had Grant with you."

"No," said Sylvia.

"That's too bad. I also lost Penelope. She was here with me, but she, ah, melted. Into the ground."

"So you're alone now," said Ralph.

"Yeah," I said.

"You have to be careful about that," said Ralph. "The melting into the ground part. We lost Fletcher that way."

"You had Fletcher?" I said. "I found him on the other side."

"We found him here. I'm sorry we lost him. He was a good ally."

"We're on our way to the lake," said Sylvia. "Want to join us?"

"Yeah!" I started walking toward them.

"Whatever you do, though," said Ralph. "Don't wade into the creek."

I was two steps away from the water.

"Don't tell me," I said. "It's acidic or something?"

"Well, I don't know about acidic, but it's not something you want to get into. It's not water. Or, at least, it's a different kind of water. It turns you green."

"Who cares," I said. "Anything else?"

"There's creatures in it. They're like the worms on the other side. You found those right?"

"Yeah," I said.

"Well," said Sylvia, "these creatures in the water, they are like the next step in development of those worms, I think. Or the previous step. Who knows for sure? They have teeth and they bite. They like to hang onto you."

"Oh boy," I said. "Anything else?"

"We have these strange growths on us," said Ralph. "You too?"

"I have a horn on my forehead. Penelope had horns coming out of the sides of her head."

"Yup," said Sylvia. "Us too. It appears to be a male female thing as to the type and location of horns."

"This is one weird ass place we've ended up in," I said. "Do you know what happened to Penelope? I mean, the melting into the ground thing, what's that all about?"

"She's gone on to the next stage," said Sylvia. "We're all going to go on eventually. We're just waiting."

"For what?"

"That's just it," said Ralph. "We don't know. We both have this feeling that we don't want to go on yet. But as soon as you fall asleep, it'll happen. So if you aren't ready, don't sleep."

"Fine," I said. "How do we get in contact with each other? I don't want to shout across this creek for the rest of my life."

"Just keep walking," said Sylvia. "We'll walk too. The lake is about a mile or two away. We've got a lean-to and some furniture. A couple of chairs and such. We've just been relaxing for the last couple of days. Trying to figure things out."

A lean-to seemed like the ultimate in luxury. "Looks like I ended up in just the right place," I said.

"Okay," said Sylvia. "Just keep walking. Downstream of course."

"Of course," I said. I stepped along the shore, being very careful to stay away from the water. Didn't want any of those toothed worms on me.

A thought occurred to me. "Say," I said. "You two aren't like a couple now, are you?"

Sylvia laughed. "Whatever gave you that idea."

"I don't know," I said. "You seem pretty chummy, and you have that lean-to and all. It's like an Adam and Eve set up."

"Believe me," said Ralph, "this is no garden of Eden or anything."

"But you're staying. You aren't ready for the next step."

"We just need a rest," said Sylvia. "It is kind of nice here. At least we recognize the landscape."

We walked in silence for a few minutes. I heard their footsteps across the creek. The creek was mostly flowing over rocks. I heard the water splash against the stones. This was the kind of place that people dreamed about, that they always wanted to be in. The kind of place that said to them: this is the good life. I could see it. But it also seemed as though it could still be deadly.

"How long did you have Fletcher with you?" I asked over the sound of water on the rocks.

No answer. I asked again. Still no answer. A chill went over me, but it didn't last. Of course nothing stays here. Sylvia and Ralph were gone already. Who knew where? I tried to keep myself from being upset. They would return. Or they wouldn't. The flip had its own logic, that was already clear, and nothing was going to change that no matter what I did or didn't do.

Now I just wanted that lean-to. I kept walking. Periodically I called out to Sylvia and Ralph, and each time I got no answer in return. The path ahead looked like it was going to be tougher going. The light was returning, so it appeared that at least day followed night here. That was nice. To have something that made sense.

Now where did Sylvia and Ralph get to? Did they stop to sleep? Were they ready to take the next step already? And without telling me? That was unkind of them. Weren't we in this together? Didn't we have the responsibility to try to stick this out as a team? The bank was gone in front of me. I came to a rise in the rock. Impossible now to walk along the water.

I would have to detour away from the creek and circle around the high outcrop and try to get back to the creek. It was my guide to the comfort of a lean-to.

I scrambled over and around the slope. It got up to about fifty feet or so. A bit of a climb, but not real treacherous. There was no path, so that meant few if any people had been through here before me. I was a trailblazer. How marvelous, I thought.

But I was alone again. People kept disappearing from this place. It was very disconcerting.

I still had the sound of the creek to one side. I kept that sound as a guide and walked around the outcropping as best I could. It was disorienting in a subtle way. I had already gotten used to having the creek to my side. It was a safety blanket that I had glommed onto in no time flat. Now the hills rose to the other side. There were trees. I was already into a forest, and I thought the forest had thinned out.

But Sylvia and Ralph mentioned a lean-to. They must have used tree branches for that. The spot by the lake sounded so pleasant. I wanted to be there. I understood I could not stay there forever, especially if everyone else had already melted into the next phase, but I wanted it for just a few minutes if nothing else. Just an hour of bliss. That shouldn't be out of the question.

Except now I was hopelessly lost again. I was in trees. I could not hear the creek. I made the deer ears that Penelope had showed me. Nothing. There was an all pervasive kind of white noise humming, but nothing else.

It was all so discouraging to keep going through this displacement of expectations. And where were we going? Were we all chasing Grant? Had he blazed the trail we were following? Was this the afterlife? Grant's afterlife?

I stopped walking. The trees were so tall all around me. Suddenly I had lost the will to continue walking. I imagined some puppeteer somewhere manipulating us all into thinking we had some control over our lives, when we did not. Could not. The script was written and in place. We were following the structure of someone else's plot, someone else's dream. Or nightmare. Daydream, maybe. Notion. Brain fart. A terrible thought, to realize that we were all just so much raw material for—something. Some *thing*.

There was shade, at least, in the trees. They had wide branches and broad leaves. They swayed in the wind.

Their sound, that white noise, was soothing in a pleasant way. I did not feel as though I would have to change my opinion of that. I was always going to have this memory of this place. If it was a place.

I put that thought out of my mind. This was something. I sense, therefore I am here. Didn't Descartes say something along those lines? I'm sure of it. He would have known how to navigate these woods. He invented Cartesian coordinates, after all. Or stole it from someone else and said it was him. One or the other. You could never tell what happened in the past and then people who might have been thieves become heroes and then you can never ever come close to the truth about what really happened.

I stepped over branches. I waded through leaves. I climbed slopes. It was hopeless now to think that I could return to the creek. Wherever it was, it was nowhere I knew. I might stumble upon it again, but I could no longer hear it, and my sense of direction was completely turned around. The ground looked inviting. Just stretch out, doze off, and I'd be in the next realm, wherever and whatever that was.

However, even the thought of maybe rejoining my friends was not enough to make me take that necessary step. Even the bliss of collegiate conviviality could not induce me to let my skin actually touch the ground here.

I looked up. The trees swayed. I could imagine their language, their leaf words speaking to me. That's what this place did to you. It made you believe things that weren't normal, maybe not even possible.

I saw that some of these trees had low branches. So low that they were within reach. Was it a sign to me? The ground beneath my feet suddenly felt toxic. Heat seemed to sear my soles. No, no. I couldn't stay here. I had to go on. But even as I thought that, the trees above me were silent and cool as ghosts. They were green like my heart. They were quiet like thoughts. They were solid. Their strength was my strength. Or so I thought.

I began climbing. It was not so hard as I thought it might be. The branches were there where I needed them. I would step on one branch, swing myself up, reach higher, where another branch would be right there at my palm, which I would grab, and then pull myself higher, where another branch presented itself. And so on.

Thus I was able to quickly climb a hundred feet or so above the ground. I looked down. This was so natural, this way of looking at the world. The bird's view of things. An all encompassing way of responding to the realm.

And so I climbed. Kept climbing for hours, it seemed. Along the way I dismissed any notion that I was doing the wrong thing. Everyone else was proceeding oppositely, but not me. Did it matter? It did matter. Because I was taking myself out of the group.

As I climbed, I found evidence of past climbers. There were scratch marks in the bark. That was animal. Which made me a little nervous. But I clung to Ralph's belief. *This place is benign.* It had kept me sane up to now. As far as I could tell.

I also found bits of thread clinging to the bark. So, I was not the first clothed climber here, which probably meant I was not the first human climber here.

A little farther up, maybe at the one hundred and fifty foot level, I found a shelter. A crude tree house of sorts, made of wood and plastic pieces. Some shingles crudely tacked on. It was nailed up. It was also old. I looked through a window. It had a floor. Uneven and very crudely constructed, but a floor nevertheless.

I also saw that it was wedged into the V of two branches that met at the trunk. So it had stability. I wondered if Descartes had ever built a tree house, would be like this? It seemed to have the sturdy structure and ephemeral setting that he would have approved. It was like his Cartesian coordinates that purported to map reality but was as imaginary as any dream.

The tree house had no door. Or, rather, it might be more appropriate to say that the windows were the doors. In any case, I entered the tree house through one of the windows by putting in one leg and following with my upper body, then letting my trailing leg follow inside. I hit my unicorn horn on the frame. Thanks for the reminder. I'm not the human I once was. Got it.

I stood by the window. I felt like I was at home, or, at least, in a home. One of my homes. Did I have so many I could no longer keep track? Is it that we all used to live in caves once that makes us like these little enclosures?

If we did live in caves. I knew there were conflicting opinions about that. Nevertheless, in the popular mind we used to live in caves. We were once cavemen and women. Is it that old cave dwelling instinct what makes us want to huddle in places like this, where the walls and roof are so close and the surroundings so rudimentary? I've heard some say that. Don't know if any of it is true. Don't know if it matters.

It can feel womb-like to be in such a place, especially if it is dark. And that is the first home, isn't it? The coffin at the end, also dark and close, the last home. In between we journey here and there, but those are nothing but detours. We have our beginning and our end mapped out for us always.

So I stretched out on the floor of the tree house. It was small, but just big enough on the diagonal so I could lie down without having to bend or huddle myself.

I closed my eyes. I wasn't tired, exactly. I didn't actually *need* sleep. And yet, there seemed nothing else to be doing. A good long nap seemed like the best treat imaginable. I anticipated dreams I might have. Plotted them, actually. Many of them involved food. I wasn't hungry, either, but the mere thought of food made me realize that I was so far removed from my former life that I didn't even care about meals.

So I made myself think about them. I tried to make myself into something that would not remain complacently passive in this realm. Other dreams involved fist fights. I wanted to find Fletcher and punch him in the belly.

Then, as he doubled over, I imagined that I would then knee him in the nose. That felt good, to think of that. It would just about take care of him. He would fall over, of course. I would kick him a few times, then fall upon him and punch him repeatedly in the face and about the neck, maybe.

I had never been in a fist fight. Only seen them on TV and in the movies, where they usually seemed ridiculous. I knew, somehow, that such an encounter with Fletcher would be good for me in a manly kind of way. And this was a mode of thought I had never indulged in, so it was strange. It was the sort of thing I had not purposely imagined myself capable of in the past. As a finish to that particular dream, I saw Fletcher's face wrecked and bloody. It was all in the abstract. I was sure if I actually saw Fletcher, or anyone, with a pulped face I would most likely be sick. But in the fantasy it was very satisfying and not sickening at all. It was more of an artistic triumph. A way to make me just that much more powerful.

Remembered his paper. Which might have been paraphrased thus: *Nothing worthwhile happens without someone dying along the way.* A perfectly ghastly notion. Would I kill Fletcher? No. He would just be wounded. Crippled up. Enough that maybe he would be disfigured for the rest of his life.

Then I would feel good. I would turn my attention to food. One needs to eat after exerting oneself. And then the third impulse. I would seek female companionship. Let word be known around the realm that I was ready to find a mate.

Would women come to me? It was hard to say. I had proved myself to be a provider and a warrior. Wasn't my reward a beautiful woman? I certainly thought so, in my strange and fevered way. The tree house was conducive to odd thoughts and fevered dreams.

I thought briefly that perhaps it was not the best place to be. I rose from the floor and looked out the window. I was considering the possibility of continuing my climb. Out the window, onto the sturdy branch, and up up up. To where? That was the thing.

It felt good to climb, but it had no end of any consequence. Once one reached the top, was there any reason to be there? I remembered how I first arrived in the realm. The floating around in the dark, a different kind of womb. More like a cocoon, which was as much a womb as anything else could ever be. That was the best part of this realm, and, now that I thought about it, the reason I climbed. I wanted to launch myself off the tip of the tree and float around in the air again. Why was I afraid of that sensation the first time? Why did I want to let it go?

I stood and looked out through the windows. There I saw other trees. I felt like I was in a tall apartment building in the city and I was looking out the window and seeing other apartment buildings. Always a lonely activity in my experience. The surrounding buildings always looked so close you could touch them. But at the same time you knew they were far far away.

And as I looked now, I saw that other trees had tree houses in them as well. Many of them. In fact, most of the trees had tree houses at the exact same level as the one I was in. This made me feel oddly secure, as though I had discovered an ancient civilization. And who was to say I hadn't done just that?

I squinted my eyes in an effort to improve my vision at least a little bit. I saw that the tree houses were all crudely built. They were also all small. None of them was bigger than mine, as far as I could tell, and many were smaller. We were a city up at this level. Why were they all built at the exact same level? Now that I looked out at them, they seemed so numerous as to be infinite. Although I knew that was impossible.

My gaze went over the array of tree houses. It was satisfying to see them all arranged so neatly, hanging in trees that also towered over them. In the distance I saw a flicker of motion, a small black dot hovering over the tree houses. It moved to my left, then to my right. It reminded me of a fly buzzing around pieces of furniture.

I watched it intently. It was not a fly, of course. It was a person. He or she seemed very capable in the realm. The dot was able to go, apparently at will, wherever it wanted to. It zigged and zagged as though browsing the tree houses. Then I saw what it must be doing. It was checking each one to see if there was anyone inside it. I briefly considered the possibility that I should hide, but that went out the window in a heartbeat. I knew I could not do that. The person was almost certainly not some kind of predator. Most likely by far was that he or she wanted to find a fellow creature. I stuck my upper body out of the window and waved and shouted. "Hey," I said. "I'm here. Over here. Hey."

The dot did not hear or notice me at first. Then the dot got bigger. It was approaching my tree house. To what purpose I could not know, but Ralph's thought was now my mantra. *This place is benign.*

Wasn't it so? Wasn't it true that I had not been injured or starved or pained? Inconvenienced, yes, but nothing more than that. If I thought about it all in a certain way, I could even tell myself that this was nothing terrible at all. It was a thrilling fun ride, the ultimate carnival diversion. I didn't really believe that, but understood it to be a plausible version of the facts.

The dot grew bigger and bigger. I discerned a female shape to the dot. Which eventually resolved itself into a familiar face and person. She arrived in a flash.

"Naomi," I said, with more than a little wonder to my voice.

"Terry," she said as she advanced right up to me. I got out of her way. She floated, or rather *flew*, through the window and lighted softly on the floor of the tree house. My tree house.

"How long have you been here?" she said.

"A few minutes."

"I've been here a few days. I've got a nice house over yonder." She gestured toward the window. "Isn't it great here? I love flying."

"Yeah," I said. "Have you seen anyone else?"

"You're the first. I found some bones in one of the tree houses. I'm systematically checking every one of them, just in case, but I think we're it."

"Oh," I said, not trying to hide my disappointment in the least. "Penelope already moved on. She fell through the ground."

Naomi looked startled, then interested. "Do tell," she said.

"It appears to be the way to go from realm to realm."

"Yup," said Naomi. "That's how I got here. Dug down for some of those worms—love those things—and dug a little too far and here I was."

"We did the same," I said. "Anyway, I found Sylvia and Ralph, too. Then I lost them. Think they probably went to the next realm."

"I wouldn't be a bit surprised," said Naomi. "Everyone always wants to go on to the next thing. Never happy where they are. Want to fly some?"

She was like a kid with a new toy. Her eyes were bright and eager. Her face was flushed.

"I don't think I can," I said. "I fell. Penelope and me both. We fell out of the sky. By some miracle we didn't die. Ended up in some leaves. Then they all disappeared and I climbed up here. What are all these tree houses doing here?"

"I think they used to be on the ground and the trees grew up under them and lifted them up."

An interesting thought. It would account for them all being at the same level.

"So someone built all these houses."

She looked at me with puzzlement. "Well, of course. They wouldn't just grow on their own."

"How do you know?"

She had no answer for that. "Are you sure you can't fly?" she said. "Have you tried since you fell?"

"No," I said. "I don't want to just launch myself into the air."

"Why not," said Naomi. "I did."

"How did you know you weren't going to die?"

"I just knew. You use your hands. You get to know about the wind. It's all about manipulating the wind. It is so glorious, so amazing. We never should have come down from the sky."

"We?"

"The human species. We should have stayed in the air all those millions of years ago."

"Naomi, what are you talking about? People were descended from sea creatures, not birds."

Naomi laughed. "A common misconception, perpetrated by our antiquated and wholly inadequate educational system. I'm surprised at you, Terry. That you would swallow such a preposterous notion. Sea creatures breathe *water*, Terry. How can water breathers become air breathers? Air creatures breathe air.

We had to come from air breathers. The only question is why give up wings? Why let flying go?"

"I can only assume that it gave some advantage. Maybe we grew thicker bones and got stronger."

Naomi looked at me with pity. "I'm not sure you are institute material after all. We want *independent* thinkers, or didn't you read your job description when you signed on?"

She was teasing me, surely. She could not seriously believe that people evolved from birds. I searched her face, looking for some sense of seriousness. A change had come over her. She was no longer the staid bureaucrat I had known her to be. I had to admit that she was a much more lively and interesting person that I had realized. How had I missed that before?

"I saw Fletcher."

"Oh, him," said Naomi.

"You knew about him," I said.

"Of course," said Naomi. "He was scheduled to meet with me the afternoon of our spoon digging."

"I thought he was supposed to meet with Ralph."

"Sure, but me as well. We were checking him out. Ralph really thought he was the cat's meow. I had my doubts."

"His is a well-respected mind."

"You think so? I read his paper you were all so excited about. It had serious flaws."

"No one said it was perfect, but the main argument seemed airtight to me."

"No. He neglected to take into account institutional precautions. There is a non-zero probability that any particular activity will result in a zero death outcome."

"I think he covered that."

"If you call dismissing something covering that something, then sure, he covered it."

"He never said that there weren't activities which would not lead to participant death. What he said was that at a certain level of complexity, there would have to be at least one death."

"But he never defined that level. That's the big flaw."

"Only if you want something outside of the scope of the paper. What he proved was that there was a level beyond which there was a certainty of at least one death."

"That's an egghead's answer. Without the level defined, it's a completely useless result. No one can make coherent policy based on such an outcome."

I saw her point, but she was missing the genius of the paper. "It gave a result to search for," I said. "Subsequent researchers knew that the level existed. Searching for something while knowing that something is there is very different than looking for something which you aren't even sure exists.

"What I'm sure of is that the result as stated is not significant. Ralph was in love with the guy. Thought he walked on water. But I was prepared to show him the door. Ralph and I were going to have a showdown over Fletcher."

I told her about my fantasy in which I delivered a beating to Fletcher. Naomi laughed. "What an odd thought to have," she said. "I didn't want his overrated smug face at the institute, but I didn't want to do him harm."

"I don't know what was going through my mind," I said. "I don't know why I wanted to hurt him, but I did. At least for that brief time."

"Maybe you're in love with him too," she said. "People in love sometimes have odd ways of showing it."

"How could I love him, I didn't even know him."

"You read his paper."

"A lot of people read his paper."

"You *loved* his paper."

"And so that meant I was in love with him?"

"That's all you knew about him," said Naomi. "You were so enamored of his work, this particular work, that you could easily have transferred your enamoration onto him, even if you had never met him. Haven't you ever read any psychology?"

"Not a lot, but it is an interesting thought," I said. "I think."

"Yeah, well, I think we've had enough talk. Let's go look for skeletons." She went to the window and put her hands out.

"I told you," I said. "I'm not just leaping into the air."

She turned around and advanced toward me. I retreated to a corner, but the tree house was so small that it did not offer me much protection. She grabbed my upper shoulder. She had a strong grip. I ducked and twisted, making her release her hold.

"A lively one, eh?" she said.

"I'm not jumping with you."

"Yes you are."

"Just go do your thing and come back. I'll be waiting for you right here."

I scampered over to another corner. She turned and advanced on me again. I put out my hands, grabbed *her* shoulders and gave her a firm push toward the wall.

"I'm serious," I said.

That stopped her. "Hey," she said. "Don't have to be mean about it."

"Sorry," I said. "I'm not used to this sort of thing."

"You're not used to fighting?"

"No."

"Neither am I."

"Maybe we should stop," I said.

Naomi retreated to the opposite corner. We were like boxers between rounds. Only without the trainers squirting water into our mouths or wiping the sweat from our foreheads. "I just want you to fly," said Naomi. "Why is that so strange? Why won't you fly with me?"

"I don't want to fall."

"You won't fall."

"I already fell once."

She sighed. "Well I don't want to hang around here."

"You don't have to," I said. "I told you I'd wait for you here."

"See," she said, "the thing is, I just really like the flying. It feels so natural, like I have been doing it all my life. Like my years of *not* flying were an interruption in the natural flow of things."

"That's interesting and touching," I said. "But I don't feel that way at all. While flying was interesting, it was also disconcerting."

She studied me for a few seconds, like I was a particularly repellent bug under her magnifying glass, and she was an entomologist who was both fascinated and disgusted by my particular species. Her gaze was a little unnerving. I wanted to step away from her but the tree house was too small for that.

"I'm not sure I can find you again."

"You'll find me," I said. "Naomi, what are you so afraid of out there? What do you think you'll find?"

"There's a lot of wildness in the flip." She paused, as though waiting for me to agree.

"That's obvious," I said.

"It's best to stick together, if we can. Safety in numbers."

"I agree that as a matter of course we shouldn't split up, but if you need to fly, then you need to fly. It's okay with me. I'm not going to try to stop you."

She turned her head to the window. But her feet didn't move. She was having difficulty deciding, I suppose. Safety versus adventure. Often a tough choice for some people. Not for me. I always chose safety over adventure and never thought it was anything to be ashamed of. I wanted to tell her to go, but I also wanted her near me. Her presence and her familiar look was something I understood.

"Fletcher could be out there," she said.

"I know. He could be anywhere."

"If I found him, you could beat him up."

I smiled. "That was an errant fantasy that had nothing to do with anything. I wouldn't try to hurt him."

"He would be the victim," said Naomi. "Like in his paper, he would be the unavoidable death. Wouldn't that be sweet justice? I'm sure when or if we ever find out what this flip is about, he'll be at the heart of it."

"I've thought the same thing. But it's not just him that you should be looking for. It's the rest of the spoon digging crew."

"Of course," she said. "The rest of us. It would be good to find them. Maybe I could get us all back together."

"Penelope is gone," I said. "I know that for sure. And probably Sylvia and Ralph as well. We need to go to the next realm if we are to find everyone."

"We don't know what that next realm is," she said.

"We'll never know until we go, but we have to go."

"I like it here."

"Yeah, I can see that. There's nothing wrong with staying here, if you want to. But give it a few days. You might get tired of flying."

She seemed doubtful. So was I. She obviously loved it so much that it didn't seem she was ever going to get tired of it. "Well," she said. "I can see I'm never going to convince you." She stepped over to the window and put her hands on the frame. She extended her neck so her nose was prominent in the air. She took in a deep breath. "Love that air," she said. She stepped out and dropped from view. I went to the window, but already she was out of sight.

I turned from the window and surveyed my tree house. It might have been better if I had gone with her. What was I going to do here? Just wait for her? But I couldn't risk falling again. Penelope and I had been lucky the first time. I did not want to depend on that luck again. I sat down on the floor with my arms around my legs. I don't know how long I was there in that position. It felt like hours and hours, but it was probably no more than a few minutes. That's when I heard a terrible ripping sound. It made me jump and pumped a shot of adrenaline through me instantly.

Next to me, one of the floor boards had been torn away, taken off like a piece of orange peel. Another tearing sound, and another floor board gone. I scrambled away from the hole in the floor and stood in a corner, scared out of my wits. Naomi poked her head through the floor.

"What the hell?" I said.

"You can't stay in the tree house if there *is* no tree house," she said. She raised her hand in a fist, then brought it down on the edge of the hole. Two floor boards splintered and fell from view. I climbed up in the window frame. She pulled out the remaining bits of floor and began tearing away at the wall. The window frame wobbled and trembled. It was not going to hold me for much longer. I looked outside. The trunk or the tree was right there, but it was too wide for me to hold onto. I needed a good strong limb. They were there too, but not within ready reach. I would have to jump onto them and I was not ready to do that. Naomi was methodically tearing the tree house apart, piece by piece. She let the pieces fall. I watched some of them drift down and begin to flutter as they neared the ground.

"You're crazy," I said to Naomi.

"I just want you to love what I love," said Naomi.

"You can't make people love something they don't love."

Naomi laughed. "Who told you that? People are coerced into things all the time. It's called persuasion. It's the way of the world, Terry."

What was left of the tree house lurched. I dropped a good foot. I was hanging on by just a few side boards now. That was all that was left of the tree house. The supporting limbs were still not quite within my reach. I hung in the air, more vulnerable than I had ever felt before.

"See," said Naomi, "the different realms all have different entry points. I've established that. You think they all go through the ground. Okay, maybe you're right. But maybe you're wrong. It could be that you can go to the other realms through all kinds of avenues."

"I never said they all go through the ground," I said as I hugged the remaining two pieces of the tree house. I could see that I was going to have to commit myself to the wind. I was trying to gain time to do this. To get my mind into a proper attitudinal frame.

"Oh yeah," said Naomi. "You said we have to go through the ground."

"Only because that's where Penelope went. If we want to have everyone together, then we have to follow Penelope."

"Now that's what I thought for a long time, too," said Naomi. She had her hand on the side board. I strengthened my grip on it. She pulled it away from the tree. I was still holding onto it, but it was in free fall and so I fell with it. Further conversation seemed futile, so instead, I screamed. I released the side boards. They fell away. Naomi descended next to me. "But the thing is," she said, "we don't know enough about this world, the flips, or anything." She grabbed my hand, extended her other arm, and pulled me up.

I lurched toward the sky with her. It was as she had predicted. I was not dragged down at all. There was lift supporting me, a lift that I could not know the origin of. In the event, I saw the trees rush by me. In an instant I was above the tops.

I looked down. The creek was off to one side, it snaked through the landscape and emptied into the lake. I saw the lake and tiny dots next to it, which was probably Sylvia and Ralph's lean-to. Naomi kept going up. I followed her. How I was doing it, I was not sure. There was an understanding in my brain that this was a perfectly normal means of conveyance. " Any fear I had was now gone.

"How are we doing this?" I asked.

"Don't question it," she said. "You need to accept it and use it."

"I accepted it before and I fell. So did Penelope."

"It all has something to do with belief. It's very complicated, I'm sure, but what does it matter? Throwing and catching a ball is complicated too, just try to program robots to do it at all, let alone efficiently. But six-year-olds do it without any problem at all. They just accept it as part of their make up. Accept this in the same spirit."

She was right about that. We talked about that sort of thing at the institute all the time. Artificial intelligence could come up with a chess-playing genius, but it couldn't even make something that could tie its own shoe without months and months of programming. Not that it would probably have a shoe, but the principle still held.

The landscape was getting further and further away. We were so high up now that the ground didn't even seem like ground anymore. It was as though it was a separate place and I could not fall to it anyway. I was no longer in an environment, I was looking at a world. Or, at least that's the way it felt to me. Above us the air was the same color as always. I half expected it to be darker, like a twilight. But now. The ground was resolving itself into a curved surface. We were so high up that its spherical nature was becoming apparent.

"Where are we going?" I said.

"You'll see."

I was in the sky. That thought made me think of being in a dream. How could this be happening? I felt air rush over me. I looked up. A dot in the distance, way over us. "What's that?" I said.

Naomi didn't answer. She increased her speed and pulled me with her. I was getting tired of her enigmatic ways. I wanted to abandon her, but at the same time, I liked being near her. She was a human being who took interest in me, even though it was an odd kind of interest.

The dot above us grew larger. It resolved itself into an elongated shape. Like a bubble, only stretched a bit. As we got closer I saw that it was a balloon. There was a balloon up here in the upper atmosphere. The flip was indeed a crazy place. Who would have thought such an object as a balloon would be waiting here for us? At least I assumed it was here for us. Or were we assaulting it?

"This isn't some kind of commando raid, is it?" I asked.

"You are so funny," she said.

"I'm funny? You're the one who tore my house apart right from under my feet."

"It had to be done so I could get you to here. It seemed the most efficient way of doing it."

"And where is here?"

She gestured toward the balloon.

"You're full of secrets," I said.

"Not full," she said. "I've just got a couple."

I studied the balloon as we approached. We were slowing down for contact. The balloon was shaped like a tear, the fat part at the top, the tapering part hanging under it. At the tip was a large shack, similar to the one I had just been in and Naomi had ripped apart. It was attached to the balloon by rope, which I imagined had to come from the trees somehow. Maybe their bark? Or were there vines on the trees? I didn't remember.

"You brought this up here?" I said.

"I wish I did. I'd like to have the ability to make something like this a reality. But no. The balloon was here, floating around. There are others up here. You can't see them because they are spaced wide apart, but they are here. You you want to find them you just have to fly. A lot of them have shacks hanging from them. Like this one. Someone attached it once. Maybe it was last month, maybe it was a thousand years ago. Who knows?"

We came to the shack. It was not exactly like the one I had been in. It was much better constructed, and it looked as though it had been repaired over the years, like someone had added components to it.

"What keeps the balloon aloft?" I said.

"Thoughts," said Naomi.

I looked at her. She was laughing. "You are so gullible," she said.

"One never knows in these realms," I said. "Who knows how anything is in reality."

"Oh my," said Naomi, "quite the philosopher."

"Helium, then."

"Most likely," said Naomi. "I haven't investigated that."

We came up to an actual door. Naomi opened it. We glided inside and our feet came to rest on the floor. It was much smoother and nicer than the shack Naomi had destroyed. It was an actual well-kept place, with furniture. A place to sit on. I noticed a bench on one wall. There was a person on it. He lifted his head. "Hi Terry," he said.

I was so shocked I didn't know what to say. "Grant?"

"Yep," said Grant. "In the flesh. Thanks to Naomi."

I looked at Naomi, who was standing—hovering, actually—next to me. I looked down at her feet. "Don't like the contact," she said. "Much prefer the air. Don't you?"

I looked down at my own feet. They were planted firmly on the floor. Grant laughed. "She's always trying to get me to love the air," he said. "I'm still ground bound, I'm afraid. Even though I'm up here."

"Enough of this indoor crap," said Naomi. "I'm going back out. You want to come with me, or are you happy here for a while?"

Before I could answer she was on her way out the door.

"I'll see you later?" I said.

She waved her hands at me, stepped into the void and dropped from view.

"She's in love with flying," said Grant.

"I see that," I said. I pulled a chair from a corner and dragged it next to the bench. "Tell me everything," I said. "Don't leave out a single detail."

"Okay," said Grant. "It feels like it all happened years and years ago."

"I know," I said. "But in reality, I think we were spoon digging only a few days ago."

Grant nodded. "We had gotten into the car and were pulling into traffic. I saw someone cross at the corner. Naomi said it was Fletcher, that he was coming to the institute and she had an appointment with him. I told her that was great, that I thought Fletcher would be a perfect addition to the staff. She wasn't so sure. I pulled into traffic. I was so interested in the *fact* of Fletcher being here that I didn't pay attention to what I was doing. Worse than the absent-minded professors we all make fun of all the time. I let my attention waver from the task at hand, and somehow let the car drift into the other lane. Then I saw another vehicle coming toward me. It jolted me to attention. It suddenly loomed up big and menacing. I knew we were headed for an accident and I knew it was going to be bad. We both swerved. That slow motion thing happened, you know, where you think a second takes a week?"

I nodded. "I've experienced that."

"Well I had time to think about a lot of things. Strange as that may sound. I watched my hands work the steering wheel, trying to get out of the way. I was completely aware of my foot stepping on the brake. And I watched the landscape. I saw it swerve around me. It was so green, the lawns. The sky was amazingly blue. There was a line separating them."

He paused. "You mean the horizon?" I asked, a little puzzled.

"Yes," he said. "The horizon. That's where the flip started. I was so focused on the horizon because it seemed like it was going to save me. I figured, for that instant or instants, that if I could get to the horizon I would be okay and there would be no collision and we would not get hurt. Of course that isn't what happened. About a million or so years later, my car collided with the other car. I flipped over, cut myself on something, I don't remember what, and was hanging from the seat bleeding. We were both stuck there. The roof was caved in. Not enough to hurt us, but enough to make the doors stuck. We couldn't get out. Naomi called nine one one then you guys. We heard the sirens screaming. The world got fuzzy all around me. The horizon, though, it didn't get fuzzy at all. It held its steady line and seemed to separate the earth from the sky with an admirable sense of duty. I heard Naomi next to me. She was calling someone. I was conscious of that, but not really interested in it. I was completely enraptured by the horizon, which had by then flattened out into a perfectly straight line, no bumps, and no valleys. Remember when you first read Plato? How it was to think of ideal things, like chairs and thoughts and such? This is what it was like. Here was the ideal line. I had never seen an ideal thing before, not in the platonic sense, but I thought maybe I was dying and this would be my last chance to do that. So I completely focused on it. It was like I was meditating. You ever meditate?"

I nodded. "A few times. Never did much for me."

"Yeah," said Grant. "Me neither. A little too woo woo for me, but I know many swear by it. It's like the only thing that keeps some people going. Hanging there bleeding to death in the car, I started to understand it. Meditation and platonic ideals really go hand in hand anyway because it's all about how you perceive the world, and they are usually ways different from the mundane day-to-day world."

Here Grant paused, as though he needed to gather up some of his thoughts. "I feel bad that I didn't have any real concern for the people in the other car. I didn't try to see where they ended up. I didn't think about what they might be going through or how they were going to survive, if they were to survive. I was just too busy building the flip."

That startled me. "Building the flip?"

"Yup. Didn't know I was doing it, but I was. Had to. My accident, my wandering mind, my focus on that line, it took the whole world with me into—well, into this. Wherever we are."

I was stunned by his hubris. How could he think that mere thoughts—*his* mere thoughts—could have made our flipped reality as it was now? I studied him, while trying to look as casual as I possibly could.

"Oh, yeah," he said. "I'm crazy."

"I wasn't thinking that."

"You should be. We're all crazy now. The sooner we realize that, the better."

"Better for who?" I said. "It doesn't do anyone any good to say things like that. And it doesn't help any of us to think we are crazy."

Grant laughed. "Okay," he said. "All of what we've experienced so far is perfectly normal."

"I didn't say that," I said. "But what we are perceiving is real, in some sense or other. We are not crazy because if we were we would all have different perceptions. But that isn't what happened. We all perceive exactly the same thing: the mossy plain, the worms, the digging, and so on. Each of us sees what the other sees."

I felt like I was making excellent points, but Grant wasn't paying much attention. He listened politely, but was much more interested in his surroundings. He didn't even pretend. It was as though he had heard this before and was politely waiting for me to go through the arguments and eventually I would see that my arguments were wrong and I would come around to his point of view.

In the meantime, there was really no reason to listen to arguments which, in his mind, were already refuted. He would wait as though he had nothing else to do.

He looked around the little shack, at the ceiling and the walls. He examined his fingernails. He ran his fingers through his hair, to straighten it out. Then he looked at the walls again, which, I noticed, were of a distinctly wallpaper mode, with flowers and butterflies all over them. Where did that come from? The ceiling was bright purple. The floor was a kind of intense green. Very different from the shack I was in. And the furniture. While not exactly the kind of thing you would find in a furniture store, the pieces were well constructed and seemed to have come from somewhere other than a dump. I could see that Grant's interest in his surroundings had some merit. It was an acknowledgment of the importance of environment, the sort of thought that would help us all in the days to come. After a while he seemed to notice that I was noticing him.

"We just found this," he said, indicating his surroundings with a wave of his hand. "This shack was just here."

"You and Naomi flew up here?"

"We were floating around, yeah. Saw a dot above us. Went to it. It was a balloon. Not this one, the first one we found had no shack. There are tons of these strung out all up here. We looked in a bunch. Liked this one the best so we moved in. Been here a day or two."

"Still looking for occupants in other shacks?"

"Yup."

"But you just stay here."

He pointed at his arm and throat. "Still recovering from my wounds."

I wanted to hear more about the flip. "About the horizon," I said. "What happened in the car?"

"Fletcher came over," said Grant. "Before the ambulance came, Fletcher was at the car, staring through the window at us. He smashed the glass with his elbow and reached inside. I remembered his paper in that moment, how steeped it was in death, especially the inevitability of death. It was like the grim reaper himself was grabbing for me. It was more than a little unnerving, let me tell you."

I had not thought Fletcher's paper particularly steeped in death, as Grant had put it, but I did see how Grant might have construed it as such, given his circumstances at the time. "I would have been scared shitless," I said.

"Exactly," said Grant. "I was scared. But not only scared. Something else, too. There was an inevitability to the whole thing. It was as though I was about to be a statistic and Fletcher was one man who knew statistics. He had made his reputation on them. So on the one hand, I was ready to die. But on the other, the guy who really believed in the inevitability of death, well, he was right there trying to save me. It gave me a real boost. Made me want to live because *he* thought I *could* live."

"Makes sense to me," I said.

"But he couldn't really do it. He said he was going to release our seat-belts, but then he couldn't reach them. And we couldn't get to them either. The angle was all wrong. I asked about the other car. He said they were fine. Spun a couple of times, but there was only the driver, no passengers, and the driver was out of the car. He was pissed, but unhurt. That made me feel better. I would have *wanted* to die if I had killed anyone else through my own negligence. You know what I mean?"

"Sure," I said. Grant was in a hypnotic state, it seemed, as though he was still in that crumpled car. "About the flip," I said gently. "Do you remember that moment?"

He kept that dreamy look in his eyes. "The horizon."

"Yes, you told me about that. What about the horizon?"

"Even with Fletcher there trying to save our lives, for what reason I'll never know, there was something about the horizon that was way more interesting. Do you remember those experiments we read about where they figured out that intense experiences often lead to altered states of consciousness?"

I didn't remember that. We read papers all the time, thousands of them, from all disciplines. "Sure," I said. "I remember that one. It was pretty impressive."

"Yeah," said Grant. "It made me think. I flashed back on that paper as I was hanging there, blood rushing to my head, the horizon still as strong as ever. Remember the point of that paper?"

"Um, kind of. Refresh my memory."

"The conclusion, Terry. Geez, that's the most important part. There were hints that if the experience is intense enough it can change the nature of reality.

Not just for a moment, or for just that person, but for everyone. For the world. And permanently."

"Ah," I said. "Now I remember." Even though I didn't.

"Yeah, the researchers had the results. They were on a microscopic scale, but so what? Quantum effects are on a sub-microscopic scale, and look what they lead to, huh?"

"Yeah, just look," I said. "So, you're suggesting that in your intense state of being, you, um, kind of made the flip happen."

"I had only the sky and the grass. Blue on green. That was my world. Fletcher was there, like a buzzing fly, but he wasn't really the focus of my attention, or the focus of reality, if you want to put it that way, and I think I do."

"But, Grant," I said. "Lots of people have intense experiences all the time. They don't flip the world upside down."

"I've thought about that," said Grant. "The thing is, you are right. Lots of intense experiences all the time. But they are all the same. People have similar thought patterns, so their similar intense experiences create a world we are all familiar with. They don't do anything we would not expect."

"Oh. But you—"

"That's right. My experience was unique."

"Hold on. People get in car wrecks all the time. They flip over in their vehicles, they bleed."

"Sure sure, but what was different with me was that I had been digging with plastic spoons."

"Yeah. . ."

"No one had ever done that before."

"I'm not so sure," I said. "You can't really prove that."

"Forget proof," he said. "We don't need proof. Or, rather, the proof is all around you. The flip happened."

I didn't care for this circular reasoning. It may be true that Grant caused the flip, but I didn't think it had anything to do with the spoon digging. Although the rest of my colleagues certainly had their beliefs on this score, and they didn't coincide with mine.

"How long is Naomi out on one of these expeditions?" I asked.

"Usually an hour or so. She likes to come back and check on me."

"I never knew she was such a caretaker type."

"She's not, really. She's desperate to not be alone here. It's too scary to her. So she looks for others for insurance, and makes sure I'm still here. She thinks I might die of my injuries, that maybe I'm bleeding internally or something." He shrugged.

"She could be right."

"Even if she is, there isn't a whole lot I can do about it."

"You're ready to just die?"

"Well, no. But it's more her issue. She doesn't want to be alone here."

"I was alone for a while," I said. "It wasn't so bad. Ralph says this place is benign." Even as I said it, it sounded lame. We've been lucky, so far. That's not the same as being in a benign place. "But who can put any stock in what Ralph says, right?"

"Ralph has always had peculiar ideas."

"We all have. That's why were at the institute. Did Fletcher remain with the car?"

"Only until the ambulances got there. I didn't recognize him. Neither did Naomi. We had never seen a picture of him, so we thought he was some random guy who just wanted to stop and help us. It wasn't until later that we figured out who he was. He was very polite about leaving. He told us real help was there and that he had an appointment and that he hoped we would be fine. Paramedics pushed him aside and talked to us through the window. Fletcher disappeared, into the ether or something." Grant laughed. "Okay, not the ether. The paramedics attached this machine they called the jaws of life. It pries open crushed metal. They use it in car crashes all the time. The sound was incredible. I thought we were in another wreck, only worse than the first one. I closed my eyes and wished I could cover my ears. The crunching and splintering went on for a while. Then it was all over. When the sound stopped, I opened my eyes and I was in the flip. Just like that. Naomi was gone. The car was gone. Hell, you know, the *world* was gone. I was all crumpled up on the ground. Moss. Whatever it was. I felt sore, but I didn't think I was seriously injured. Except for the cut. Which healed up pretty good. I wandered for a while. Not sure how long. Looking for something—*anything*—that would tell me I was in some kind of normal place. Naomi found me. We dug and ended up here. I'm guessing you have a similar story."

I was about to tell him my tale when we both stopped, frozen in place and silent. There was a large rumbling below us. Far down below us. We felt the floor of the shack tremble a little, the same way a building will shake in an earthquake, though, of course, there could be no earthquake shaking us up here in the shack.

"Is that the balloon?" I said.

"It hasn't done that before. At least not while we've been here. Why don't you look out the window and see what's going on?"

I went over to the door and pushed it open. I stuck my head out while holding onto the door frame. I looked up. The balloon looked perfectly intact. I looked down at the surface of the earth, way way below me.

How to describe what I saw? Great blotches of ground were fading and wavering. It was as though there were patches of watercolor eating away at the ground. Trees were falling. The giant trees. They crashed and shook. That was what was making the shack shake.

As they fell, they melted into nothing. As I watched, the ground was disappearing. There was no other way to describe it, and I knew that we were in another flip situation. We were about to be propelled into something else. Again.

I closed the door and stepped back towards Grant. "Come look," I said.

He struggled up out of the couch and stepped to the window and looked down. He was as awestruck as I was. We were witnessing the end of the world. A world. Some world we did not know, but it was still a terrible feeling in my heart. I saw from his face that he must have been feeling the same thing. He was pale and looked frightened.

"Where's Naomi?" he said.

"She can fly, so she'll be safe."

"None of us are safe," said Grant. "This planet is disappearing. The atmosphere is going to diffuse. We'll soon be in a vacuum without the gravity of the planet to keep the air around us. He looked down again. "The destruction is accelerating."

He got up on the window frame.

"What are you doing?"

"We have to fly into the ground."

"Are you crazy?"

"Maybe," he said.

"If we fly into that mess, we'll die for sure."

"Don't think so," he said. "You told me yourself that Penelope went through to the other side. Through the ground. We have to do that, and we have to do it while there still is some ground down there to go through."

I looked down again. The trees had almost completely disappeared. I had the sense that Grant was right, but the decision to fly into that morass was still not an easy one. Grant was still perched on the sill, like a waiting bird. He was being patient with me, allowing my slower thought processes to catch up with his. He knew what he had to do.

"Okay," I said.

"Good going," he said. "It's the right decision. We would eventually suffocate here."

I got up on the window sill with him. I had an impulse to hold his hand, but suppressed it. We weren't that friendly. Although I thought maybe we might be. Or should be. Was it necessary to keep an emotional distance between us?

"What about Naomi?" I said.

"She can take care of herself."

"She might come back for us."

"Nope," he said. "We had a plan. If something drastic happened while she was out looking for people, we agreed that I would do whatever I thought necessary. She trusted me to have good common sense."

"Do you?" I said.

"Not sure," he said as he dropped from the window sill. I looked down. He waved and grew smaller very rapidly. Against the backdrop of the world crumbling, he was an eerie sight, dwindling, shrinking, wavering.

I took deep breaths. The air already seemed thin, but that had to be my imagination. I stepped off the window.

It was not exactly the same as before, when I flew up to the shack with Naomi. Then, it was more like we were going to something magical, a kind of castle in the sky, and that was the most appealing kind of journey.

This was a descent into hell, and I wasn't completely sure I should be doing it. It might have been better to die in that shack in the sky. Surrounded by comfort, at least, and a sense of security. Of a kind.

This descent was something else entirely, a mad rush to a conflagration, which had to be the mark of a crazy person, at least. As Grant had hinted at, we were all some sort of nut now, some kind of altered reality had gripped us, as we had gripped it. The rumbling still reverberated through the air and through my bones. How could that be? I did not know. It was as though the ground was reaching up and grabbing me. I wanted to resist. But dared not.

I looked off to the side. Grant was still falling. He ripped through some dust clouds. I felt particles of dust myself, in my eyes and peppering my arms and face. I put my hands over my eyes for protection. My fingers got sprayed with particles. This was not going to be easy. I tried to peek through my fingers. A great broiling mess awaited me. I increased my speed. Needed to meet my destiny quickly, didn't want to end up floating around in a void.

I entered a trance state, of sorts. Was this sleep? Penelope went through when she fell asleep. Maybe the land made her sleep, and then took her down into itself. Maybe that's the way it was for everyone, or anyone. If Grant was correct, then Naomi was probably already through. She would assume Grant would follow and that he would take me with him. Penelope should also be there. Wherever *there* was. And Sylvia and Ralph? What happened to them? Did their lean-to fall through, taking them with it? No way to tell yet.

The dust was getting thicker. I no longer felt individual particles, instead it was a steady pressure. I pushed against it. It was warm, like bath water. It was soothing, a curious sensation, given the circumstances. But I accepted it and pushed on. There was a moment when a dreamlike state, kind of hypnagogic, seemed to want to grab me and crush me. An even more curious sensation than before.

Then there was nothing but heat. A searing as though I had opened a hot oven and put my face in the escaping heat. The heat was everywhere. I saw nothing but redness, my own eyeball lit up like a flare. Then all was white.

I think time passed. Not sure. I felt like I woke up to a gently rocking motion. I heard tiny splashes somewhere behind me.

I opened my eyes. I saw wood grain in front of me. I blinked. My hands gripped wood. I raised my head. I was in a boat. Not a large one. A kind of lifeboat.

"Hey," said a familiar voice. Fletcher.

"What are you doing here?" I said, more than a little irritation in my voice.

"I'm your rescuer," he said.

"Rescuer? Rescued from what?"

"If you have to ask."

"Yes. I have to ask. What exactly is going on?"

"Well, we've been drifting for some time. Everyone was on board. It was cozy and very family oriented. We had meals together and told each other about our day. Now, the sad fact is that there wasn't much to tell, really, since we were all drifting on this boat with nothing to do, but we ate our raw fish which we had caught and we talked. That was the point. Not the subject, but just the fact of talking. So supportive. But then the fishing got bad. We couldn't catch a thing. We speculated as to why. No one had a definitive explanation, but we had lively discussions about the migration, pollution, warm water, predators, and so on. All very interesting, but the fish, even after all that discussion, just weren't coming back. Very distressing. Not to mention discouraging and depressing, since catching and eating fish was just about all we had. Oh, and you were in a coma or something. Maybe not a coma. I'm not sure, except that I knew you weren't responding to anything any of us had to say. We treated you as an art object and put you in a corner where we imagined visitors coming by and admiring your fine lines and exquisite composition. Which was okay by all of us. We didn't need to feed you at least. But the others of us were getting kind of hungry. And very thin. We saw the end coming for all of us and we didn't want everyone to die, so we did this lottery thing based on pure chance to decide who would get eaten first. That was difficult in itself, let me tell you. A boat load of intellectuals trying to come up with a fool proof randomizing system. So many ideas. The short straw, classic, except that it wasn't exactly random because the person holding the straws knew which was the short one and could give unconscious clues to the others. Coin flipping? No one had a coin. And so on. We finally decided on birth-dates. We took our birth-dates and added up the digits. Then kept adding the digits until we got a one digit answer. Whoever had the lowest digit would give themselves up for the betterment of others. Everyone agreed to this. Okay, so we put it into play. Let me tell you, I could write a paper on what happened next. Very ugly. We had all agreed, but when we got down to it, see, Ralph was the first to go and he didn't want to go. Big fight. We had to hit him a few times to subdue him. Why did he make us do that? Very unsporting of him, plus, his body was getting damaged with the beatings, which meant he might not be as good to eat as he should be and we might have to go the lottery sooner than necessary. All very complicated, as I'm sure you can tell from my description. We got him pliant enough to toss him overboard and held his head down until he drowned. That was no fun either. Took a long time, for one thing, and we were tired. But also, especially for the others, this was someone we knew. It's hard to kill someone you know. Much easier, for example, to have the death be part of a large group, where everyone has the idea that they might die, and then fate takes over. Like in my paper, which I'm sure you've read and debated. But I'm getting away from the story. Ralph thrashed around quite a bit, but we told each other it was for the good of the group and we needed to do what we could. Always better to provide for the many rather than pander to the wishes of the few. Then we hauled him back up and started eating him. That was tough too. So much blood! And we had no cooking supplies, so it was raw. Very unappetizing, to say the least. I retch just thinking about it. But we learned. All of us. We knew we had to eat, just to survive. There are basic needs in life, you know. This sort of situation makes that more plain than anything else possibly could. So, yeah, it was awful, but we did what we had to do. Isn't that what everyone does? We went along like that for a while, drowning and eating each other. One by one they all gave themselves up. It was all done by lottery. Though not the birthday thing, since everyone knew their place after that. Instead we resorted to birth country, assigning a number to each letter, then adding up the numbers repeatedly until we got a one digit number, just like with the birthday situation, and the lowest number was food. Again, these are activities we would never have participated in if we didn't absolutely have to just to survive. I assure you it was completely fair and everyone was on board with the decision. No one had any reason to feel they were coerced or forced into this in any way, so don't get all moralizing and such about lifeboat ethics. There is no world outside of here, just as there was no world outside of the moss world or the hanging from the balloon world or any other world, okay. Back to my story. After Ralph it was Sylvia, then Naomi, Grant, and Penelope. I think. Yeah, that was it. After birthday and birthplace, we used hire date, mother's maiden name, and, just to be fun, date of first sexual experience. That was a fun one, except most of us didn't know the exact *date*. But we figured it out. It was beautiful, if you want to now the truth, how they all gave up themselves so that the rest of us could live. And now you. Just me and you left. I hope you will continue the tradition of benign altruism and agree to participate in the lottery. I would point out that we did not include you in the original runs of lotteries, since you were comatose and could not consent. So you have been the beneficiary of a system that extended a significant advantage to you by not asking you to participate. I believe that this should instill in you a gratitude that would make you want to now participate, although that is certainly not my call and you are a free agent, of course, to do as you please. Let me point out, however, just in passing, that you do look a little thin. We will not be rescued. Or, let me put it this way, there is only an infinitesimally small probability that we will be rescued, so small that we may as well say that we will not be. By the way, just to satisfy your no doubt morbid curiosity, Penelope was the most tender and tastiest. Sylvia, strangely, was the toughest and least tasty. Odd, I suppose. But then, who can say about such things before they actually occur? I have never had experiences of this kind before. Well, I've written papers on survival strategies. It's all kind of a game, you know. But again, I won't bore you with my professional obsessions, as I'm sure you have many of your own. Maybe we can talk about them some time when you're feeling better. I see you holding your head. No doubt you have a terrible headache. Some water might help. You can drink from the ocean around us. It's not salty at all. We drank from it all the time. Oh, and just to elaborate on our survival strategy, we found that if we didn't eat the drowned one in a day or two, they went really bad and were inedible. We actually had to throw some food out because we waited too long. Although that was at the beginning and we learned from our mistakes and pretty much didn't throw anything away after that. I have also tried to keep a fit ship. That is very important, as I'm sure you know. Boats, even small ones like this, accumulate a lot of junk. It's important to keep everything as shipshape as possible. Don't you agree? I see you aren't talking.

That's fine. I'm sure you need some time to get yourself together. We can wait for the lottery thing. Grant just provided me with a pretty good meal only a day or two ago. Or was it three days? It's hard to tell, you know. One day being just like the next. Who can keep track? We tried to wait a long time between meals. Just to make the food last longer. It's strange to think of yourself as food. But then, we have been prey for predators for many thousands if not millions of years. You can't go through life without having some intimation of that. They say, whoever *they* are, that the adrenaline that shoots through us when we are fearful makes us tastier. That would have been interesting to experience, but we were in a position where we didn't have the adrenaline. Because there was no surprise, you see. We all agreed to this and we all knew all of us, except one, would not survive the process. But I do go on, don't I? All this was by way of letting you know what has happened on this boat, the history and present circumstances. I don't have to remind you of the importance of history, I'm sure. It is really the only discipline. From history springs everything else. And what is history? Memory. What we think about the past. What has gone before and what is likely to occur next."

I listened to Fletcher's long speech, the most sustained piece of irony I had ever heard. He had told it with a completely straight face. "There's no blood," I said.

"I beg your pardon."

"Blood. If you ate all those people, or they were eating each other or whatever, then there should be blood all over the place. Blood everywhere."

"Well, I know I said a lot, so you might have missed a few things, but I did mention that I kept the place clean. I am aware of the need for cleanliness, let me assure you."

"There would be stains. Something. You can't possible keep a boat like this as clean as it is if there was cannibalism going on."

"I must say," said Fletcher, "this is a side of you had not anticipated. That you would accuse me of lying. Well, that's just hurtful."

"What was the point of that story, anyway? You didn't think I would believe any of it for a second, did you?"

Fletcher shrugged. "Entertainment. In case you didn't notice, there isn't much to do here."

"How long have I been out?"

"Days. Or minutes. Time is getting slippery. I'm not happy about it. I was always very well aware of the passage of time. Before the flip I always knew what was going on. Now I have no clue. Less than no clue. I really hate it."

"Did you see any of the others?"

"No. But I wasn't kidding about the fish. I caught many early on. With my hands. They just came up to the boat. Bite size. Just dropped them down my throat. They have the same color as the worms. Maybe a different stage of their development? Who knows."

He didn't say it, but I heard it anyway, the final "who cares" as silent punctuation.

"So what do we do now?" I said.

"Just a second," said Fletcher, "I'll check my itinerary for instruction. Oops. Must have dropped it somewhere. Along with the first aid kit and the lunch I packed." He grinned.

"You losing it?" I asked.

"Already been to the lost and found to check for it, placed fliers around the neighborhood, and put an ad in the paper asking if anyone has seen it."

I had to admit he was kind of entertaining in a very limited way, the way you find embarrassing people entertaining if you are in a particular frame of mind. "Have you seen any land?"

"I look up and see the sky. I look down and see water. That's it."

Positively Zen-like observations. I remembered Grant telling me about the sky and the moss, two pure color realms separated by the horizon. "What about a current?" I said. "Have you detected a current?"

"Just drifting."

There was light everywhere, but no source that I could see. "Where's the sun?" I said.

"Haven't seen it," said Fletcher.

"Is there a dark period?"

"You mean night?"

"Yes."

"No night phase. Just this kind of bright—I don't know—*twilight* I guess you'd call it."

"Other boats?"

"Nope."

"Flying creatures?"

"Uh uh."

I ran out of questions.

"How about storms," said Fletcher. "Aren't you going to ask me about storms?"

"Um," I said. "Okay. Seen any storms?"

"Nope."

"Ah."

"Now ask me if the water ever changes temperature."

"Fletcher, I was just trying to figure out our situation. You don't need to get weird about it."

"No, really. Ask me."

I sighed. "Has the water gotten any warmer or colder?" I said.

"No," said Fletcher. "Keep going."

"Keep going with what?"

"With your questions. There's a million things to find out."

"How did you get on this boat? How did *I* get on this boat?"

"Don't know. Just woke up here."

"No oars or sails, I see."

"We could remove our clothing and sew them together and make a sail."

That didn't sound too bad, actually. "Yeah," I said.

"Except we don't have a mast."

Ah. He has thought of these things.

"Go on," he said. "Try me with anything else you want."

I was tired. "I don't think I have anything," I said.

"Too bad. I have answers for everything. I really do."

"No doubt," I said. I leaned over to one side and trailed my hand through the water. It felt nice. Not too cold, but not exactly hot, either. It would be glorious to take a swim. The water was pretty clear. I could see down what looked like a long way before it took on that green shade that water does at depth. I leaned back, and considered the ways of the flip. "We have to go overboard," I said to Fletcher.

"What?"

"Down. Every transition has gone down. We have to swim to the floor."

"We have no idea how far down the floor is."

"We have some idea. It's a long long way down, from what I can tell just looking at it."

"You're crazy. This boat will drift along until it finds land."

"How do you know?" I said. "Maybe there is no land in this realm. Maybe we're on a water planet. Have you thought of that?"

"No," said Fletcher. "This is a completely new concept to me."

"And besides that, even if there is land, there's no guarantee that we'll get to it. On the Earth, pre flip, people have drifted in boats for months and months without ever even sighting land. All I'm saying is we can drift around, maybe forever, or we can take action and go to the next realm."

"What's so great about that? Why should we go to the next realm? What's wrong with right here?"

"We don't have anything here. We have no freedom."

"The next realm may be worse. We don't know."

"It could be better. It could be substantially better."

"It's not worth the risk."

"Staying here is a risk."

He shrugged.

I looked away from him, scanned the horizon for motion. The sea was calm, but there was still some motion, a slight up and down. I thought that I didn't really need him. I could just take the initiative on my own and swim down through the depths to the sea floor. Why not? But I was getting tired of being alone.

"It might actually be just a few feet down there, you know," I said.

"You're wrong. I can see that."

"Maybe it's an optical illusion. Water behaves strangely in water, you know. It always has."

"Even if you get to the bottom," he said, "you haven't solved your problem. How do you lie there long enough to sink into it? You'd be covered in water. You'd drown."

I had no answer for that. He was right. My hand was still trailing in the water. I felt some *things* touching it and pulled my hand out with a great splash. Fletcher laughed.

"That's the worms," he said. "In their fish incarnation. Don't worry. It's fine. They taste pretty good."

I put my hand back in and waited for the sensation to touch my palm. As soon as it did I quickly closed my hand into a fist, trapping at least one fish, possible two. They struggled against my skin as I raised them out of the water and popped them into my mouth. Yep, tasted just like the worms. Sweet and refreshing. I put my hand back in and pulled out a few more. I offered some to Fletcher who shook his head. "You on a diet or something?" I asked him. He actually smiled.

"Something like that," he said. "Hope you don't mind."

"No skin off my elbow," I said.

"It's knee," said Fletcher.

"What?"

"No skin off your knee, not elbow."

"Actually it's nose. I was just doing a variation."

"Nose?"

"Yep, I think so. That's the expression I remember."

"Nose? Really?"

"Yes, nose."

Fletcher grunted, as though that was the most interesting and dumbfounding thing he had ever heard. I was a little mystified by his reaction, though I understood how memory can scatter you all over the place. You think you know what's going on, and you don't really, because what's going on has no anchor in your brain. It's all just a theater of the absurd going on all around you and you have no way into it. There is no guide or script except your own brain, and your brain is having trouble keeping up. I put my hand into the water again, pulled up more of the fish. I took the time to look at them before I ate them. So pretty. They were a deep deep red. I never thought I would be okay with eating raw fish, indeed, still living fish, but these weren't bad at all. It was actually quite a culinary experience. I thought that when I got back to my regular life on my regular world, I would maybe confine my diet completely to living food. That would be a way of improving my life after all this arduous nonsense in the realms, flipping from one insanity to the next.

"I would have eaten the others," he said. "If I needed to."

"I suppose we would all do things we wouldn't normally do," I said. "If it meant we could survive. We are survival machines."

"Although," said Fletcher. "Surviving is sometimes not all it's cracked up to be. This realm is very boring."

I couldn't argue with that, and chose not to try. "I am intrigued by this boat," I said. I ran my finger along the edge. "It's made of a wood I don't recognize."

"Look at it again," said Fletcher. "Examine the grain. See how it kind of looks like scales."

He was right. The wood had the look of fish skin, tiles of pale tan overlapping each other.

"Remind you of anything?" he said.

"What should it remind me of?"

"Think back to the previous realm. The trees."

Now I saw it. The wood was from one of the tall trees where I had a tree house shack for a while until Naomi destroyed it.

"The point is," said Fletcher, "we may not be in a different realm at all. We could just be in a different part of the big trees realm."

"Which is why you think we'll strike land."

"Yup," said Fletcher. "This boat could not have been built on water. It must have been constructed on land."

I liked his logic, though I wasn't sure he necessarily made any sense. The wood could have come from the water. Maybe there are trees growing under the water. Still, how could the boat have been constructed? It did seem as though land had to be around somewhere. Unless the boat was built in a previous realm and brought over to this realm. Then the fact of it being in a landless realm wouldn't matter. "Then our task," I said to Fletcher, "is to find land?"

"That could be a task," said Fletcher. "Another task we might want to be doing is to make sure we don't find land."

Fletcher was always full of surprises. "Why would we do that?" I said.

"Land is dangerous. It leads to other realms. Here, we just float along.

It's like a vacation. We should enjoy it, not make it seem like we are in some terrible situation."

"But we are in a terrible situation."

"Only because you can't wrap your mind around how nifty it all is. We are pioneers," said Fletcher. "We have the world at our fingertips."

"I don't want the world at my fingertips. I just want to get back to what I had. These things must have a path, a way to get from beginning to end, and we don't want to circumvent that path, I don't think. We should follow it."

"Then follow it," said Fletcher. "Whatever that means."

"It means—" What did it mean? I wasn't sure. Except I knew it couldn't mean that we simply drift around aimlessly like this, with no goal in mind. We should be doing things. We should be taking action to make ourselves participants in our own destinies. Isn't that what human beings should do? Isn't that what makes us who we have been for so long? For ages and ages. From the time of the cave people? "Well," I said. "I don't know what it means."

"Neither do I," said Fletcher. "I'm getting kind of sleepy."

"Sleep is nothing to be doing right now."

"Says you," said Fletcher. He put his head down on the deck of the boat and curled himself into position with his arms tucked against his chest. He closed his eyes.

I watched him falling asleep, as though it was the most interesting thing in my world, which, in a way, it was. His sleep breathing came quickly. It was eerily familiar to me. I'd seen many people at the institute take afternoon naps like this, just putting their heads down on their desks in the afternoon and letting themselves drift away.

Some of them swore by it, said it was when they got their best ideas. Just thinking about it, I felt kind of drowsy myself, but did not want to sleep. Not now. Didn't even know why I was so against it, but it felt like absolutely the wrong thing to do. Was there anything I could do to improve my place in this realm? What did improvement even mean here?

I leaned against the railing of the boat. Fletcher had a point, of course. This was something he could do. Maybe dream of something. That could be interesting, in a strange kind of way. To dream. Wasn't there a realm to be learned about in dreams? Wasn't there something that made sense when you thought about dreams? At least it made more sense than what was happening here.

I wanted birds. I wanted land. I wanted people. I ached for other people. People besides Fletcher, who I was beginning to think wasn't a person at all, just some kind of odd construct built by our imaginations.

Fletcher coming to the institute. Fletcher trying to help at the crash site. Fletcher seeing the spoon digging. Fletcher telling us death was inevitable.

What powerful nonsense. There was nothing inevitable about the demise of a life. It was just a habit we all got into some time a few million years ago. A habit many of the creatures picked up. But there were sponges and single celled creatures that essentially did not die. We didn't have to die either. None of us did.

Look at us in the realms. We got along fine in all kinds of dangerous circumstances which would have lead to death by injury, starvation, thirst, or suffocation in our original home. But not here. We went through all that and have done just fine. Still alive. Still experiencing the world for all it was worth. Was it worth anything? Did the world want us? Were we going from realm to realm at its whim so it didn't have to deal with us at all? We were on an odyssey, of sorts, but one where the world controlled everything.

I sighed. None of this mattered. Fletcher let the natural urge to sleep overtake him. Nothing wrong with that. We had our coping devices. *This world is benign.* As indeed it seemed to be. So far.

I scrambled up from the deck and stood on the rocking boat. Fletcher, still asleep, shifted and muttered. I didn't care if I woke him. I looked down at the water all around me. I stepped to one side, took a deep breath, and dove in.

There are times when it seems particularly right to do something that makes no sense. This was one of those times. I pushed against the water, going down toward the bottom.

Those fish swam around me, bumping into me. The water covered my eyes, but I kept them open, just like my ancestors must have done years and years ago. I was mostly water, isn't that what we all learned back in school? Seventy percent, was it? Think so. I didn't want to dissolve here, but if I did I would be going home, wouldn't I? In a metaphoric sense, at least.

But none of that was really relevant now. I was holding my breath, but knew I could not hold it much longer. Still I swam down further. I touched the bottom. It was hard, like firm ground. Not at all what I expected, which was squishy mud or soft sand.

I was a little disappointed. It meant I would not be able to dig into it, which I was really looking forward to. Was this an ocean, or a lake? There was no salt. And yet, it had the feel of something much bigger than a lake. It felt like the ocean of the world. This world. I touched the bottom with my hand. My lungs were burning. Bursting.

And then I let the water in.

Opened my mouth wide and flared my nostrils and inhaled for all I was worth. My instincts did not fail me. The water filled me up, but did not make me cough or blubber. Nothing ever felt more right than my immersion in water and the water entering me and molding itself to my interior. How was it that no one ever told me how marvelous this was? Surely others knew of it. Was this what suicides were seeking when they plunged themselves into water? The sweet embrace that never let you go?

My only wish then was to continue living in this water realm. My only desire was the need to hold myself to another standard, the standard of water retention. Now I was more than seventy percent water. With that lungful, I must have been up there close to eighty. I breathed water out, breathed water in. The ocean cradled me in comfort. Not bad at all. I wish everyone else had this. Maybe they had. I looked up to the surface. The bottom of the boat had things stuck to it. Shells. So it had been in the water a long time, I supposed, to have collected all that.

I put my back to the bottom of the ocean and stretched out my arms and placed my palms against the bottom as well. I felt as though I was pushing against the world. I saw a shadowy form beside the bottom of the boat. Fletcher, I supposed, peeking over the boat's edge. Looking for me? Maybe. He must have gotten up and wondered where I was. Jump in, I thought. Swim down here. Breathe water. It's what we were meant to do.

But the shadow retreated. A disappointment. For me and the shadow? Maybe. I wanted him to take a chance, but I suspected he never would. I had appeared, then I had disappeared. Probably figured I was the inevitable death he was always going on about. How did someone keep living, knowing that he had proved the inevitability of death? It must be hard on a person, to come to that kind of realization. Then all of life was futile. People couldn't live long with that kind of conviction. No wonder he was so hard to be around. No wonder he had terrible social skills. Not that people at the institute were much better in that department. We all kind of behaved like misfits. It's probably what got us into the institute in the first place. There we could indulge in our silly notions without having to be part of the normal social interactions that human beings are naturally prone to.

And now here I was, at the bottom of the ocean, as far from human contact as was possible, and I was thinking about how silly it was for people to go against their natural tendencies to socialization.

I laughed, but laughing under water is not nearly as satisfying as laughing in air. An interesting fact I filed away for future reference. Maybe that's why we crawled up onto land and started gulping air instead of water in the first place. Who wants to live without laughter? Many did, I knew, but really, once you have laughed, who would want to live life without it? Even if it wasn't one of the three Fs?

Fletcher, probably, but he didn't count. He was too weird. He would rather think about dying than do any laughing at all.

I wanted to sink into the bottom of the ocean, but it wasn't yielding to me at all. So it appeared my idea was wrong. I waited a few minutes longer. Then a few more minutes after that. The fish swam above me. They no longer bumped into me. I guessed it was because I was now a part of their world and they didn't need to keep investigating me. Or they were just bored by me. Which, I thought, probably amounted to about the same thing.

The boat was drifting away. I saw it gliding past me. I had this urge to try to keep it from deserting me, but then thought better of it. What did I need it for? Fletcher's companionship? No. That was a joke more than anything else. Fletcher was the guy with the black robe and the scythe. Fletcher had no need of the three Fs because his credo was that death was all there was. If you had life, then you would get death. It was inevitable.

Other boats drifted into view.

At first I didn't understand the significance of this. I just thought I was observing an interesting fact. "Oh, it looks like the bottoms of other boats are visible from here. They must be collecting above me."

They must be collecting above me.

There were four of them. They traveled slowly, bumped hulls. It was a slow motion ballet above me. Should I go up and meet them? What if they were hostile individuals? What was I saying? There were no hostile individuals here. But I was born of a hostile world. So I have been told. We evolved defensive strategies and mechanisms because we needed them. Wasn't it just that simple? But I didn't have to worry here. As far as I knew. There were no other people, just the seven of us. Six if I didn't want to include Fletcher, which I kind of didn't. Except, someone had to have built the shacks, the tree houses, and the boats. Such things do not arise in and of themselves. And it wasn't any of the spoon diggers that did that. What if they were up there in those boats, the people who made these things? What if they were looking for me? Suddenly the benign world didn't look quite so benign anymore.

It is sometimes difficult to understand another's fear. If spiders fascinate you, then trying to come to grips with another's gut wrenching fear of them is more than difficult. It is close to impossible.

I felt as though the fear that had gripped me, completely unwarranted, was owned by someone else. It was exactly as though I was watching another's deep agony and I was powerless to do anything about it.

Not that it mattered. I couldn't do anything about anything down here, and that was the way I liked it. I was fascinated by the hulls. They all had shells stuck to them, just as Fletcher's boat did. And now I noticed that the shells were red, or at least redd*ish*. So the fish that were once worms were once these shells. Or would become these shells. Their life cycle was being paraded in front of me, but I could not understand how one step fitted with the rest. What order did the stages come in?

Shadows appeared at the edges of the hulls. I saw they were round, like heads. Had to be heads. The occupiers of the boats looking for me? A blurry length extending from one of the hulls, wavering and trembling in the water. Then the bulbous white intrusions as they all jumped out of the boats and plunged into the water. I counted four of them. One for each boat. Okay. They were obviously looking for me. They had found me, somehow, and now were coming down to meet me. I saw as they approached that they were people I knew. The plastic spoon diggers. Penelope, Ralph, Grant, and Sylvia. My colleagues and fellow travelers through the realms. The only one missing was Naomi. Had she not been able to get away from the giant tree realm? Was she still there, floating among the balloons? If so, she was probably dead. As Grant had pointed out to me, the air was going to dissipate there, and she would be lost in a vacuum.

I lifted my hand to wave at them. They did not wave back. They swam determinedly in my direction and grabbed me roughly.

Oh. So this was not to be a pleasant reunion, then.

Two of them on each arm. They weren't fooling around. They lifted me from the bottom and pushed/pulled/yanked/shoved me up to the surface, where I promptly exhaled water, coughed at the thinness of the air—how could people *breathe* this stuff?—and found myself tossed into one of the boats. I touched my head where it had impacted on the hull. There was going to be a good-sized bump there. My colleagues hung on the edge of the boat, four faces looking at me.

"And a very pleasant hello to all of you, too," I said, then retched, coughed, and gasped for air. Needed not to talk for a few minutes.

"What were you thinking?" said Sylvia.

"I was relaxing," I said in a whisper.

"What?"

"Thinking about the next realm," I whispered again.

"We're all in this realm," said Grant.

"Yes. . ."

"There's no reason to go on."

"There is if I don't want to float around on an ocean the rest of my life."

"He doesn't know," said Penelope.

"Know what?"

"We're back," said Ralph.

Now I was confused. Were they saying we were actually back on Earth?

"No," I said.

"Yup," said Grant. "Believe it. We are back on the original realm, the earth realm. Where everything we grew up with is there, and the institute is still operating and and and, well, it's all here, that's what. We made a complete circle."

"But we're on boats. We're in the middle of the ocean. And where's Naomi?"

"She decided to go on."

I blinked. I was still lying on the bottom of the boat. I pushed myself up and stared at each of them. "You're telling me Naomi didn't want to stay here?"

"Nope," said Grant.

The rest of them, Penelope, Sylvia, and Ralph, had retreated to their own craft. They pulled themselves up and over the sides of their boats. We all had our own boats. Wasn't that interesting? Grant pulled himself up and into mine.

"But that's crazy," I said.

"Maybe so. Naomi was always kind of different, though, don't you think?"

"Not that different," I said. "She wanted what everyone wants."

"What does everyone want?" said Grant.

"Yeah," said Sylvia. "What does *everyone* want? There's no way to know that. We're all different."

They had oars. They began pulling them through the water.

"Hey," I said, "where'd you get those? Fletcher had nothing."

"Fletcher's a nut job," said Grant. "He wants to drift. He probably threw his oars away so he wouldn't have to make a decision about where to go. Do you want to drift? Or do you want to get your life back?"

Everyone was lining up and following Penelope, who, somehow, had emerged as the leader. She rowed and the others rowed after her. Grant rowed at the end. We got into a rhythm, and the boats stayed fairly close together. I had a million questions, but could not summon the energy to ask a single one. Instead I laid on the deck and let the sky pass over me. Occasionally I got up and let my hand trail in the water.

"Do you know where we're going?" I said.

"To land."

"Yes, but where? Where are we going to end up?"

"Not sure," said Grant.

"How do you know we're going to touch land? How do you know anything about this place? It sure doesn't feel like earth."

"We've been studying it," said Grant. "All the observations point to this being earth."

"What observations?"

"The length of the day, the temperature, the feel of the air, the water color, the clouds. Everything."

"Haven't you all noticed that there isn't any life on this world, in this realm, except for the worms, which are the fish, which are the shells?"

"Sure, we've noticed."

"So this can't be earth."

"I didn't say it hadn't changed. There has been some kind of event that has altered things on our home planet. Probably related to our going on this trip through the realms. The flip. I don't know." Grant shrugged.

"You talk about Fletcher drifting."

"What does that mean?"

"You don't know anything. None of us do. It's all just guesses."

"Penelope has some ability in this area. She knows how to find things. She knows how to get to things."

I looked up at the string of boats. Everyone rowing. Sylvia waved at me. I waved back. Penelope had pulled ahead of everyone else. A large expanse of water lay between her boat and Ralph's boat. Ralph glanced over his shoulder and yelled at her to slow down. Penelope raised her hand and waved at him. I couldn't tell if it was dismissive or an accepting gesture. We certainly were determined to go *somewhere*, I thought, wherever that might be.

"You really think Fletcher is crazy?" I said to Grant.

"I used to think he was a profound thinker. He discovered stuff and made connections I had never thought of and probably never would have thought of. But that was before. Now I just think he's a pessimist who got some editors to listen to him."

"Huh," I said.

"What," said Grant. "You disagree?"

"Not exactly. I think he's pretty much of a jerk, myself. But I wanted to give him a chance. Just because he discovers something we don't like, doesn't mean that he's evil or anything."

"I never said evil. That word gets thrown around way too much."

"Okay. Not evil. Let's say less than altruistic, maybe. Or let's say he's not the kind of guy you would invite over for dinner. How's that?"

"Fine," said Grant. "I'll grant you that."

"In any case, he's crunched some numbers, attained an insight that was counter to intuition, and published his findings. That's what we're all supposed to be doing."

"Maybe," said Grant.

Suddenly he didn't want to talk about it? "Just because he discovered something we don't want to believe is true does not mean there's anything wrong with him. Come on, you have to give me that, don't you?"

"Sure," said Grant.

He was obviously distracted, looking ahead to the other boats. "What's so damned interesting up there?" I said.

Grant pointed. I followed his finger. It was immediately obvious that we were in trouble. The sea ahead of Penelope was bubbling up like soup in a pot. We all stopped rowing. Black clouds moved over us and it began raining. Cold tiny drops that pierced my skin. We all huddled down, trying to protect our faces. The drops stung bad. A twilight seemed to descend on us. I looked toward the boats. They were out there, but they looked like ghosts now, gray and misty. A wind picked up and blew around us. "We need to get together," I said to Grant.

"I know," he said. Waves started lifting us up and dropping us down. I gripped the sides of the boat. I had been in the water, but it was still disconcerting to think the boat would upend itself and I would fall overboard. *This realm is benign.* Grant put the oars into the water and began pulling with all the strength he had. The others had turned around and were trying to escape the bubbling ahead. It was hard to tell from this distance, but it did appear as though the bubbling was resolving itself somehow. The bubbles were spreading out in a circle, which might have meant that the bubbling was dissipating and all was about to be safe again, but that isn't what was going on. Instead, it looked like the center of the ring was caving in. A large whirling hole had opened up in the ocean. The other boats were desperately trying to row away, but they could not. They began circling the depression. At first slowly, then more and more rapidly.

"We're not going to make it," I shouted to Grant.

"I know," he said. "He pulled the oars into the boat. We're going to leave this realm after all."

"The flip has its own rules," I said.

Sylvia jumped out of her boat and tried to swim away. She made some progress, but in a few seconds she was pulled into the whirlpool along with the boats. All of us were being pulled inside. There was an inexorable necessity to it. It was as though we were fated to this and we needed to understand the ways of the world if we were to survive. The ways of what world? Grant insisted this was the realm we knew. I was not so sure. Even if a change had occurred, how could it be that the ocean was no longer salt water?

Grant had stopped rowing. He held onto the sides of the boat. "We're going in," he shouted.

I could see that. I vaguely wondered what all the shouting was about. I heard Ralph's voice. "We need to stick together," he said. "When we get to the other side, we need to find each other."

We were all swirling around the whirlpool, like floating bits of trash. The center of the whirlpool was a very marked depression now, very deep. I could look into it and saw only a solid blackness that stunned me. I was going to fall into that? My insistence on the benign nature of this realm was taking a severe beating. Could I not be torn apart? I still had sensation. I could still be broken.

Grant grabbed me. I held onto him.

"Should we jump out of the boat?" I said.

"Then it'll just become an object that could strike us," said Grant.

"So we stay."

"I don't know," said Grant. "I don't know."

The boat was listing. Eventually we would not have to decide, the water would decide for us.

I saw across the whirlpool that our colleagues were about to fall into the water. We were going to follow them. I reminded myself that I was able to breathe that water. I was on the bottom of the ocean for a while, with no ill effects.

"We might forget," said Grant.

"What?" I said.

"We might forget all of this. The next realm might be so different that it might affect our brains, our memories."

"Why do you say that?" I said.

"Just an intuition."

The boat seemed to slide out from under us. It flipped. The hull loomed over us, then we were under water. We released our grip on each other. I surfaced long enough to grab air, then plunged under water again. The current was as strong as anything I had ever felt. I got pulled way way down in a split second, and then I was breathing water again. I had my eyes open, but it was so dark I could see nothing. All was black. I saw brief flashes of bubbles and red things. That was all. I was not even sure if they were real or just things my eyes were doing.

It didn't matter. The water was cold, and getting colder. I wondered about hypothermia, but figured that wouldn't happen. Even if I wanted to die on this world, in this odyssey, it wouldn't happen. Circumstances would not allow it. After a while the current grew weaker. I lost the sensation of being pulled along so strongly. Now I was more in a lazy floaty kind of mode. This was as I had expected. The realms give you fear, but never follow through on it. In the end we always have calm and peace. Hasn't it been proven again and again, from realm to realm?

The water grew warmer. Yup. That was to be expected. Then soft light began to return. Uh huh. Yup, yup. I was close to the bottom. Very good. Until a few moments ago, I didn't know there *was* a bottom. But the bottom was not the hard surface I had been on previously. It was sandy and very nice. My feet were wrapped in the essence of softness. The sand was more like mud. Or perhaps a smooth cheek. Warm flesh of the earth.

And then I was walking. Taking steps through the softness. The light grew stronger. It was coming in through the surface above me. The water was getting shallower. I took short steps forward, not knowing why, but needing to move.

No, not needing. More like *wanting* to move. There was something ahead of me. I looked for the others. The water was clear again, and suffused with light. I could see a long way, and was very disappointed to find that I could not see any of the spoon diggers. So they had either been directed to some other shore or they were just out of view.

I imagined us strung out along the ocean floor, like beads on a long string. The surface was just above me now. I looked up. Waves broke at my head and I poked through the surface. More retching and coughing, as before, while my lungs got used to air again. It was what made fire burn! Why would we choose to breathe it? No matter now. We didn't choose, our ancestors chose for us. We were just following a hereditary protocol. And had gotten used to it. Had decided there was no other way to be in the world. But these worlds showed us different.

Once I had cleared my lungs of water and returned to some semblance of comfort with the air, I looked around. The shore was ahead of me. Water stretched out for miles on either side. Sunlight sparkled on the surface. The water was a lovely blue and the shore, well, it was a long way off. There were these shallows that seemed to go on and on. I was going to have to walk a long way to get to the shore. I thought about turning around and walking back to the deeps, but rejected that idea pretty quickly. None of my colleagues would have done that, I was sure. They would go to land. So I went to land.

The walk was slow and plodding. I estimated, by the look of the land, or what I assumed was land, and the look of the water, that I had about a million miles to go. Give or take a few thousand. Perfectly accurate estimates were next to impossible, of course, but I was pretty sure I was in the ballpark on these numbers.

So I had some walking ahead of me. I put one foot in front of the other and walked. Time passed. A few hundred years. Then I put the other foot forward. Another few hundred years. I watched the shore change. Vegetation sprung up, trees rose to the skies, then fell, toppled by wind or cut down by rot. Insects, maybe. The shoreline changed, moving in and out, dancing like water spatters on a hot pan.

I had to remind myself that all this was happening at a furious pace, with events which normally took eons, occurring in a few seconds or less. How did I get to have this sense of drawn out time? How did I get to have anything in the flip? It has all been given to me, unsolicited gifts that fill me up with dread every time I think about them. And why? Even though they are disconcerting and throw my world out of kilter, they have not yet done any permanent damage that I can see.

But there is no perception difference. I see what I see. The light enters my eyes and paints pictures, somewhere, that I pull out of the ether and examine. So simple a process, but so unnerving in its implications. I looked over the ocean. I could see the individual waves frozen in place.

This is not the way we should be seeing things, since we have all been through the flips. We have gone from one extreme to the other. I called out to my colleagues. "Grant," I shouted. "Sylvia, Naomi? Ralph? Penelope?" My voice echoed over the water. It seemed to move over it and crash on the shore.

Yes, my voice. How was that even possible? I watched it. Then shook my head. The voice did not matter. We were all granted the ability to see what we could not have seen previously.

I saw other voices skimming over the water. Ah, yes. Now it was clear, to some extent. We were not to see each other, at least not now, not in any way that we would have understood in our previous life. The voices were words personified, a kind of color stance that held the information in gobs of solidified air. Clouds of meaning floating on the surface of the ocean. We pushed through the air, all of us. My words were clouds, similar to the clouds from the first realm, when we were wrapped in them and did not know how to continue our understanding. The way of the clouds had followed us from realm to realm.

The colors were amazing, and I assumed there was meaning in the different hues, but did not know how to discover those meanings. I had never been trained in such things, so how could I now discover what they meant? I needed my spoon diggers to bounce my ideas off. I needed them all in a group so we could work this problem and come to some conclusions.

And don't tell me that they were already there. I could see that they were there, or at least their words, translated into cloud, or represented by cloud. But that was no good. I had no cloud/English dictionary. It wasn't my fault.

Grant used to say that there was no meaning in the world. All of what we called meaning was simply the prejudices of our brain attempting to survive in a meaningless environment, swirling with motion and a tendency to clump.

Tendency to clump. What a way to describe existence.

I considered that some of the clouds I now saw were probably representations of Grant's words. So what was his tendency to clump telling me? What could anyone's tell me? There was nothing that we ever wanted to see that we couldn't see if we convinced ourselves it was there.

How was that for making ourselves into gods? That was one of Penelope's. We all had different ways of understanding the world, and we all tried to make the others believe that we knew what we were talking about. Was it true? Was it that simple? The art of persuasion was what we needed everyone to understand. The tendency to clump applied to ideas as well as objects.

Dust had a tendency to clump. That was how we got stars. Ideas had a tendency to clump. That was how we got thoughts. Which leads to words, and then the flip happened. How would we ever find our way through the flips?

The clouds seemed to flow in from both sides of me. I put out my hands for them. They flowed over and through me. There was something there, but I felt next to nothing. It was more a way of refreshing myself than learning anything.

The clouds felt cool and warm at the same time. Good. Holding contradictions was the mark of a genius. Or so I had been told. Others considered it the sign of a seriously unmoored mind, one lost in meaninglessness. I wasn't that person, I was sure. I liked the feel of the water around me, hugging my legs and spreading out like a mirror in all directions. What could be more amazing? Nothing, nothing at all. And the shore. It was there, I could see it. It was still a long long distance away, and it would take me a long long time to reach it, but I was already in love with that shore, imagined myself on it, could see a civilization arising there and wrapping us all in benevolence.

The sun ate the clouds. The word clouds, I mean. The sun swooped down and scooped up all the word clouds, then returned to its place in the sky.

How amazing!

I had never seen this before, but then, I had never had a slowed down sense of time before, so it stood to reason that I would never have seen it.

More word clouds came. I occurred to me that maybe they wanted to hear me. So I opened my mouth.

"Where are you?" I asked. In a whisper. Don't ask me why. I was testing it out, seeing how it worked. As soon as I said the words, a thread of smoke emerged from my mouth. A thin thread, hardly even worthy of the concept. It flailed about in the breeze for a few seconds, then dissipated.

Ah, I saw. I needed more volume? I opened my mouth wide, cupped my hands around my lips and shouted. "Hello! Where is everyone?"

This time the smoke was thicker, with many more colors and it seemed to fill the air. It kept its shape. Or at least it kept itself clumped together. Everything clumps. Everything always will clump. It's how we are made. It's how everything is made. The clouds of my words rose, caught the wind, and scooted away. There. I had added to the conversation, even if I did not know what the conversation was. None of that mattered. I had to be in on the exchange. That was how things were determined in our world, even in the flip.

The shore was still there, and I assumed would be there for a long time to come. Perhaps the whole purpose of the flip was to get me here in this one place where I could watch time unfold on the shore.

Grant would shake his head at this and tell me I was suffering from a very common delusion and that we were luminaries at the institute and were supposed to be bright and should do better than that. The delusion was that everything revolved around the self.

But without the self there is nothing. He would listen to this rubbish politely for a few minutes and then cut me off with a flourish. None of that esoteric philosophical mumbo jumbo bullshit here, he would say. Or words to that effect. I may have exaggerated just a little. He wanted evidence. He wanted facts. That's all that Grant was ever interested in. Was that my fault? No.

So, okay. If the flip wasn't here for me, what was the flip all about? Ralph would say we were just chance occurrences in a chance realm. That at least had the virtue of being understandable. Short and sweet. We could all understand such a stance. But Ralph had the burning conviction that every realm we went through was benign. I was not so sure of that. The flip could be an accident, I was fine with that.

What it could not be was benign, at least on a permanent basis. I had felt discomfort and even pain in some of the realms. I retched. Surely that meant that my demise was possible. I was not some immortal and untouchable being because I was here in this admittedly wondrous place. Neither was anyone else.

I had a lot of time to consider these things, that was for sure. It was a question we sometimes mulled over at the institute. How would we spend our time if we had infinite time? If we were immortal. I never believed any of us could be immortal.

But what I had now seemed to come pretty close in a strange way. I had all the time in the world and I was thinking about where I was. That was it. Kind of anticlimactic.

I was still walking. Very slowly. More slowly than I had ever thought possible.

The land beneath my feet was shifting. Slowly, I grant you that, but shifting nonetheless. It was as though the entire planet was moving. Which it was. I knew that. Everyone knew that the planet was not the stable object it seemed to present itself as.

But the movement was so slow over such a long period of time that no one ever really noticed. Well, that wasn't true anymore. Now I noticed because I was the super slow one. My body was a geological collision of forces.

"So how about that?" I said to Grant as loudly as I could. The clouds erupted from my mouth. They gathered up the colors of space and tattooed the words like stained vapor onto the air. Then the wind took up the clouds and spread them around over the water. I watched them disappear over the horizon.

One foot in front of the other. It's slow but it's steady. What else could anyone want or look for? We are about survival. Nothing more. If you think there is more to life, then you are deluded.

I tried to remember who said that one. Penelope, maybe? No, she was too idealistic for such pessimism. Just as well.

I shouted their names. All of them. Penelope, Sylvia, Grant, Naomi, and Ralph. Said them over and over again. Each cloud was different. Penelope's was iridescent, blue. Sylvia had flecks of green in her cloud. Grant was mostly gray, with streaks of red. Naomi's was a subdued maroon. Ralph's a kind of peach, but not so dull, maybe tending to the orange a little. I repeated their names in different orders, enjoyed watching the clouds puff away in various combinations of letters. It was like playing music.

My legs were almost like separate parts of me. They moved on their own while I occupied myself with the amusements of the clouds.

Fletcher. His name nagged at me. I didn't want to say it, but then decided

I should. I sighed. And I moaned. Not Fletcher. Yes, Fletcher. I opened my mouth and said his name as loudly as I had said the others. Louder.

His cloud was the dullest of them all. A sickly brown, weak like diluted tea. That made me feel oddly happy. I said Fletcher again. Added his name to the others and said them all several times. Clouds puffing into the air.

Then from over the horizon came a string of clouds. They had the same colors as mine had. Ah ha. A smarty walks over there. Had figured out that the names were unique.

"I'm coming over there," I said. The words puffed out and went on their way. I started walking parallel to the shore, to reach the speaker of those words.

"I don't know who you are, but I know you must be one of us," I said.

I hoped it wasn't Fletcher. I could go another few million years without having to deal with him.

"I like being in the water," I said. Stupid thing to say. "I like being in the water and feeling the mud on my feet." I slapped my head. What was I saying? Where was this coming from? "I like the feel of the water hugging my legs," I said.

The puffs went out like they were propelled by jet engines. The speed was enormous and it was enormously satisfying that I had the ability to make them go like that. "I like it all," I said. "I like everything and everybody. Is that so bad? Isn't that what we were put here to do, love everyone? Whoever is seeing this, listen to what I'm saying. There is no reason to fear anything. If that's Ralph, then you know. If it isn't, then listen to Ralph."

These were not things I believed in, and yet I was saying them with calm conviction. What was happening to me? This was all wrong, in so many ways it was wrong. Except that I was saying it was all right. It was the way things should be.

I looked up as I walked. The clouds were above me, my clouds as well as the ones that came from the horizon. They skitted along the water, it appeared, and then rose up on thermals where they accumulated. How long would they remain there? Impossible for me to know, but it made me think I should be more careful with my words. Wouldn't want to fill up the sky with my ramblings and mutterings. A kind of pollution that we really didn't need.

The water was getting colder. And deeper. Where a few minutes ago the temperature was pleasant, just right in fact, and the surface was at my knees, now it was definitely chilling my bones lapping at my mid thigh. Each step took me a little deeper. I saw that there was a trench ahead of me. I could see it through the water, the bottom sloping down precipitously. Huh. Hadn't expected this. Did this realm allow me to breathe water? Even if it did, did I want to breathe this cold water? Wouldn't I get hypothermia or something? Probably.

And now, here comes Fletcher. Again.

He loomed up out of the water ahead of me. He dragged clouds through the air behind him on strings that he held in his hand. Like they were balloons and he was the clown at the circus handing out balloons. He waved at me. I waved back. The wave took about a few hundred years to complete.

I didn't much care for him, but it appeared he didn't much care for me either. I stopped walking. He kept going. He held his breath and disappeared under the surface. Huh. That was easy. He didn't seem to worry about not coming back. Well, good. Then I wasn't going to worry either. The clouds on strings followed him into the water, disappearing, but not, as far as I could tell, dissolving. They remained clouds under the water. How odd, and how amazing. A few millennia later, Fletcher rose up from the depths and stood in front of me.

"Never thought I'd see you again," I said.

"We haven't time for delaying," he said. He puffed out clouds. The wind picked them up and took them aloft to join the rest of them. He still had clouds on strings. He looked so absurd I had to laugh.

"What's so funny?" he said.

"You remind me of a man who used to stand on the corner selling balloons. He couldn't have made much of a living, but he was there, every day for years. He became part of the landscape and on rare days when he wasn't there, I felt like something was missing."

"Now see, this is what I'm talking about. You wander into nostalgia when there is important business to attend to."

"What business?"

"Have you looked at the sun lately?"

"What about it."

"It's getting bigger. Noticeably so."

"All right," I said. "That probably means it's getting closer."

"Think again. We *may* be getting closer, a little closer, but that wouldn't account for the observed size."

I stole a glance at the sun. It *was* quite a bit bigger. In fact, it was so big I was a little shocked by its size. It was at least ten times as wide as I remember it. I looked back at Fletcher. A deep fear had lodged itself in my belly.

Which annoyed me. Why was I still so fearful of everything? I had lived a long life. A very long life, now, longer perhaps than any other creature had ever lived in the universe, as far as anyone knew. And I was fussing about the sun exploding. Because that is what it was doing. It was at the end of its life span and it would expand, burn up all the planets, then contract. We were witnessing the beginning of the process. Which meant we would soon be incinerated. Just great. Oh yes, that was just *peachy* keen.

"The sun's going nova," I said to Fletcher.

"Bingo," said Fletcher.

"What can we do about it?"

"Plenty," said Fletcher. "We have amazing powers none of us have dreamed of."

"Like breathing under water."

Fletcher waved his hand. "Sure, that one. But it's about the most minor one of all. We can spread ourselves out over the whole globe. Just by thinking it, we can diffuse our bodies to such an extent that we become the atmosphere."

"Of course," I said.

"You sound skeptical. Watch."

So I watched. Fletcher began to expand. Every part of him got wider. His head, hands, torso, everything. At the same time he lost some of his color, as though he was fading, which, in a way he was. Dissipation is a kind of fading, isn't it? I stepped back from him. He laughed at my nervousness. The laugh was small, as though it too had lost some stature. It was coming from some place other than Fletcher. Or so it seemed to me.

"You don't have to run from me," he said. "Just stand there."

Against all my natural born instincts to run from this odd apparition, I did as he requested.

"There," he said. "Much better."

Better than what? What did he want from me?

As Fletcher grew, his color faded. His surface got more diffuse. His boundary was intersecting with me. I felt nothing. It was as though he was the most ethereal of concoctions. Lighter than cotton candy, which is what he reminded me of. He began to take on the appearance of the clouds that came from our mouths. We were clouds, now? His voice was so quiet, so strange, because now that I was located in Fletcher's interior, his voice seemed to come from everywhere.

"What is the point of this?" I said.

"Survival," said Fletcher. "As the sun goes, so goes the planet. We will burn up if we don't do something. By spreading ourselves very thin, we can avoid the demise of our bodies. We become gaseous creatures, as it were. We live, but we don't live. Now you try.

"Live, but don't live? Are you serious?"

"It's the only way. The sun is a cloud, really. A cloud of gas. Look how long it lasts. It's a perfect survival scheme."

"But if we spread out, we won't have any coherence. Will we?"

"Just try it," said Fletcher. "Stop being so annoying and just do what I did."

"How?"

"Oh for heaven's sake," said Fletcher.

Then I felt a rumbling around me, and a kind of shift in the air. A *presence* in my brain. Right there, just a few inches under my skull. I tried to step away from it. Took two or three steps. The presence was still there, a form of blockage. Overwhelmingly cold and solid, like a piece of my brain had become frozen.

"What?" I said.

"Just helping you along," said Fletcher.

I was about to tell him I didn't need this kind of help when something happened. I knew how to do what Fletcher wanted me to do. I hate that saying "it's like riding a bicycle." But it was. It was exactly like that. One minute I didn't know how to diffuse myself, the next minute I did. And further, I knew that I would know it for the rest of my life. It was something that *could not* be forgotten. Ever. How marvelous.

"Okay," I said. "Here I go."

I turned something off. I was instantly aware that I had done so, even thought I had never done this before. There is something in people that keeps them confined in their accustomed forms. I didn't know that. I don't think anyone ever knew it. But it is so.

And further, it is very easy, once you know you can, to turn that function off. Which is what I did. Right there. Right then. And with my form gone, I was as free as I was ever going to be. I became more than a fixed body in a time and a place. I became something I had never expected to become: a free floating notion.

I expanded myself as quickly as I could. I heard some rumblings, which I recognized as Fletcher, his words, I supposed, though by that time I didn't care. Fletcher was just a petty annoyance. Was that even possible? Fletcher was less than an annoyance. He was more or less an idea. As, it appeared, so was I. A floating idea. Which was disconcerting, but still fascinating.

Fletcher was a distant memory of a time and place I could no longer fathom. He was there, a kind of inclination in the ether, but not that that mattered. What truly mattered was that I had now become an ethereal being.

Oh, what wonder.

The sun continued to expand. Uh huh. I saw it. Or, rather, I felt it. The heat and the particles flitting about and through me. They did not burn or warp, they did not maim. Instead, they kind of jostled up next to me. That's how the sun is at this level. It grows and grows, seeking more space, trying to fit its bulk into something else, and so it does. It fits into all the nooks and crannies of the immediate cosmic neighborhood, of which I was now one. A neighbor.

I felt others around me: the whole crew, all the spoon diggers were diffuse dust clumps now. How did they learn? Maybe from me. Did I expand and intersect their presences? It appeared so. I had taught them what they needed to know about the process. This puffed me up even more. I was a teacher. I was able to show others the way by my mere presence, diffuse as that presence was. Hah! We all existed like this. I wanted to talk to them, but what is talk at this level? Any ideas, anyone? I sent out the thought processes.

Answers came back. *We'll think about it: we'll understand some other time:*

we'll eat the ether and let you know: who cares for now let's just have fun with it: talk is for the other time the old time: we are not separate beings anymore and talk is for separated beings.

I could not identify the thinkers who sent those thoughts, but just feeling them course through me was as wondrous as anything I had ever felt in my life. Do you suppose, I said to the ether, that we will be like this the rest of our lives?

Lives don't matter: we'll loop back on our lives: time is bending and so are we: lives are superfluous when you have all eternity.

It is difficult to convey how this all felt at the time. It was as though we were seeing the wind in all its color and firmness. We were flipping our perceptions and trying to learn how it made us who we were and who we might end up being. Because none of us had ever experienced anything like this before. The universe dissipates, I thought, eventually it just spreads out to a thinness we can't imagine, in which everything is at a low energy and nothing happens. Just infinite dust. What do we do about that?

Silence.

Come on, people, how do we survive? It's a simple question, the kind we asked at the institute all the time.

Not how do we survive but rather why do we survive: the institute I remember but would prefer not to: the institute made me what I am: hey we should put that on a T-shirt: it would have to be about a few million miles wide: hey no need to be a buzz kill.

So, frivolity ensues. We are here to have fun, is that it?

Silence again. I remembered many times at the institute where we began talking about weighty matters, which, after all, was our job, and then continued in a comical vein when that got just a little boring. That was pretty much how the spoon digging began, and the spoon digging was exactly what got us into this mess in the first place. In any case, no one seemed particularly interesting in discussing it. I had the impression everyone was ready to move on other things and were impatient with me for continued to harp on this subject. But I had to know what was coming up and what was going to happen to us. Didn't I?

Fletcher was still there. I felt him. And the sun was there, as always. Steady presence, now expanded so large that it could not be fathomed on any level. It was bigger than any of us, quite literally bigger than anything the solar system had ever seen. It had done it's thing. Incinerated the planet, I supposed, and was now contracting. I forget my stellar evolution. Would it now be a dwarf star or a black hole, or what? Who was the astrophysics expert? Ah, yes, Grant. I want to ask Grant a question.

White dwarf, said a voice. I assumed it to be Grant.

Thanks. What does that mean for us?

The planet's toast. We're done with Earth.

So where do we go?

We don't go anywhere. We're right here. We're everywhere already.

No, no. I don't mean on the basis of that religious neo new age crap. I mean for real. What are we going to have to do?

We could coalesce back into our bodies, but who knows where we would end up? Or we could just continue as we are, with our essences strung out around the cosmos. It's kind of fun, don't you think?

I had to admit it felt good to not have to think about how we were going to get back to earth. That had become tedious, getting back beyond the flip.

We've gone a long way since the beginning, I said.

Yes, said Grant, *from our perspective. But there's still a long long way to go. We've only covered a fraction of the life span of the universe. Unfortunately, it was the interesting fraction. From now on we're just particles floating around. Proton decay will set in and eventually we won't even be particles. Just tiny islands of intention. And the islands will be separated by so much space that there won't be any connection.*

We need to reverse this trend, I said.

We could try contracting again, said Grant. *I don't know how well that would work. Plus, we don't have a planet to get back to.*

Because the earth is incinerated?

Something like that.

How can we even be communicating? I said.

An interesting question. Anyone else want to tackle that one?

A toughie no doubt: need further evidence: need a hypothesis: need to rest.

Come on, everyone, I said. We're supposed to be the smart ones, remember? Come up with something.

Their determined silence was beginning to annoy me a great deal.

Later, probably a few million years later, after I had grown tired to waiting, I made an announcement. I don't care what you are all going to do, I said, but I'm going to turn off my diffuser. I'm going to contract and be on a *planet*, the way people were meant to be.

Planetary living was only ever a temporary option. Someone. Maybe Fletcher?

Who said that? I said.

Doesn't matter. I'm no one you know.

A pulse of interest snaked through me. Someone new. There was other life out there. How interesting. You know this for certain? I asked.

Yes.

Who are you?

I've been around for a while. Started out much like you. I've been watching all of you. You think you're the first ones? No no. We've been here for ages and ages. You're just the latest additions. Lost your home, eh? So sad. Well so have we all. We stay here in the empty places because it has become habit. Not that we would have it any other way, not any more. Energy runs through us all the time. Do you feel it? Of course you do. Or you will. We're connected with all of it. All of the stuff that ever was and ever will be. Sound amazing? It is. But also just normal. As normal as anything could ever be. Here's the thing. Most of us are very happy to be clouds. Thoughts as you put it. But there are a few who, how shall we say it, feel out of their element? No matter and no surprises there. We've all been around people who seem out of place. It happens. We can see that there are enough of them, with enough mass between them that if they all joined together and coalesced, they would create a planet. Not a particularly large one as planets go, but enough for a solid surface, a biosphere, and a semblance of normality for any, um, inhabitants that would care to live on them. What do you say? Do you want to join them? They are massing for contraction now.

If I understood what this—*voice*—was saying, I could become part of a planet.

Would I still be alive? I said.

You'd have awareness. Whether you were alive or not is something else entirely, and a subject I am not qualified to pass judgment on. People have debated what being alive is for a long time. We still wonder about it.

The voice was right. I remember many a session at the institute in which we asked that very question. What is life? No one had a definitive answer.

It's all semantics, isn't it? I said.

In a manner of speaking, said the voice, *it all depends on what you mean by that.*

Ah, a cosmic jokester. That was fine. Where do I find these ones that want to become a planet?

You already have them. Just cast your attention to—

Oh! I said. There they are.

Right, said the voice.

There's a few billions of them, I said.

The voice seemed to consider this. *Cast out again,* it said. *I think you're missing some.*

I extended my awareness again. Still felt the same billions. Maybe about ten billion, if my estimate could be considered in any way even close to accurate. I only see about ten billion, I said. What am I missing?

There's more like trillions, it said, *or quadrillions. Anyway, a lot.*

No, I said, that can't be. There haven't been that many people born in the history of the world.

Of course not. But people aren't the only creatures that die.

Ah. I tried again. This time I felt them all: the trillions upon trillions of animals that have lived and died, now floating in the void. So cats diffuse? I said.

Yes, of course.

And dogs? Horses, bears, sharks, hummingbirds, badgers, worms, fleas, whales, crabs, dragonflies, turtles, ospreys, ducks, chipmunks, aardvarks, baboons, bats, buffaloes, crocodiles, elephants, goats, coyotes, parrots, horses, hamsters, snakes, lizards, camels, cows, armadillos, beavers, kangaroos, stingrays, skunks, frogs, wolves, giraffes, iguanas, cheetahs, moles, ladybugs, rats, crows, shrews, mice, parakeets, spiders, and salamanders? All of these creatures can diffuse themselves.

Sure. Some of them knew long before we did. Others learned from us. We'll need them all. You need a lot of mass to get a planet going, you know.

That seemed reasonable. And they all want to make a planet with us?

Some do, some don't. Those that do will join us, those that don't won't care.

I tried talking to them all. They answered. Every one of them. I could tell that all of them had a voice and they all greeted me at the same time. It was like the entire cosmos had woken up in the morning and they were trying to make me see how they saw things. And I did see things that way.

Join us, they said, *be a part of us. We could use you.*

I tried to find my spoon digging crew. They had to be out there, somewhere. Were they? I couldn't seem to connect to them. They were lost in the chorus. I hoped they were there.

Hey, I said, have you seen my friends, the ones who came with me?

That was a long time ago, they said. *We've all kind of forgotten who you came with.*

I really miss them, I said. I want them back.

Not sure we can really help you there, said the voice. *Search around. Maybe they'll come to you.*

While I was pleased to see that there was more to the diffusers than just humans, it also seemed like now there was too much. Too much to take in. All those creatures. All that life floating around out here. My friends were just tiny little insignificant nothings, or so it seemed. It was like looking for needles in haystacks. Worse. It was like the needles were too small to see and the haystacks filled the universe.

Their coalescing, now, said the voice.

Are you god or something? I said.

Something, said the voice. *I'm something. Or I used to be. Not sure what I am now. I heard that I might be the collective of all the diffused entities. That sounds about right. You have any other ideas?*

You're asking me?

Sure, you learned to diffuse. You know stuff.

I don't know anything, I said.

Well, okay, have it your way. Each entity accounts for a very small bit of matter, but when you put them all together, you get a very large mass.

Like a planet.

Exactly. Come on.

Come on? What did that mean?

It took only another instant to find out. There was a feeling like I was in a whirlpool, rather like the time Fletcher and I circled that depression in the water a couple of flips back. An inexorable process had begun, or so it felt to me. I also saw that I could opt out of it if I wanted. I had an opportunity to just flick my mind in a certain direction, perpendicular to all directions, and I would not be in the whirlpool anymore.

Did I want to do that? I had the inclination, but did not know if it was the best thing to do. I needed to know about the spoon diggers. Where were they, and what decision had they made about all this? I didn't know. I put my mind out. I intersected with a vast amount of energy that wanted to be friends with me. Fine, fine, but I was onto other things right now.

They flitted by me. It was like being in an infinite carousel, only stepping away from it, and standing on the outside looking in. Who would have thought such a thing was going to happen to me or anyone? None of that mattered, exactly, but it still made me think that there was way more to things than I had ever thought possible. Well, obviously, why would I ever have thought otherwise? Open up the world to myself, that was what was happening. Opening up the entire universe.

Um, said the voice.

Yes?

Your kind of gumming up the works here.

Me?

Yes. If you want in, then get in. If you want out, then stay out.

Excuse me.

You're excused.

I was being sarcastic.

I know. I was going along with it.

How long will this coalescing last?

A few million years. Haven't you been paying attention?

I miss my friends.

You'll feel them, you'll feel everyone once we've collapsed into the planet.

But I don't know if they are opting in.

Then you'll find other friends. Really, doesn't it seem as though friendship is an outmoded concept anyway?

Not exactly, I said. Without friends there isn't much to life, is there?

Friends are transitory.

Not really good friends. They stay with you forever.

Now the voice laughed and laughed.

What's so funny? I asked.

Nothing lasts forever, not even eternity.

I'd heard phrases like that at the institute all the time. They seemed profound or amusing, even witty, but they didn't make sense. I never let them go by at the institute, and I wasn't going to let this god or cosmic voice or whatever it was get away with this one. That's a stupid statement, I said.

Silence.

Did you hear me? I said.

Well, it wasn't just that this voice was silent. It was way more than that. It was that *every*thing was silent. All of the cosmos was completely and utterly quiet.

It was more than eerie. It was unnerving.

I was completely alone. I was so alone and it was so quiet that I didn't even want to say anything for fear I would break some cosmological constant or way of being on this scale. All because I insulted the voice? That voice wouldn't have lasted two minutes at the institute. No sirree. Much too touchy. There was more to being a cosmic voice than just blathering on about this and that. There was more to interacting with life than making silly statement.

I wanted to fill all of existence up with something and all I had was my voice, as far as I could tell. Everything else was empty. The coalescing was gone. Finished. Or if it was going on, I wasn't a part of it. Fine. It would have been fun to be part of a planet, but I could have a rich existence here without it. Couldn't I?

Well, no. Not exactly. There were no rich existences anymore. There was only the void and some hints of something else, something that could once have been called me. My identity was no longer wrapped up in a physical presence in the physical universe.

Wasn't that something? Couldn't I have found better ways to understand the world?

So the coalescing was going on. A planet? Sure, if they felt the need. But a planet is small potatoes. We can do better than that, can't we? We can find a lot more to do, the spoon diggers and I.

I was guessing that none of them was going to go along with the planet-making scheme. There were bigger things to do, much bigger. A planet was tiny, a little thing. A planet could be compromised by a plastic spoon. Not even a silver one. Plastic.

We could go after bigger things. Like change the universe. How about that? Wouldn't that be better than making a piddly little planet? Where are you, spoon diggers? We were taking apart a planet, spoonful by spoonful. Once you do that, what is the point of anything else?

But there isn't a way to go on from there. That was the problem. It was why we veered into the flips. You can't just dismantle a planet, or even try to. If you did that, all the inhabitants would be cast adrift. And that, as we might have said in the institute, presents unresolvable moral hurdles to the enterprise. Hurdles you couldn't really go around, which is often the way these things were resolved in our discussions. But none of that mattered now. We couldn't cast the entire life of the Earth adrift. Could we?

It's kind of how I was living now, wasn't it?

The universe balances out in the end. And the beginning. That was the thing that we didn't understand. Or didn't want to understand.

We in the institute thought we could find the secret of life, but it never really worked that way. Never could, in the end. Or the beginning. Because that was the whole point, wasn't it? The end and beginning are not really different. They're the same event seen from different perspectives. Especially when you consider that our perspective is more or less arbitrary, taking into account that vision is an accident of eyeballs. Yes. Without them, there is no vision. So if all the eyeballs are gone, where does the vision go?

A good question, or a silly one? Isn't like the tree in the forest? If no ears, where's the sound. I always said of course there's sound. You don't say there isn't something just because you aren't there to witness it. How egocentric! The silly questions are the one's children ask, but they are often the most penetrating and insightful, aren't they? What's the difference between a silly question and a profound question? No, really, what is the difference? Does anyone know?

"I do."

"Who's that?"

"Fletcher."

I groaned. "Not you."

"Something wrong with me?"

"I don't like you," I said. Strange to be petty about people at the end of time and space, but there it was. I wasn't proud of it, but I couldn't deny it. Fletcher bugged me. Got on my nerves. Always did, from the moment I met him.

"A lot of people don't like me," said Fletcher. "I'm used to it."

"How marvelous for you."

"The thing I noticed is that people have their own reasons for not liking me. And it's different from person to person. For example, some don't like my looks."

"What's wrong with your looks?"

"I have a slightly elongated face, but that's irrelevant. What's important is that the reason you don't like me is not about my looks."

"Okay."

"But that's interesting, to find out the reason for your dislike."

"Maybe to you, who seems to keep a list. Do you categorize them? Do you list them alphabetically?"

"I make mental notes, but I don't keep an elaborate list, no."

"It's good you don't have a physical list, because it would be gone now, wouldn't it?"

"I suppose so. Is it the smugness?"

"What?"

"The reason you dislike me. I've been told I have a smug attitude. Like I know everything and like to lord it over people. Is that the reason?"

I thought about it. It was a valid question. Not a silly one, although in another context it might have been considered silly. But he was being genuinely inquisitive, as far as I could tell. Not snarky at all. So I thought about it.

Fletcher could be annoying, but that wasn't the reason I disliked him. It was more than that, and a little less than that too. It was that he wasn't one of us. He seemed to want to try to be one of us, but he never could be. He was just too foreign, too much the loner to be a team member. I could not see him joking around with us after work, or finding a funny cartoon and showing it to everyone, maybe even posting it on his cubicle door. He just simply wouldn't do that, and that made him distant from us. He was always going to be the one who was separate from us. Too elitist.

"You think you are better than us," I said. I felt like I was in high school. Wasn't it Ralph who pointed out once that the institute was a lot like high school and we should maybe have a prom one night just to seal the deal. Sylvia agreed. She said we have cliques just like in high school and we sorted out the social hierarchy just like high school kids do.

I thought they were nuts and told them so at the time, but now, talking to Fletcher, who was the new kid in town, it kind of made more sense than I was comfortable with. The idea that we were these insignificant beings who had set up the rules and didn't let anyone else come close.

"Well," said Fletcher, "I do think if I was in charge of things, we wouldn't have been so freaked out about the flip."

"Freaked out?"

"You all behaved like the flip was the end of the world. But it wasn't so bad. Isn't so bad."

"You don't know anything about the flip," I said. "You fell into it just like the rest of us."

"I know that the flip would have happened no matter what any of us did. Or didn't do."

"Ridiculous," I said.

"Consider," said Fletcher. "You were digging with plastic spoons. Very charming, by the way. I found it endearing."

I didn't think he was being sarcastic, but I couldn't be exactly sure. I let it go.

"But plastic spoons are insignificant in the long run. You were scarring the ground, but again, the ground has been scarred any number of times. No, the big difference is that you were all working together. No, scratch that, not working together, but *thinking* together."

"I'm not following you," I said.

"At the institute, you all get together and mull over weighty problems and questions, yes?"

"And little questions, too. Everything is fair game."

"Fine, but you get together, that's the important part."

A lot of places like ours had the people separate, but with us that was the exception. We spent most of our time together, that was true. Naomi said it had been proven that small groups make better progress on problems than bigger groups or individuals. About five or six seems the best. All meetings of any kind should have no more than that many people. Seven or eight at the absolute most. Any more than that and people start to hide in the crowd. You don't get the full participation of the best minds.

Also, there are communication difficulties with so many voices. If you want to say something, often you can't, so your contributions are lost. There are all kinds of studies conducted and papers written about the dynamics of meetings. It all boils down to a few things: Start on time, stay small, keep it short. We tried to do that at the institute as much as we possibly could. "Yes," I said to Fletcher. "We get together."

"So don't you see?" he said. "You created a group mind with enormous power. You probably didn't even know it."

That didn't sound right. "You make it sound like no one had ever done this before," I said. "That just isn't true. Groups have been getting together forever. Maybe even longer."

"You don't want to listen to me, do you?"

Oh, there was the smugness and the elitism and the loner, non-team-playerism. We really worked to eradicate that attitude at the institute. We conducted conversations. In conversation people got interrupted. That was the way things worked. We all needed to understand that. If someone didn't then maybe they needed to do something else with their time and ours. Now how simple was that? "No," I said.

"We're here cast adrift in time and space," said Fletcher, "and I'm about the only voice you can hear, the only entity you can have interaction with and you refuse?"

"Something like that," I said.

"Well, I'm going to tell you anyway."

"Yeah," I said. "I thought you might."

"There are these spirits," said Fletcher.

Oh my. Here we go.

"They float around in the cosmos. Mostly we don't know about them, but sometimes they interact with us. They're kind of like those tiny particles that stream through us all the time and we don't know about them."

"Neutrinos?" I said.

"Exactly," said Fletcher. "Neutrinos. Anyway, these spirits manifest themselves as ghosts, sometimes, but as other things as well. Errant thoughts. Notions that you don't know where they came from. All that sort of thing. All the mysteries of life that you attribute to chance or god or whatever, that's these spirits. They're everywhere. They were created in the big bang, kind of left over from it actually, and they've been floating around ever since. They kind of are amused by us. People. They get on us at times and they will find ways to make us seem ridiculous."

"That isn't too difficult," I said.

Fletcher had the grace to laugh. "This is what I was getting on about when you asked the difference between silly and non-silly questions. If it involves the spirits, then it isn't silly. Get it?"

Fletcher had lost his mind, let's get that out of the way first and just accept it as a working theory. Accept it as fact, actually. And in doing so, he had gone a bit nutsy, going on about spirits and ghosts and such. Never a good sign in any case, for Fletcher it meant he was too loopy to humor any more.

"That's the most ridiculous thing I've ever heard," I said. "How do you know any of it is even true?"

"I had an inkling of it when I was very young. A boy, actually, barely able to speak. They presented themselves to me. Then, when I got a bit older I learned some science and began investigating them. I was able to attract many of them. They found me amusing, I think, and told me about themselves."

I interpreted this to mean that he had gone off the deep end and heard voices in his head, like any self respecting crazy person would, and that he thought of these voices as profound and really a lot of fun. So Fletcher was like one of those people you see on the street, talking to the air, while thinking he was talking to these spiritual beings.

"What do you call these spirits?" I said.

"I don't call them anything. They talk to me."

"What do they call themselves?"

There was silence. "Ha," he said. "Good question. I've never thought about that before. What would they call themselves? I think they have no need for names."

"Of course they don't"

"Well," said Fletcher, "you see, it's simple. They, um, they, well, they're the first beings. The first with anything on the ball, speaking in terms of mental acuity. They are pure thought."

His way of talking about them, made me think of ourselves, the people at the institute. Did we have similar notions of grandeur? Did we think we were the elite of the universe? In a way, I suppose we did.

We earned our bread by thinking about things and discussing them. Then we consulted with industry leaders and just about anyone else that would talk to us or try to get information from us. That's what we did. We behaved as though we knew the secrets of the universe, when we really didn't. No one did. Except Fletcher, if you were prepared to believe him. And Fletcher was more than prepared to believe himself. Sylvia used to laugh about it. She said we were part of the lazy economy. Our whole economy was based on people doing things for us that we didn't want to do. Like other people grew our food. Lazy economy. Other people educated our children. Lazy economy. Now, other people (us) were thinking our thoughts. Lazy economy.

Grant, who had a background in math, didn't see a problem with that. He always said mathematicians were the laziest people around. They were so lazy that they invented stuff so they wouldn't have to do things as strenuous as adding up a column of figures. "All the theorems of math were invented so mathematicians could do things more quickly and with less pencil marks on paper." Or something like that. The specialization of everything.

So now Fletcher was saying that we don't have our own spirits. These energy creatures, or pure thought, or whatever it is, they live in the ether for us. They make it clear that we don't have anything for ourselves. Is that it? Is that what Fletcher was saying?

"If we have no thoughts of our own," I said, "then how are we communicating with each other?"

"You ask the most obtuse questions," said Fletcher.

"There are no obtuse questions," I said. "Any question is a fair one. The most ignorant questions, the ones that children ask, are the most penetrating."

"I've heard that one all my life," said Fletcher, "and I never believed a word of it. Children know nothing. A good question comes from someone who knows a lot and needs more. A good question is supported by knowledge already gained and assimilated. A good question is more than just a quest for ignorance quenching."

"Ignorance quenching?"

"Yeah. A phrase I invented a long time ago. Like it?"

I had to admit it had a certain charm. "It's a pretty good description," I said.

"In any case," said Fletcher, "you're displaying appalling ignorance right now."

"How's that?"

"You don't see the truth of your situation."

Okay, so now Fletcher was being the mysterious oracle at the end of time. I wanted to tell him I had no patience for his crazy machinations, but that wasn't true at all. I had all the time in the world, all the time in the known *and* unknown universe, actually. "The truth, as far as I can determine," I said, "is that we are floating around in the void and being made to listen to ethereal mutterings of former corporeal beings and pretty much getting bored in the process. How's that? I got the truth of the situation down?"

"Yes, but only to a certain extent. You haven't taken the final step."

"Final step?"

"We, all of us, we're not just what we were. We are more than that now. We are the energy beings. We are pure thought."

Ridiculous. Fletcher was again being the crazy man on the corner, wailing about the end of the world. I had not been around since the big bang. I was not about to believe that I was some spirit being with all the answers. Or even any of the answers. I didn't even know the questions.

"I wish," I said, "that I was conversing with someone else. Anyone else."

"No," said Fletcher. "Listen to me. We are the conglomeration of events which led to physical manifestations. We are the start of it all. We're like the grain of sand in the oyster, only we're a grain of sand stuck in the cosmos.

Around us grew everything. We're smaller than atoms, smaller than anything. We can't even conceive of what it is that we're smaller than."

"Why don't I remember any of that early stuff?"

"Well," said Fletcher, "actually you do. You just don't recognize the memories as what they are. Ever sat outside under the stars? Ever feel that kind of awestruck ache, that wonder?"

"Sure," I said. "Doesn't everyone?"

"Most do. Those that let themselves realize it. Not everyone though. They're like amnesiacs."

"You've got a whole hierarchy set up on this stuff," I said.

"Not me," said Fletcher. "I invented nothing. It was all there in front of me, in front of anyone. I just started paying attention."

"We all pay attention," I said. "Everyone."

"You can't believe that," said Fletcher. "There are all kinds of zombies walking around. Surely you've noticed them. They are everywhere."

"They're paying attention to different things," I said. "Just because they don't interest me doesn't mean they aren't valid for them."

"The insaniacs are the true geniuses, eh?"

"Well, I wouldn't' go that far. Anyway, genius is a relative term. We shouldn't throw it around willy-nilly like we know exactly what it means."

"Oh, genius has a definition. It's the ability to make connections. The more connections you can make, the higher on the genius scale you happen to be."

"We're getting away from where we started."

"That's kind of the definition of the universe, isn't it? We start with the big bang and we keep moving away from it. That's how everything came to be, after us."

I knew a little cosmology. I was aware of the temperatures and pressures in the infant universe. It seemed impossible that anything supporting thought could be there in that primordial singularity.

We used to ask why there was anything instead of nothing. No one had a good answer for that. It was the strangest thing that our own existence was a mystery. Why did we exist? No one knew. No one at the institute wanted to know. It was one of those spiritual questions, best left to the realm of religion.

Only now we were nothing but spiritual beings. Shouldn't now, at least, be a proper time for such inquiry?

"So we just kind of float around here," I said. "Is that what we have to look forward to?"

"You're still not getting it. There is nothing to look forward to. We are it. There's nothing else."

"Weren't some of the others going to make planets or something?"

"A planet is nothing without a sun."

"Then they'll make a sun, too."

I almost heard him sigh, even though I knew that was impossible. "You're still not getting it," he said. "You can't remake the universe like that. What we need to do is reverse the big bang. Create a big crunch and start the whole thing up again."

"While we're at it, why not create life and find the answers to the riddle of the universe?" Ha. Had him there.

"Well, yeah," said Fletcher. "Now you're getting it. That's what I've been on about all this time."

"I was kidding."

"Why kid? Why now? There's nothing left. There's nothing to kid about."

"That's certainly one point of view," I said, "but really, if you can't laugh, then there's nothing left."

"Laughter is the last refuge of the demented, the crude, the ignorant, and the ridiculous," said Fletcher. "Sometimes even the first refuge."

That seemed to explain a lot about Fletcher. Who could be against laughter? "Some people think we aren't even human without laughter," I said.

"What people?" said Fletcher. "Haven't you been paying attention? There are no 'people' left. Or very few. At any rate, almost none."

"We're still here."

"We're insignificant."

And here I tumbled back to a place I hardly remembered existing way back when, when I was younger than the primordial universe. I was hardly able to speak, didn't know how to recognize faces and spent most of my time gurgling and waving my arms and legs around uselessly. We've all been there, I'm sure. We all have that in our background, though few of us talk about it and some of us may even be embarrassed by it. But why be embarrassed? It's just a natural thing, a kind of natural progression of the world, isn't it? Well, isn't it?

"What?" said Fletcher.

Oops, didn't want that leaking out quite like that. No matter if he heard. He was just Fletcher. And that's another thing, how did I end up at the end of time with Fletcher of all people? Weren't there billions of other dead people around? Why Fletcher?

"Because we were in the whirlpool together," said Fletcher.

Wow. I really had to rein in my thoughts. They were leaking out all over the place.

Okay. So the gurgling. I always thought baby talk had a lot more on the ball that people gave it credit for. It was pure thought, unrevised by the culture. There was nothing we could add to it to make it more pure.

So, also, with the big bang: pure matter, unrevised by history. Or rather, not the big bang, but the singularity immediately before the bang.

Once at the institute we talked about that big bang thing. How the term was originally meant as a mocking name, but then it stuck. "People like explosions," is what Ralph said. "I do. They're cool."

"As long as someone isn't hurt by them," said Sylvia.

Ralph rolled his eyes at that. "Yes, of course, that goes without saying."

Ralph did have a point. Explosions are very popular entertainments. To call the beginning of the universe an explosion was tantamount to saying that here was the ultimate explosion, the ultimate entertainment. Of course the term caught on. It created expectations and a certain kind of picture of the universe. It made people believe we were made in violence and that violence was the natural order of things. One of the three F's is what Ralph would say about that.

I wasn't so sure and I didn't want to get into that argument, but fighting was a part of us, a part of many of us, so he might have had a point, though there was fighting long before we knew about the event that came to be called the big bang.

Still, there is the collective memory, the wellspring of myth. It had to come from somewhere. Maybe we all remembered the big bang and played out its drama in our lives without even knowing it. Blowing our tops? Letting loose? Screaming? Throwing punches? Are they all related to that initial explosion?

But it wasn't an explosion. That was the point. We had all been laboring under false assumptions and false history. An explosion instantaneously ejects matter into an existing medium. What the original expansion of the singularity did was quite different. It *created* matter. It was an inflation, if anything. It made space. Before the singularity expanded, there was no space. There wasn't even nothing. Less than nothing, if you can imagine that.

Grant suggested we call it the original sigh. That had a certain whimsical appeal, but it was wrong too. A sigh introduced exhalation into air. That isn't what it was about. That wasn't what happened. Grant's term softened the image, but only by degrees. A sigh was very similar to an explosion, and really only differed in intensity. The mechanism was essentially the same.

The best term, in my opinion was expansion. Not that original, but it didn't have to be. It just had to describe what was and what was going to be.

"You onto something over there?" said Fletcher.

"I'm thinking."

"Think out loud. There isn't much to do here, it would be nice to listen to something."

"You don't want to hear what I have to say."

"Try me."

"I'm trying to relate the expansion of the singularity to how people first learn to talk."

"Go on."

At the institute, that was our term of high praise. If someone said something interesting, we would often say "go on" to encourage them. It was a way of acknowledging that they were speaking of things with substance. On the other hand, if what they said sounded kind of boring, or if we could not see where they were going to go with it, we might say something like "huh" or "interesting," which did not mean what it said at all.

Ralph, especially, was maddened by this. "Why say 'interesting' when you mean the exact opposite?" he would often ask. "Will someone please explain that to me? Please." So Ralph did not understand, or want to understand, irony. That was fine. He was a literalist. Kind of simple minded in a way, but that was good. We needed people in a discussion who just said and understood things on their face value. It could be very clarifying.

"Hey," said Fletcher. "I'm dying over here."

"I think," I said, "that we're already dead."

"You know what I mean."

I did, but I didn't want him to know I knew. I also didn't want him to know why I didn't want him to know. "I was just thinking that maybe we were looking at the origin of the universe all wrong."

"Yes, yes, I got that from you already."

"Well, here's the thing," I said. "You know about the three Fs?"

"Feeding, fighting, and fucking. Sure. A very cynical view of human nature, indeed of all of nature."

"Right. Cynical, but also, in its narrow way, kind of accurate. So I was trying to relate it to the universe. The big bang is like an explosion, so it's fighting. You know, how when you get filled with fighting rage you kind of explode into the world. Then the big crunch, like you've been talking about, it's all about getting closer, contracting, kind of intimate. It's like fucking, sex. As intimate as two people can me."

"Huh," said Fletcher. "And the feeding?"

He didn't exactly say "Go on," but it was close. Didn't like that "huh" that preceded it, though. "Well," I said, "the feeding is all the stuff in between, the interacting with the universe, the taking in of matter, and light, heat. It's all a kind of feeding, where matter gets interchanged and moved around and reshuffled ad infinitum."

"Okay," said Fletcher. "I can see a loose connection. But where does that leave us? What do we do now?"

"I brought all this up because I was kind of agreeing with you about the big crunch. We need to take care of that. How do we make that happen for us?"

Fletcher shook his head. Or I imagined that he shook his head. "The big crunch. Yeah. That was my area of expertise, did you now that?"

"I didn't really know anything about your background," I said. "It all seemed kind of vague."

"Well, the big crunch is purely theoretical, you know."

"Sure."

"But there are experts in theoretical events. You can get a degree in exobiology, did you know that? Hell, I've personally known two PhDs in the subject. A subject which, as far as anyone knows, doesn't exist. Never existed. Now sure, there might be living creatures on a world other than the Earth. There's lot's of people that say it's inevitable, but that's just faith, no different than saying there's a white bearded god sitting on a throne manipulating human events. Faith. It may be very probable that other life exits, it probably is likely, but no one can say that for sure because none has ever been detected, much less studied. And yet, these guys got advanced degrees in it. They are experts in something that has not been shown to even exist. Isn't that funny? Doesn't that make you laugh?"

I was back to the babbling babies, thinking Fletcher was beginning to go off the deep end. Where do crazy people go at the end of the world? What is there left once you have survived the demise of everything else?

It's a wonder I wasn't crazy. When I was a baby there was everything to learn. Now here I am at the end. I've learned it all. There wasn't anything else to learn because there wasn't anything else. Now wasn't that a kick in the pants? And what did all that learning get me? Not much. Here I was, waiting for something. Death, I suppose. Final dispersal. I couldn't maintain this network forever, could I? I didn't even know how I was thinking words and hearing Fletcher's words. Eventually we would have to just pull apart completely and then there wouldn't be any connection and all of consciousness would be dissolved. Wouldn't it?

"What," said Fletcher. "I'm not worth answering now?"

He was getting touchier all the time, like I was always supposed to be entertaining him and if I wasn't then he had to pick a fight with me. "Yeah," I said. "It's funny about the exobiologists. They're like theoretical mathematicians, I suppose."

"Exactly," said Fletcher. "You've got it. They should maybe have degrees in Math. Statistics, or something. Not biology. Biology is like the messiest thing you can get into. It's all squishy tissue and blood and everything. But they don't do that. They sit around and think about theoretical creatures and imaginary ecosystems, and planets with weird plants and stuff. Well, that's math. That's probabilities and extrapolation and speculation. Yeah. They're mathematicians.

Frauds with biology degrees. I mean, really. Come on. You got anything else for me? I feel in the mood for rants."

"Don't let me stop you."

"Come on. What have you been thinking about?"

"Language."

"Oh, yeah, that's a good one. What about language?"

So he wanted to fight? Was that it? "I was thinking about how we acquire language. How babies start talking."

"Babies. There's something. Who needs them?"

Oh good, I found something he could go on about. "The human race needs babies," I said. "People die. We need babies to grow up and replace them."

"Yeah, of course, that's the way it *used* to be. But now? Bah."

"Yeah, now. But weren't we talking about the world before the flip, before all of this? I mean, *nothing* is needed anymore. We're all just lost in the void."

"Except I remember hating babies," said Fletcher.

Why was I not surprised? I was generally suspicious of those that disdained babies. It was like saying the human race was not worth anything. "Are you serious?" I said. "Do you really and truly hate babies?"

"Don't you?"

"As a former baby myself," I said, "I can't in good conscience even consider the idea of hating babies."

"I had a kid once. With my ex. She wanted children so bad. I didn't. But I went along with it because I loved her. Or something. I don't know. Does it matter? After the baby was born, it was terrible. I got so depressed. She was so happy. We couldn't go on that way. It was as though we were on different planets."

"So you left her?"

"Yeah. It was best for everyone involved."

I wasn't sure about that. "How old is your kid?"

"14. She's a whiz in school. Really smart."

Amazing that we can forget that there is no kid, no school, no being smart, because there is nothing left anymore.

"So you didn't really hate her, I mean when she was a baby."

"Oh I adore her now. Think the world revolves around her. The trouble was, when she was a baby, *she* thought the world revolved around her and that was hard to take."

What an odd thing to think, much less say. Of course babies think the world revolves around them. They don't know any better. "I really don't think babies have the capacity to consider that sort of thing," I said.

"Oh don't they? You aren't up on your latest infant research. They're a lot smarter than we give them credit for. They are like crows that way. They know how to manipulate the environment, let me tell you. And they leave their environment a mess, a true and unholy mess, with everything everywhere out of place and in the way and just dirty. Filthy, actually."

"That's just the way babies are. They don't know about cleanliness."

"That's my point," said Fletcher. "If they were truly worthy human beings, they wouldn't allow themselves to behave in such a way."

It was truly amazing that Fletcher had such thoughts. How could he think of babies as being able to rework their environment? It was ludicrous. "Are you okay?" I said.

"What do you mean?"

"Your thoughts on babies. Well, they're just a little unrealistic, you know. You give them way too much power. They can't actually *do* anything. They just kind of float around while everything happens around them."

We both paused, the silence covering us with devastating effect. There was nothing left for us, we suddenly realized. Fletcher's daughter was a loose collection of atoms floating in the void, if she was anything. More likely she was gone. Just like everything else was gone now.

I didn't pursue Fletcher's thought about hating babies. He clearly didn't hate his daughter, just disliked the mess of babies, the way they create chaos. Which was fair. No one *liked* the mess that babies create. But come on. You can't blame babies for being made the way we make them. Unless you were Fletcher. He was not one to abide by chaos, and not one to let chaos go. Too bad, since so much of life was chaos. Or had been chaos, at any rate. Although that kind of chaos seemed welcome now, an ordered chaos of sublime beauty compared to this new chaos that was upon us, in which we were like babies again. No power.

"Do you think they've made their planet?" I asked.

"No," said Fletcher. "They can't."

"They can't?"

"The building blocks won't stick together anymore. That's what happens as the years pile up. The atoms won't adhere to each other."

"I've never heard that," I said.

"Again, you haven't been reading the literature. You know there was all kinds of research going on about the end of the world. Lots of theorists were working on the problem. We came up with some interesting results."

"What about the crunch?" I said. "How can we make that happen?"

"The crunch. Yeah. I'm not sure it's worth it."

"Are you crazy?"

"Quite possibly."

"Without the crunch, we're doomed. There's nothing but a dissipated collection of atoms. Or partial atoms."

"Even with the crunch, we're doomed. We'd just be crushed to nothing. There would be no life."

That didn't sound right. "I thought you said that the crunch was the reversal of the big bang. That it would all bounce back again."

"Well, sure, but there's no predicting the nature of the reversal."

"Like the flips?"

"Only worse. At least in the flips we recognized stuff. After the crunch takes everything through the singularity again, there's absolutely no telling what would come out the other side. There may be atoms, there may not. Even if there are atoms, they may all be hydrogen and never cohere to make stars. No stars, no metals. No metals, no galaxies or planets, much less people."

"But it happened once before. At least once before."

"Sure, but it might have been accident. All the parameters fell into place and they made people. Great. But it could be a one in trillion chance. Maybe there are infinite universes and big bangs, and ours was the only one that had life. It's possible. Maybe even probable. Got it?"

I got it. Fletcher was saying we were most likely doomed no matter what we did. That sounded worse than terrible. It was as though the entire universe had suddenly flipped over and now lay dying on the ground in front of me.

"All because we dug dirt with plastic spoons?" I said.

Fletcher laughed. "You are so fixated on that," he said. "Why don't you let that go? It is so long in the past. It doesn't matter a wit with what's going on now because you can't do anything about it. That's the most important thing to know: we are now completely and utterly helpless."

Like children. Babies. We could not do anything to influence our future. That's what Fletcher was saying, in his laconic and depressing way.

"So what *are* you going to do?" I said.

"What?" said Fletcher. "I just told you. Nothing. I'm not doing anything because I *can't* do anything."

"It's like that paper you wrote, the one that said any sufficiently complex activity entails deaths. Only this is a complex activity that entails the death of everyone from all time."

"Now you've got it. Every living creature was terminally ill."

"That's a terrible way to look at things."

"Maybe. But how can we do otherwise? We don't have anything anymore. We're all gone. Dead and gone."

"Then how can I hear you? Why do you have a voice?"

Fletcher didn't say anything for a while. I thought maybe I had lost him completely this time and I was truly alone. The thought frightened me more than I had ever been frightened before and for an instant I wanted it all to end. I was prepared to have my life completely and utterly over.

"Maybe you're crazy," said Fletcher.

A fair possibility. Maybe I was crazy. Could I prove that I was actually talking to Fletcher and not to myself? I did not immediately see an obvious way to do so.

"If you're just a voice in my head," I said, "then how about telling me how you got there."

I thought that was a pretty good one. Fletcher *was* there. I could doubt anything I wanted to, but I couldn't doubt my own self. And that meant Fletcher was there. He was in my head. He practically *was* my self.

Only he wasn't answering me anymore.

"Fletcher," I said. "You still there?"

I waited a long time. On my perception of things it was a few minutes. On the way of the universe it had to have been millions, even billions of years. The dissipation was proceeding as expected. So all the voices were gone now. All except my own. I was still here, somehow, thinking thoughts, while the rest of the universe and all living things had simply—evaporated. There was nothing to see because there were no eyes. There was nothing to understand, because there was nothing to interact with. Actually, nothing left *to* understand, except some components of atoms flung hither and yon.

So I was alone? It hardly seemed possible that anyone could be this alone, did it? If I was as alone as I thought I was, then it would have to be the case that my aloneness could not be mitigated in any way.

Now here is where the instant of my perception flipped over. It is impossible to describe but I will attempt to do so. Do you recall ever being in a car with other cars in multiple lanes, waiting for the light to change? Then, what sometimes happens, is that the car next to you will begin moving, ever so slowly, anticipating the light about to change. The movement is almost or barely imperceptible, but what will sometimes happen, is that you think *you* are moving instead. Then an instant later, the truth of the situation asserts itself and there's this kind of flip in your perception and you realize, with some dazing involved, that it really is the *other* car that moved.

It's a very eerie sensation. It happens on trains, too, when you are stopped at a station with another train stopped on the next track. The other train starts moving and you think it is you that is moving.

Most people probably don't notice this, but for those that do, there are two reactions: *There is something wrong with me*, or *Isn't that interesting?* The latter are people who take delight in having their preconceived notions turned upside down. I used to think I was one of those. But at that moment, the universe tipped back. I thought I was moving out, but I began moving in. There is no other way to describe it except through analogy. It was exactly the sensation of seeing the other thing move while you are actually doing the moving.

So I don't know what exactly happened in that instant. Did I move, or did the universe move? In any case, the flip happened in that instant. Instead of dissipating, I was now contracting. I had been through so many flips before this, all of them disconcerting on a deep and fundamental level, even on a violent scale. All the flips before this were cataclysmic in scale, for me, if not the universe. But this one. This one was different. Had to be different because it was on a much bigger scale. It was the whole universe, all of existence that just reversed course. And I was there, not only to witness it but to be a part of it.

Now followed many millions of years. During that time I lost the thread of things sometimes. I had time perception that was off kilter, in its way, and that told me things that could not be. How could I be contracting? How could the universe be contracting? It was as Fletcher said, we were heading to the big crunch. What was I to do now? Could I jockey for position in the next universe? Should I try to arrange my atoms so as to be ideally poised for when the crunch occurs? Fletcher said it was impossible, but how did he know? Maybe there was something to do.

Another million billion years passed.

I occurred to me several times during that phase to think about how the contracting had happened. Why did we start coming back? We had discussed cosmology at the institute. Many times. There were theories about how the universe would expand, then begin to contract at some point when the slowing down happened because of the mass.

No one knew when or how that would happen, because no one really knew how much mass there was in the universe. Well, now we knew one thing. Or at least I knew one thing: there was enough mass to begin the contraction. The universe did not expand forever, as some had theorized. At least not this universe, at least not on this flip.

It is not something you prepare for, this way of seeing the universe. It can only be something you stumble onto. The power we have to observe, is really no power at all. Passivity is its own drab incompetence and ignorance combined. It was taking such a long time. So long.

As the time passed some more voices came into my head. Fletcher's might have been there, I wasn't sure. And the spoon diggers, they might have been there, too. But I could not discern any of them. They all combined in my head to create a cacophony.

They were people, animals, planets, stars, and trees. They were everything: all the creatures, the living and the dead, and the never living. All of creation was going through me. I imagined that it was going through everyone else as well. Very probably. I was just part of the multitude, the all encompassing voices, which became one voice, a kind of roaring, at first.

As time passed the roaring grew more pronounced. In my feeble sensibilities I saw it as a kind of cheering for the crunch. Go crunch, go crunch, yah yah yah. We cheered because we knew that the dissipation was over. The coalescing was upon us.

But that wasn't it completely. There was no cheering, really, except in my own interpretation of things, the way that I wanted it to be. After a few million years, it became clear that what I thought was cheering was actually singing. Sounding a single note, sustained for eons. It was the sound of the universe.

Call it the background radiation if you will, or the background accompaniment. Call it anything you want. What we had was a sonic lifeline, a path of sound that we all could hitch ourselves to.

And we did.

We had no other choice, because there was no way to shut it out. I spent some time trying to separate the threads of sound, make their components plain. But there were so many, and that was a problem. As soon as you plucked away one strand, another was there in its place. You pulled at them like unraveling the strands of a rope, but the rope was too robust and resilient, it never allowed itself to *be* pulled apart. It never allowed itself to become separate.

It was as though the universe was completely contained in the interweaving of all the strands. The universe was not the strands, it was the accumulation and braiding of the strands. There was no universe without the relationships there. How can I convey the immensity of this realization?

We were floating on a sea of temporal foam, all of us, all of life. And what was life? Nothing but the relationships between atoms and the accumulations of atoms. The flips were rearrangements of the relationships. It was disconcerting and even maybe a little dangerous, but it was not the end of the world. Literally. It was a re-imagining of the world and what it could be. We flipped so many times that the world had become more than the sum of any of its parts. We flipped to be life. The flip was the fourth F. The first three were only preliminaries, the squabbling and groping for each other. The raw need to go on. That was the first three Fs. Like the first three dimensions, it was mundane and ordinary.

But the Fourth F, the flip, was the crucial one, the one that made everything make sense and be real. It was the way time was to the first three dimensions.

The dimension of time could only give the first three dimensions a stage and make it all make sense. That was what the flips did: they made feeding, fighting, and fucking make sense, because after all the first three Fs were over and done with, the flip was still there. The amazing flip from expansion to contraction. Without it, there was no life. Without the flip the entire meaning of existence was less than nothing: it was void.

A millions years passed.

Another million.

I had learned the secret of the universe. Now what? The voices, which I had kind of forgotten about, were still there. Background, didn't I say? The background of existence. The most comforting sound ever devised. The most beautiful feeling ever felt. By anyone.

We lived for that, for the press of the other against us. To be part of another was all there was, in the end, and all that the universe understood, on any level you would care to name and understand.

And so now I was riding creation backwards. Instead of traveling away from the big bang I was going towards the big bang, its mirror reflection. Where were the others? They had to be around here somewhere. Didn't they?

Didn't they?

And how would I even recognize them?

The voices were resolving themselves, now. Slowly. I heard ones I could not possibly recognize. I thought they might be creatures I knew nothing about. That seemed plausible. I did not argue with my instincts. What was perception, anyway? A co-mingling with one's environment, and then a tickle in the brain to make one see/hear/feel/taste/smell something. It's all just atoms shuffling around here and there.

Then something I could understand. Another roaring. It came from somewhere I could not determine. It wasn't from inside me, and it wasn't from outside me. It was from everywhere all at once.

Time is the ultimate mystery, in its own way. I did not know how long I had been circling this flip. It could have been an instant, and it could have been forever. It was just simply impossible to say and I wasn't going to try.

Instead, I answered the sound, in my own way, the only way I knew possible. I sent out my own sound, trying to make myself heard above the cheering of the universe.

And here is where things got so strange. We had all been indoctrinated in the cult of the big bang and the expansion of the universe. We had all gotten that training and that brainwashing for a long time. Brainwashing? Yes, that's what I said. We accepted it because it was there. Try to say it wasn't real, just try it. No one would have taken you seriously. None of us could escape it. The steady state theorists were more or less mocked and even when their theory was modulated, there were no real adherents, no on who would stand up and be counted as believing in such a thing. None of the theories could come up with a plausible explanation for what was there before there was a there there.

You see? It's all a conjuring trick, pulling rabbits out of a hat, flowers out of a sleeve. What were the alternatives?

God made everything. Ho hum.

Matter appeared spontaneously out of the quantum foam. Are you serious?

An immensely dense singularity began to expand. Oh! Yes! Now you've got it. That makes way more sense.

But whether it did or did not didn't matter. The big bang was it. There was no other option. And now we saw that the big bang was simply a reincarnation of the past universe and that we were on our way to another flip, another step in the progression.

How many had there been, and was there a way to tell, or was it all just guesses? No way to understand this, no way to make ourselves see how it was. The flips erased everything, didn't they? Once you crushed everything to a singularity, surely there was no information left. To be a piece of information floating in the void, well, there had to be other ways of looking at things, didn't there?

But there was no other way. There could not be another way. We were only information. Wasn't that what the physicists had been telling us for years? That matter was a notion? Nothing but an idea that manifested itself, in, of all ways, strings and sub atomic particles, and then particles, atoms. Such a crazy way to make a universe. And what about proton decay? Weren't we scattered long enough for that to begin to kick in? And without protons, or a depletion of their numbers, what did we have left? What could we expect to actually *be*?

When we all coalesced back into molecules and planets and people again, what were we going to be? I hesitated to even try to understand that. I was something, some sort of energy, or tilt, or something. A yearning? A random collection of stuff, or thought that seemed to bring something into being?

What a notion. That I was a tendency to something. The tilt was like the flip, wasn't it? The tilt. I tilted to something. Or the universe tilted to something that made it seem as though I was a person. My thoughts were getting jumbled, but I had the kernel of something, I knew. The universe was contracting around me. Instead of infinite space, I was being given boundaries. Was that such a bad thing? No. It defined, didn't it?

Without boundaries we—I—was nothing that could be understood as a separate person. And still the voices. Why voices? The big bang seemed to be there still. The singularity haunted us all, didn't it? We were all haunted by the universe. That may be as good a definition as anything: the universe is that aspect of reality that haunts our minds. But that still didn't tell us what it was. We didn't know what it was. Even the name was a guess. It may not have been a singularity at all, but a kind of multiverse, where there was not one thing, but many things, indeed, all things, everything, the infinity of things collapsed into itself. Have you ever had the feeling that there is much more than you think there is? It's true. There is so much more.

And here things changed.

I had been talking to myself for so long that at first I didn't notice the change. Eventually I couldn't *not* notice it: The voices that had been floating around like a singularity of sound, were now accompanied by images. Where did that come from? I had been viewing nothing for many billions of years. Less than nothing. It had been a void of featureless and epic proportions. The sort of thing that we would invent to explain the horrible indifference of creation.

Only we did not have to invent it, it was there. In all its inglorious indifference. There was comfort in it, I will not lie to you. It was fine to think that the universe had no interest in you. By that measure, you were not special except to yourself, and what was wrong with that? We had nothing to add to the depletion of the big bang. We were just riders along for the sight seeing. Only there was no sight seeing. Not for a long time.

We came from the singularity. That fact was enough to confuse us into thinking we had significance. But a steady mind tells you something completely different. I was in the singularity, but I was less than a speck of dust. That is the comfort of creation. You don't have the great responsibility that something bigger would entail. Can you relax now? Can you just enjoy the fact of existence?

It should be easy now that you know. And not that I knew a whole lot. It was intuition guiding my mind, if it could be called a mind. And the jostling of the images now, the colors and the shapes. They were indistinct, no features, only vague and blurry shapes. But not unwelcome.

They were a feast, in fact. The pure look of pure images. We had seen to it that we could take in those visual cues. Despite our never having had the training necessary to see the universe, we saw it. It was a marvelous thing to be able to take in the atoms of the universe and make pictures in our heads.

I did so for a few million years. The shapes were extraordinary. So simple. Round, fluid, bending, and flowing. The colors cycled through all the hues of existence. There were countless numbers of them. I wasn't even sure I believed in infinity anymore, and yet, there they were, the infinity of colors, wrapping themselves around objects like they were its skin.

And then the resolving. I had to understand that we were going from chaos to order. The reverse of entropy. We were on the other side of the flip. Entropy decreased.

Oh, it was all so nuts. We would have to rethink everything, if there even was a we anymore.

At the institute we always spoke of the way of the world, that the bigger was modeled in the smaller, that the different scales of the universe were congruent with one another. Nothing one scale did was not reflected in another scale. That the deep structure of existence was probably some form of fractal. And so, now, my scale was the collection of these images in my mind, whatever that was. And that was just a reflection of the greater singularity of creation that had made all of this up in the first place. The images and the voices.

I was not sufficiently complex to understand them. They were more like random firings of everything everywhere, and I was here to take it all in and try to make sense of it. That was the human way, wasn't it? Try to make sense of creation. Why were we so interested in that? Wasn't it enough to just be a part of creation? Wasn't it sufficient to allow ourselves to just *be*? Why all the other features of life? The yearning for something beyond when there wasn't anything beyond.

There was just us. That had to be enough, and yet, it was not enough. Had never been enough for most of us. We wanted explanations. We stood before the tide of creation and demanded explanations of it, as though it was a recalcitrant child we needed to discipline. Why this way of arranging matter, huh? Why does life require this particular mix of circumstances? Why does the gravitational constant have this particular value and if you alter that value by even a million billionth of a percentage point, then the universe is not viable? Why are things arranged so? Tell us.

But there is no telling. We had to find out on our own. And you couldn't look it up in the index at the back of the book. You had to go out and discover it. And if you couldn't discover, then you had to make it up. That the was crux of the whole thing.

We made things up and told ourselves that was the reality of the universe. It was just the reality of imagination, no different that religious faith, which came from our own minds as well. Then we went on from there. We could not interrogate, so instead of interrogation, we chose dissection and rending. We experimented and pulled things apart and didn't know how to put things back together. And how could we? There was no plan to it all, it just happened.

If you want to see what the universe was like, you had to take the universe apart, like a clock. That was the paradigm for a long time. But the universe wasn't a clock. It was much more random than that, and out of the randomness came some kind of order, or what we perceived of as order.

But order is an subjective notion. The big bang was a kind of chaos that we saw as order. No one knew what to do with that order. We still don't, because we cannot understand it. Not in the way that we understand how two plus two equals four.

When we were the spoon diggers we didn't know what we were doing. How could we? It was an insane whim, nothing more. We wanted something that might be called recreation. A way to relieve the pressure. But we didn't know. We had no idea. We set something off. I still didn't know what, but the evidence was difficult to ignore and there was no reason to ignore it. Somehow the spoon digging changed our perceptions, put us through the flips to the ultimate flip, the point where it all came back on itself.

And now we, or at least I, since I wasn't sure there were others, at least not yet, I, I say, was on the downhill slide. Careening towards the big crunch. How many times did we discuss this very thing at the institute? Too many times. I eventually grew weary of it, but there were some, notably Grant and Sylvia, for whom this was the most important subject they knew. It was all about how the big bang and the big crunch play themselves out. There was nothing else.

But they were such remote concepts that they held nothing for me. Eventually. I admit I was intrigued by the questions at first, but they led nowhere, and it seemed that they could never lead anywhere, by the very nature of their substance. Like arguing about religion, such arguments never really led to any kind enlightenment. Rather, they reinforced entrenched notions and made for hard feelings between opposing adherents.

Not that that was necessarily a bad thing, but it did make lunch in the cafeteria a sometimes awkward affair. For my part, I had come to terms with the essential mystery of the cosmos and my spoon digging suggestion was mostly in the way of fun, nothing more. Now here I was. Playing the universe's evolution backwards. I anticipated that time would settle down for me. I would come to a place much like I had known before, in which the universe was a benign arrangement of planets and such, where I could live on a surface and take part in the exchange of energy that characterizes so many biospheres. That was a simple existence, to be sure, and yet the only existence that we could hope for, or so it seemed. It was not enough to be a tilt, a mere tendency of matter to have some kind of subtle emphasis to order. What a definition of life! A subtle tendency to order. Is that the best I could come up with?

"Evidently."

Ah. Finally. Another voice. One I thought I recognized. "Naomi?" I asked.

"Close," said the voice. "It's Grant."

"Grant? Is it really you?"

"As far as I can tell," said Grant. "I haven't run any tests yet."

I laughed. Ever the experimentalist. "What are you?" I asked.

"What a question," said Grant.

"You know what I mean," I said. "We rode the wave of the big bang to its edge, and now we're on our way back. That's what I did. Didn't you do the same?"

"Yes."

Of course he answered yes, there was no other answer to the question. "Well, there's no telling what we are now," I said. "It's like waiting for birth, to see what we are going to become. What we are to be."

"I suspect we're templates," said Grant. "We're blueprints from which a life can be constructed. Think of us as free floating souls looking for a biological entity to inhabit."

That seemed like a fair assessment. A kind of cosmic reincarnation happening? "There may not be biological entities."

"Agreed," said Grant. "Or at least none that we would recognize as such. We may end up as the templates for something else completely. You could view biological entities as elaborate machines, so sophisticated that we hardly even recognize them *as* machines."

So the endless speculation and thought about destiny survived the ultimate flip. "I don't mind living backwards," I said.

"What?"

"We're hurtling toward the big crunch. It feels ok."

"Well, sure," said Grant, "but we aren't living backwards. Matter is converging, but time has not flipped over."

I could see that this was to be a topic of conversation and speculation. While not exactly looking forward to it with anything approaching keen rapture, I imagined I would enjoy a bit of such talk at some point down the road. "Where is everyone else?" I said.

"Oh I feel them," said Grant. "They're out there. Don't you have a sense of them?"

"I'm not sure," I said. "For a while I thought I felt everything, all of life. Then that kind of went away. Or I became numb to it. Not sure which. Now it's like there is this infinite blank canvas upon which we all have dropped ourselves like dollops of paint. And the canvas is getting smaller, but as one of the dollops I can't really tell where the other dollops are."

"That's too bad," said Grant. "I just have to kind of let my mind slip into a searching mode and I trip over all of them."

"Where are they?" I said. "Where are *we*?"

"Now that one I can't answer, much as I would want to. As we expanded, we lost a lot of things so that by the time of the ultimate flip we had nothing except, as you termed it, tilt. A subtle tendency to order that had been much diluted. One of the things we lost was location. Since everything was uniform, location had no meaning. Now, as we decelerate on the other side of the flip, we are gong to get back some of what we lost. Eventually I believe we will get back location. But not yet."

"It makes you think about what intention is," I said.

"Sure," said Grant. "Not only intention, but all kinds of other things as well. We will never know the extent of what we lost, I believe. How can we?"

"Here's another thing," I said. "Why can I hear you?"

"Another mystery," he said. "If it makes you feel better, you can just believe that I'm not really out there. I don't exist. The voice you hear is your own thoughts, disguised as me."

"I'm tired of all that," I said. "Isn't there something we can do to become what we were?"

"It'll happen. Something will happen. It will all get resolved. In the meantime, can you explain to me exactly what all that nonsense with the spoons was?"

I laughed. "I don't know. Fletcher said we can't all survive, remember. We thought he knew what he was talking about. If so, that means at least one of us is going to die. Doesn't that make you sad?"

"I haven't got sadness back. Or impatience. I did get acquiescence. I am as pliable on that score as probably any living being has ever been or maybe ever will be."

"I think I got impatience back. I'm ready for the next stage. When will it happen?"

"No telling."

"I know. That's what I get too, but I'm getting tired of that answer. I want a different answer. I want a different stage."

"Better dollops?" said Grant.

"Something like that."

"I wish we had more power, but you know, even if I had the power, I don't know if I would know what to do with it."

"Neither do I," I said, "but I almost don't care about that. It feels better to think that I could do some thing. Some *thing*, no matter what it might be."

It was strange to wait for the universe to come to some kind of decision. That's what we were doing: riding the flip and waiting.

"I sometimes feel like all of life is waiting," I said.

"A lot of it is," said Grant. "But we do things while we wait. We don't simply exist. We grow up, we fall in love, we have children, we do work. We move atoms about. That's what it all amounts to. We assign meaning to certain clumps of atoms and dismiss other clumps, but in the end, that's all we do: we move matter from one place to the other."

"Which is what the universe does," I said.

"Well, it does that incidentally. What the universe does mostly is create the atoms. Big difference."

"And a big step," I said. "Without it—"

"Without it, we're nothing," said Grant.

"Without it, there is nothing."

"Exactly," said Grant. "Now you've got it. The universe creates itself, which, inadvertently, creates us. Then we do our thing, bing bang boom. And the universe keeps going along, like we hardly even exist. Then it spreads way way out and it seems like it's about to disappear into a poof of nothing, but then it gets this crazy notion in its head that it needs to go back. Turn backwards to what it had been."

I had this insane picture in my head of two crazy guys floating around in the void, talking to each other. Speech balloons sprouted above our heads, containing oceans of text in tiny type, too small to read. I imagined myself pulling out a giant magnifying glass, big enough that I had to build up my muscles just to lift the thing. I held it over the speech balloons, each one in turn. The text exploded, each line blooming like a row of sunflowers. But the words were unknown to me. I needed a translation of them, but I did not know where to find a translation.

"There is no translation," said Grant.

"Oh," I said. "You see them too?"

"I've seen the speech balloons for a long time. They are not so much a record of what has been said as they are a blueprint for what might be said at some future date."

"Why aren't they in a language I can understand?"

"The future might not have a language you understand. It actually might not even have a language at all."

"That's impossible. You can't have existence without language. That's what DNA is, that's what the flitting about of atoms is."

"You sure about that?"

"Information," I said. "That's all language is, and matter is nothing but a big pile of information."

"I think you can have information without language."

"If you know about the information, then you know about it by language. It's really very simple."

"So the speech balloons have to have language because they have information? Is that what you're saying?"

"That's it. If I had my office I could find the references and prove it to you."

Grant seemed to want to say something, then waited for me to catch up. I wanted to tell him that we could not go to the end of this ride if we had no idea what was going on with the hope that we would return. That was the crux of the matter, wasn't it? We had only ourselves to hang onto and that really wasn't enough without the background. We could be matter, tilt, recognition, ripple, or thought. We could be all of these things, in turn or simultaneously, but we could not be any of them without a stage.

"I don't know how to tell you how I know what I know," said Grant. "The knowledge just seems obvious to me. Painfully obvious. We are in an empty transition era. There is nothing, so there can be no record of anything. So if we see something, it must be something that is to come."

He stated it like it was an airtight case, but I didn't see it that way at all. It was mere speculation. "Those are guesses on your part," I said. "You can't possibly believe that it is obvious or proven that that is the way of things."

Here Grant drifted away from me a little. It was as though he wanted to be more of a mystery than he actually was. Who was I to make him feel like he wasn't that at all? "You are wise," I said in as solemn a voice as I could muster. I wanted to burst out laughing, but suppressed the urge as best I could.

"You mock me," said Grant.

"A little," I said.

"Have you ever walked a labyrinth?"

"You mean a maze?"

"Similar, but not the same. A maze is a game where you try to find a path to the center via deceptive turns designed by the maze builder. A labyrinth is laid out so there is only one path in and one path out. There is no ambiguity, no attempt to trick, no decision to be made, beyond the one as to whether you want to walk the path or not."

I searched my memory for any mention of a labyrinth and came up empty. "I've walked mazes," I said, "where they grow corn, but I have never walked a labyrinth."

"Well, we're in one now. We don't have a choice, beyond the non-choice of deciding to opt out by killing ourselves."

This startled me. "You know how you would kill yourself?"

"Sure. It's not that hard."

"Tell me."

"You're missing the point. I'm trying to explain about labyrinths."

"Later, later," I said, too excited by the prospect of opting out. "Tell me how I can kill myself."

"You don't want to know that," said Grant. "Killing yourself is not an option."

"Of course it is. Free will dictates that I have that choice."

"Fine," said Grant.

"Then tell me how."

"Free will dictates that I don't have to tell you if I don't want to."

I groaned. "Come on. Just knowing I have a way out will make me feel better. I'll feel like I have some options. I want options."

"I want to tell you about labyrinths."

"Fuck labyrinths. Tell me how I can suicide."

Grant said nothing for a long time. Maybe a couple million years in objective time. At least a few minutes in subjective time. I tried to remember my question the whole time, tried to keep it in my mind as long as I could. I didn't want to forget. And I didn't forget.

Even while Grant was taking more time than was almost humanly possible to consider his answer. I didn't know about labyrinths, that was true, but I knew enough to know more or less what he was going to tell me, and I didn't want to hear. Didn't *need* to hear it. The universe was like a labyrinth where you go in one way and come out the other way. And there is only that way. Yawn. I was much more interested in ending it all: just cutting out of the race. Like skipping over the twists and turns in a maze, and flying to the finish. Express lane. Yeah, that was for me.

I think I was almost falling asleep. That's how long it had been. I was made of atoms strewn across the cosmos and I was getting sleepy. But I was jolted out of my drowsiness in an instant. Grant appeared, looming over me, a scythe in his hand. No, it couldn't be. I closed my eyes, then opened them again. He was still there, dressed in black, eyes gleaming, and his scythe lifting over his head, then beginning to arc toward me. It was fast. Too fast for me to get out of the way. I just stood where I was and waited. The scythe picked up speed at a frightening pace. It blurred against the background, then stopped. Just a millimeter or two from my flesh, it stopped in mid swing. I remained frozen still, not wanting to disturb anything because it seemed like that was the important thing to do.

"There you are," said Grant.

"There I am? What does that mean?"

"That's how you end it. You conjure up a picture of me, or anyone, really, and imagine them cutting you down. Chop chop. And you will be ended. Taken from this realm and passed on to another."

"Another realm? What other realm?"

"It's just a figure of speech," said Grant. "I don't think there is another realm. Not really."

Now I knew he was joking. "How can there not be?" I said. "Every time we've flipped, we've gone somewhere else. There is no nothing. There is always something."

"Wow," said Grant. "That sounds almost profound."

I listened to my own breathing, which had ratcheted up quite a few notches.

If I had a corporeal being, I probably would have been hyperventilating. Instead, it was like I was making the most sound in the universe that anyone had ever heard. Sound. That meant waves, which meant a medium to propagate the waves.

"Hey," I said.

"What?" said Grant.

"It looks like I have a body. Or something."

"Congratulations," said Grant. "What's it made of?"

"Not sure yet, but I definitely have some boundaries. I'm not flung all over hither and yon."

"'Hither and yon?' Who says 'hither and yon?'"

"Never mind about that," I said. "Let me see if I can figure it out."

I tried making a fist. Couldn't. Didn't seem to have hands. Or arms, for that matter. Okay. That's a little distressing. Let me see what else I don't have. Ah. No limbs at all. Even more distressing. And disappointing. I was hoping for a renewed life something like my old life. Something I could actually understand and maybe get good at.

"You can't relive your life," said Grant. "You can't just hope to correct the mistakes you made before the flips. It just doesn't work that way."

"Says you."

"I'm not an ignorant party here. I know some of what's going on."

"You make guesses just like me. Some of your guesses pan out, some don't. It's mostly all a matter of dumb luck."

"The whole universe is dumb luck. Haven't you heard? It's all random at its most fundamental level. We get order on a random basis."

"Yes, of course," I said. "Quantum fluctuations. But that doesn't say anything about what we become, does it?"

"You just have to pay attention to what's going on to know what we become."

"That's all we've been doing for close to eternity, now, is paying attention."

"Yes," said Grant. "That's what I've been saying."

I continued my inventory. No limbs, but an enormous midsection. Or where my midsection would have been. In this guise I seemed to be *all* midsection, if you can believe that.

I was round. Very round. Huh. So I was an overweight slob? That was a let down. Where was my TV? And my chips and beer? Not to mention my stained yellowish T-shirt?

No. Wait. The scale was all wrong. I didn't know how to adjust myself to it. I thought small, like I used to be, but those thoughts didn't fit anymore. It was as though I had outgrown my thoughts. Or that my thoughts were somehow too small to fit what I had become. No, that wasn't it either. My thoughts didn't have a size. I just made them think they had a size. So I released that notion, somehow. Not sure how.

I let my thoughts roam around. It was quite roomy in there. Labyrinthine turns and chambers. A maze, no matter what Grant said, because it was a puzzle. It was not some simple thing where the path was evident just by walking it. Now I saw. I was not fat. I was just big. Which—if I was correct in what was happening to me—is what I was supposed to be. Because—drum roll please—I figured it out.

I was a globe.

A large globe. I was, in fact, a planet. I let that sink in for a while. I was a planet. An odd statement, but sometimes the truth feels as odd as anything one could imagine. But that's the thing. It wasn't really odd at all. It was so *right*, given my sensations, that nothing else could make any sense. Once I had that, everything else fell into place. I identified continents, an ocean, and volcanoes. The volcanoes were pinpricks of heat, like a hot needle stuck into me. Surprisingly, it was not unpleasant. It had the satisfying pain of a healing scab, when the tingling gets to the point where the danger of bleeding is pretty much gone.

"Oh," said Grant. "I see."

"What do you see?"

"Everything. I appear to be a star. Solar type. An ordinary, garden variety star. I wonder if I have a solar system?"

A star! It was cool to be a planet, but to be a star. That was something else entirely. The engines of the cosmos. Stars were much more important than planets. Without stars there could be no life. They heated up everything, made photosynthesis possible. They were the power plants of the universe. Why was I a planet and Grant a star?

Planets were much more complex, with all the elements and metals and systems, life, oceans, tectonic plates and so on. Stars were so simple: hydrogen atoms squished together. That was it. But the simplicity was beautiful. It accounted for the complexity of everything, and it was so basic.

"Yup," said Grant. "Six major planets. Three minor. And a whole slew of dwarf planets. An asteroid belt. Some comets that are just plain humdingers. They are whizzing around me like tornadoes. Oh, man, this is cool. I'm a star, Chris. Can you believe it? I'm a star."

"That's great," I said. "Is this our reward for all that waiting, all the flips? I'm a planet and you're a star?"

"I don't know about rewards," said Grant. "It's just what happened."

"You think everyone else is something?"

"Probably," said Grant.

"You think you're the only star?" Silence. "Grant?"

"I think I know what was in those speech balloons," said Grant. "It was a representation of the language of the universe, the natural language that arises from the random arrangement of matter."

"We're not random arrangements," I said. "You can't still believe that. We were put inside astronomical bodies on purpose."

"Come on Chris. You have no evidence of that."

"Where's everyone else? I want to talk to others."

"Okay," said Grant. "Hang on a second."

I don't know what he did, but in less than a second I heard such a roaring as I had never thought possible. It was so large, so all encompassing, that I had trouble even recognizing it at first. It just seemed to be part of everything.

It was the voices of all the stars, their chorus filling all of creation. It was white noise and static and an orchestra, all at the same time. It was the harmony of the ages filtering through my ears to my soul, whatever that was. The metal core under the mantle? The miles and miles of rock, some of it molten? The surface of water and rock? Where was I now?

"Grant?"

A voice swimming through the morass. "Yes?"

"Can you turn it off?"

"Man you are fussy," said Grant.

I could tell he was joking, but I wasn't in the mood to laugh. The sound diminished. I felt better. Like I wasn't about to be obliterated by the energy of it all.

"How's that?" said Grant.

"How did you do that?" I said.

"I just opened you up a little. You got about a millionth of one percent of the universe there. It's a big place."

"I just never expected this," I said. "I never thought such a thing as becoming a planet or a star was possible."

"My guess," said Grant, "is that we didn't become anything. Our consciousness floated around looking for something to snag onto. Before the flip, on the uphill side of the universe, we snagged onto biological clumps of atoms. That was fine. We adjusted ourselves to that, as we had to. Now, after the flip, on the downhill side, we have snagged onto astonomical objects. We'll have to adjust ourselves to that, eventually, too, I suppose."

"This is all speculation," I said.

"Maybe. But you have a better explanation?"

I did not. It didn't mean there wasn't one. "It feels right," I said, "but it feels like an illusion, too. How can I be a planet? How can you be a star?"

"Just wait until I go nova," said Grant. "I'm not looking forward to that. I'll pretty much die."

So Grant had some fears. That was refreshing in a way. I always thought of him as fearless. He seemed like the one of all of us that would go anywhere and do anything and not ever worry about the consequences. No, that wasn't right. He took into account the consequences, but he planned for every contingency and so did not have to be concerned that he was going to get into trouble.

"We're not active participants," I said.

Grant's voice came through disappointed. Not a mode I was accustomed to hearing from him.

"I know," he said. "That's kind of discouraging. The good news is stars last a long time. Maybe I can use some of that time to figure out a way to extend my life."

"What about me?"

"Planets last a long time too."

"They get fried in novas. I'll die when my star dies."

"Well, there is another view of the matter. We didn't die in the big flip. We're probably not going to die now either. Somehow our essence has remained. That's kind of comforting, don't you think? We lost our bodies, lost everything that ever was, really, and yet we remained. It's a kind of reward for patience."

Oh no, Grant was getting mystical. Even he could not resist, given the power of our situation, to get all woo woo. How could anyone, in these circumstances? "Sounds like you're talking about reincarnation," I said.

"Ah," said Grant. "Yes. That concept had to come up at some point, didn't it? I have never given much credence to reincarnation. The thought that we have many lives, well, it was just crazy. Life comes from biology. When you destroy the biology, you destroy the life. It's just that simple. The atoms can re-congregate into other biological forms, but then that new form must have a new life."

I nodded. This was all pretty standard theorizing. "I'm with you," I said.

"But now this blows all that out of the water. Life, or at least consciousness, seems to live on after everything else is nothing. We are more than biology."

"We aren't even biology anymore. We're something else."

"Yes," said Grant.

"If I was a religious person, I might say that we are God. Or gods. Something."

"Well, that's about the most slippery concept there is. God was invented to explain things that had no explanation. Anyway, in the general conception of God, he she or it is very powerful. I don't think we have much power. We hitch rides on clumps of atoms. That makes us passengers, not gods."

He had a point. And yet it felt so amazingly invigorating to be able to feel myself as a planet. To feel that the ground beneath my feet *was* my feet, and that I had a stake in how everything came out in the end because I was strong enough to sustain a planet. An entire planet. It was more than simply amazing, it was truly out of this world. But then we had been through many out-of-this-world moments recently.

"You ever think about what it all means?" I said to Grant.

"The ultimate question, that," said Grant.

"Yeah."

"I don't pretend to know the answer or even how to go about finding out the answer to that. It's a very personal thing, don't you think?"

"I heard someone say once, when they were trying to decide which of the religions was real, she said that all religions had equal validity, because they were all personal to the person who believed. If I believed that we went to hell after death, then I went to hell. If you believed you turned into a cockroach in your next life, then bango, that's what happened to you. It's a very comforting view of things."

"And," said Grant, "like most religious proclamations, there is absolutely now way to prove or disprove it."

He had a point. At the institute we were always looking for proof, or at least sure knowledge. So often we fell short of that. There were so many views of reality, that picking from among them according to if they were real or not, well, that just seemed impossible. "I like to think that we become vines," I said. "Plants. We curl around and up buildings. That always seemed like such a marvelous life. To be so vulnerable and soft, and yet to be mated with solid brick. Protected from pretty much anything."

Grant had drifted away from me. I felt the absence of his presence. I didn't want that. I tried to reach for him, but he was gone. Well, where did he go? "Grant?" I tried calling to him, but I felt the smallness of my voice. I could not compete with the great universe at large. It was too big, and my voice too small, stuck inside a lowly planet. A tiny planet, as it appeared to be. I tried casting about, looking for my star. I had to have a star nearby. Every planet had a star, didn't they?

But, alas, it appeared I was the exception. I had no companions with me. All the space around me was empty of planetary and stellar bodies. I was, in fact, in a very dark region of space. I saw very little light anywhere. Or, rather, felt very little light anywhere. Radiation was foreign to the region of space I seemed to be inhabiting at this time.

This was disappointing, to say the least. It meant that I probably wasn't going to have any life on my suface. I was doomed to be a dead world, and who knew for how long. The volcanoes were something, but they weren't life. They were just molten rock moving around and burning me. Interesting, but ultimately it didn't mean anything. Have you ever been in a place where you knew you were going to be miserable and you had no way out? There is something especially depressing about such a situation. I was in that place. I had no way to find a way out, because there was no way out. Couldn't be a way out. We live our lives thinking we have some kind of control, but that was not the case at all.

"Such a buzz kill." A voice. Not Grant's or Fletcher's.

"Who's that?"

"Don't you know? Can't you recognize your boss when you hear her name?"

"Naomi?"

"Right you are. And you're making me sorry I kept you on. How can you be so defeatist? So whiny, if you don't mind me bringing that up."

"No," I said. "It's true. I'm whiny. Not my fault, really. I don't know how to live in this new situation."

"Like all the rest of us got the manual for it?"

"What rest of us?"

"The spoon diggers. We're all here. Sylvia, Penelope, Ralph, and me. You and Grant somehow drifted off to somewhere else. You know where he is?"

"What a second. Where are you? *What* are you."

"Oh yeah," said Naomi. "Pardon my ill-bred manners. I appear to be a cloud of dust. I will coalesce into something, planet, star, or something else. Don't know yet, but I'll have plenty of time to enjoy it when it happens. Or curse my fate. One or the other. Ralph is a single-celled creature on some comet somewhere. He'll probably impact a planet and start life. The planet of the slobs. He's sanguine about it. Sylvia eats radiation for dessert. And the main course, too, come to think of it. She's a black hole somewhere. How about that, huh? She rides the singularity to the flip, and then comes back to become a singularity. Irony or what?"

This was a lot to take in. "What about Penelope?"

"Ah, yes, Penelope. She's the oddest of them all. Penelope is not inside an object. Oh no. That would be too mundane for our Penelope. Instead she has been fortunate enough to find haven in an idea."

I wasn't sure I heard her correctly. "Idea?"

"Precisely. She is the idea of being. The very essence of life, as it were. She is not animal, vegetable, or mineral, but she kind of partakes of all of those things because she inhabits the idea that animates us all."

I tried to understand what Naomi was tying to tell me. How can someone be snagged by an idea? An idea had no substance. It was just the secretions of the mind, empty waves of something—who knew what—but it had no strength of its own. It couldn't possibly find a way to actually hold onto something. Could it?

"Are there other ideas?" I asked.

"Sure."

"Do they have life associated with them? I mean, are they harboring networks like me and you?"

"You mean, are there other Penelope's out there, enmeshed in other ideas like love, hate, compassion, greed, and so on?"

Is that what I was asking? It appeared so. "Yeah," I said. "Is there more to the universe than just a bunch of objects careening about banging into one another?"

"And what's wrong with banging into one another?"

"Nothing, as far as it goes. It's pretty much the definition for sex."

"Ah, yes. Sex. One of the three Fs?"

"I think actually there's four of them now."

"Four Fs? It does have the benefit of alliteration. Which can be good. What is the fourth one?"

"Flip. That's what life is: Feeding, fucking, fighting, and flipping."

"Flipping out?"

"Maybe. That's up to you I suppose. I'm just trying to get a handle on the universe. What are we right now? What have we become?"

"Let me put it to you this way," said Naomi. "We're on the downhill side of the flip. I think you already know that. We all know that. We have come to a place where we can communicate with each other again, even though we are all different than we once were. What that says to me is that we have retained a certain connection that we had established earlier. Now, I don't pretend to understand that connection and we don't have to try to get into it right now, but we are nothing more than vibrating strings, after all. Remember that? Remember those discussions? We have also a strange sense of time. Have you noticed? We've essentially become immortal. Now isn't that a kick in the pants? But even so, our immortality has not made us bored. Why? Because apparently we have a sense of time that is about the length of a human life. Even though we have now lived for billions of years, we still feel as though we are right there in middle age and have about the same length left to us as we have so far traversed. I can't explain any of this and I won't try. At least not for a while. I suspect that we have a time image the same way we have a body image and that our spiritual sides latch onto that image and won't let it go. In any case, it's fortunate we didn't experience all that passage of time in literal terms. We would almost certainly have become crazy from the waiting. No one can be patient for that long, no matter how much we try. In any case, we are left with the task of building a universe. You think you are up to it? Before you answer—because I think I know your answer—please consider that whatever we build is going to be temporary. That should take some of the pressure off. But even given that, we shouldn't then conclude that there is no importance to the matter. We all are important. One thing this has shown me is that existence is much more complicated and much more important than we could ever imagine. But that's the thing, you see, we can imagine it now. We can hook onto all these constructs that the universe made for us and we can manipulate matter and energy in ways we never thought was possible in the past. Are you with me so far? Don't answer. At least not yet. I want to get this out. After the first flip, I saw some of us were discouraged and upset. That was to be expected. Then the flips continued and I was a little disgusted by what I saw. We were giving up. We had found ways to be passive and relinquish our power. That was not acceptable. We were better than that. I saw it at the institute. We had our intellect and our will and we should have been able to do something. So what I did was I extended the flips. Again, please don't say anything, at least not yet. Here's the crux of the thing: the universe goes in one direction. I wanted to get back to the construct I knew, of course I did. But that was not possible. You might just as well have tried to push water uphill. Could try it for centuries and never get anywhere. Same thing with time. You can't make it go backwards. So, ok. We go forward. I expanded my mind. Made it take in as much of the surroundings as possible. And then I tweaked it. Not a lot, but just enough. The flips continued. We slipped away from matter, but kept our integrity. It was as though I had found the fulcrum from which I could move way more than the Earth. I was a spoon digger, thanks to you. I used that skill to dig more than dirt. I dug the entire expanse of creation, and sent us on the journey to the ultimate flip, which you also know about. But you see, that was a fulcrum as well. It was the pivot point on which everything else balanced. And when I say everything, I mean exactly that. All of existence. Anything you can imagine or try to imagine, it was all there, balanced on that moment. And here's something else you need to know. The universe never forgets. Everything is still there. All of it. Remember at the institute we talked about a universal recorder? We were daft. The universe is already a universal recorder and we should not have to try to invent anything else. Maybe that's the ultimate message I'm giving you here. There is no need for invention. Everything has been invented that will ever be invented, because the universe is not a set of results, but a catalog of all the possibilities all at once. So what it comes down to now, is that the institute, represented by the spoon diggers, have come to inhabit a disparate but unified system of constructs. We don't have to change the world, because the world is changing on its own. What we need to do now is reconnect with each other and reclaim the institute as our portable community. We are separate, but not really. Our separateness is a function of our place in the timeline of the universe, but that changes. It has changed and it will change again. Here is the best way to look at it: we moved the universe. It responded by moving back and taking us in. It has encompassed us in all our differing aspects, and more than that, it has retained our identity. That is the most amazing thing. Through the dissipation of matter and the almost death of the universe, we kept our integrity intact. That is the ultimate purpose, don't you think? Our identities, all our identities. It's what we never managed to create at the institute, but it turns out we didn't have to. The universe loves us so completely and it will never ever let us die."

I would like to say that at this point all the disparate threads fell into place and I saw the light. I really wanted to. But the light was fading, in its way, even though things were heating up and the universe was getting brighter. There was something not right in what Naomi was saying. We were way past middle age, for one thing. We had hit our peak at the flip and now were accelerating toward the end of time, or the end as far as we knew it. The atoms were emitting radiation, but they were doing so on a smaller scale and for a shorter length of time. The big crunch was there before us and with it the contraction of everything. There was no way to view that and think that we were becoming more. More light, more enlightened, or more lighthearted. What we were now was a collection of some things becoming swept up into a more dense something else. The singularity was eating us alive.

"You have nothing to say?" said Naomi.

It was a question, but it might just as well have been a statement. It perfectly summed up my point of view.

"Why say anything at all?" I asked.

"To learn. We have a duty to understand."

That sounded familiar, but I couldn't place it. Was it something we said at the institute? Probably now. We didn't much think about duty there. Fun was more the operating principle. We were there to amuse ourselves. Which we did. We amused ourselves mostly to death.

"I wonder if any of this would have played out the way it did if we hadn't begun digging that dirt with those spoons."

"Don't think about that," said Naomi. "There's no way to tell. It's entirely possible that the whole shebang would have happened the same way whether we dug or did not dig."

"I wonder," I said.

"Don't do this," said Naomi. "It will only make you sad. You think senior citizens don't think about the end? You think they can't be happy?"

"Well, I'm the most senior of citizens I have ever known, and I'm not happy."

I felt her pulling away. It was as though she had tried to get me on her team, but she sensed an unwillingness that she didn't need to fight. Only, what was her team? She was dust. I was a planet. What exactly did she want?

"I've got other fish to fry," she said.

"Are there fish? Is there anything left anymore? Naomi, is there anything for us except emptiness? Can you answer that one for me?"

"If you could see me right now," she said. "I'd be shaking my head."

"I'm not trying to be difficult. I really want to know."

"You eggheads, you're always thinking too much. We are what we are. If we try to go beyond that, we run into all kinds of difficulties."

"But," I said, "but but but."

"But nothing." And then she was gone.

Just as well. We weren't really getting along anyway. Dust and planets. She was dirt. I was Earth. Or something like Earth. You would think that would mean we would get along famously. But no. I wanted life. I was a planet and I wanted to be overrun by life. Why wasn't that happening?

I contrived to move myself into a zone where things were whizzing around all over the place. Was I really doing this? I don't know. I was working blind. That was the disconcerting thing, really. I couldn't actually *see* anything. I just knew things were out there by the way they felt and by listening. I was hearing it all, in a way, the sound of the universe closing.

Was there a more lonely sound? I couldn't think of it. It was so subtle as to be almost not there, but I felt the sound in my core, my rocky molten core. I remembered a phrase: the music of the spheres. I think it had something to do with the way the planets swung around in their orbits in harmony. It was what some of the ancients thought about the universe, how it would all fit together perfectly. They were a little mystified by that, I think. How could things work so well together? Wasn't there more to the universe than harmony? The harmony was an illusion, wasn't it? It was our own minds that demanded harmony so we found some that wasn't even there, simply so we could say we had it. I never gave much credence to such thoughts. The ancients had their points, but they also fretted about a lot of stuff that really didn't matter. Like I was doing.

I saw how it was. I had a satellite. How about that? By moving it around in its orbit, I was able to move myself. Pull myself along, as it were. That was fine. It was slow, but I had some time, at least. I wasn't about to die, as far as I could tell. I found a place. Or I invented a place. Hard to tell which. I was as much an idea as Penelope was. My idea was survival.

I entered a region of space where comets congregated. They were like tornadoes of ice. They were like whiz bang drops of energy. They made me think that there was more to it all than just my melancholy thoughts.

I put myself in the fray. In no time at all the comets began bombarding me, inflicting bruises, bumps, lacerations, breaks, and tears and cracks. It was beyond glorious. It hurt like nobody's business, but it was something alive. I felt like I was being welcomed to the fray of life again, after I had been absent for too long. For years. Eons. Ages and ages.

And now there was something else. The build up of matter. I had dirt, but now I had even more dirt. I was collecting it the way an old primate collects memories, encrusting its brain with decaying images. Only I wasn't decaying. At least not yet. I had a kind of reprieve from that. We all did. We were every one of us on a slide to something else. Which was a way of saying that we had more than we thought we had. Or at least more than I thought I had. I couldn't speak for the others, flung around the universe now, in a diaspora that was, curiously, the reverse of diaspora. We were separated, but we were getting closer. The universe was contracting. Slowly, but it was contracting. I wondered why things didn't feel any different.

Why was it that I felt almost exactly the same as when the universe was expanding? At the institute we were always discussing the possibility of time travel. It was a major area of dispute. I usually argued that time travel could only go in one direction. You went into the future, but you could not go into the past. Or, conversely, I could imagine a universe in which you went backward, but if that was the case, then in that universe, you could not go forward. Seemed simple enough.

The paradoxes were what sold me. You could not have time travel in which one went willy-nilly backwards and forwards, because the paradoxes would negate causality and you would get these impossible situations like killing your parents before your were born, or being born before you parents were conceived. Stuff like that. It made you crazy to think about. Or it made *me* crazy thinking about it. I didn't have much company. Everyone else at least entertained the idea of time travel, and most of them thought it was not only possible but *inevitable* on the grounds that anything that might happen, will happen, given enough time.

I countered that such a view only begged the question. You can't speak about "given enough time" if what we are debating is the very nature of time, in other words the crux of what we are discussing. To which I was told, essentially, "blah blah blah." I never moved anyone at the institute to my point of view. In fact I was treated as being somewhat unimaginative and stodgy. The ultimate insult in such a place, where everyone was supposed to be on the edge, looking at things in completely new ways and so on. Blah blah blah. But now it appeared I was wrong, at least in some sense. I was on the other side of the flip. That made all the difference. We were replaying the history of the universe, except we were doing it backwards. Time travel? As good an explanation as any, I suppose.

As I was thinking about this, as I was running the words around in my mind, I was also running the worlds around in my mind, everything was there. Many have thought that the whole of existence is contained in the smallest subset of the universe. The tiniest bit of matter or pre-matter or non matter or vibration has the great vast mystery wrapped up all inside it like a little model of the universe. We are holographic entities. We are made of holograms and we construct holograms. The multitudes inside me were not some game. They were everything and would be everything for some time.

But now, here is the thing of it all. The spoon diggers were back. Yup. My planet—me, in effect—had attracted them all. Sylvia crawled out of her black hole, Grant left his star to burn unattended, Naomi dared to leave her dust unattended, Ralph made sure he could get back to his amoeba or whatever he was, and Penelope, well, she kind of floated out of the ether and landed on me.

They all said hi.

"Hey," I said. "Is it really all of you?"

"We're all here," said Naomi. "I rounded them up to make you feel better. You feel better yet, Terry?"

"I'm working on it," I said.

They all laughed and started digging.

"What are you doing?"

"What we started out doing," they said in unison.

"We are what we are," said Penelope. "There are no three Fs or four Fs or anything except one B. That B is Be. To be. The art of being. Human being, planetary being, whatever."

Even Fletcher was there. "Hi," he said.

"Fletcher?"

"In the flesh, as it were. Or in the spirit." He laughed.

"What are you?"

"Me? Why isn't it obvious? I'm radiation. I flit about the universe, landing here and landing there, more or less randomly. I may be part of the big bang. I feel very ancient, like I've been around forever."

They all answered in unison. "We've all been around forever."

Fletcher laughed. "When this contracting universe gets small enough to spawn scientific journals again I have an idea for one."

"Yawn," said Ralph.

"I second that," said Naomi.

"I'll third it," said Grant.

"Give him a chance," said Sylvia.

"He is what he is," said Penelope.

"You've got two minutes," I said to Fletcher. "Then we go back to what we do best." I sent a mental gesture Penelope's way. "We dig and we be."

"Ok," said Fletcher. "Two minutes. Anyone else have a subjective notion of time? Anyone else notice that?"

"What I notice," said Ralph, "is that I miss those damned worms. They were pretty tasty."

Feeding.

"You remember my previous paper. I said any sufficiently complex activity will result in at least one death. After riding the universe to the flip and then back, I have revised that theory. I now believe that any sufficiently simple activity will result in at least one immortal being."

"Oh, man," said Grant. "That's crazy. You can't prove it. We disposed of that a long time ago."

"You didn't do it right," said Fletcher. "You missed a lot of important factors."

"You're crazy," said Ralph. "You're stark raving nuts."

"Says you," said Fletcher.

"Yeah," said Ralph. "Says me."

Fighting.

"Children," said Naomi. "Do we have to do this? Why can't we behave in a more civilized manner? There is no need to name call."

"She's right," said Sylvia. "We can't get laid anymore, but there must be a substitute for it. Why don't we find that, instead of rehashing old ideas."

Fucking.

"I'm all for that," said Fletcher. "But first, let me just get this off my chest. The grand flip, where we went from expanding to contracting, it changed everything. We're going backwards now. The ultimate 'be' is to be forever, and now we can do that because life has been turned upside down and we're all on the path to something else."

"One minute," said Naomi.

"One minute or one million eons. It's all the same now," said Fletcher. "It's all about the Flip."

mn

You just have read **The Institute** by Emen. Copyright © 2019 by Emen.

ISBN: 978-1-949644-52-4

This book by Emen. No fair for you to be copying this book, so don't do it, okay.

Picture of spoon © Jamroen Jaiman | Dreamstime.com.

Emen no dedicate books so don't ask him for to dedicate book to you, okay.

About the author:

What, you not read back cover? Why not? Is all there. Nevercare. I repeat here: Emen not always writer. But now is. Where Emen was born? What you care? Emen was many things before writer. Emen work in call center. Was terrible job. So Emen write books now. Emen don't have pets. So what? What you care if Emen have dog or cat or bird of paradise? Emen don't have facebook or twitter. No social media. You not go online for experiencing Emen. Just read books, okay. That's all. One more thing. Not have here picture of Emen. Don't need.

www.ingramcontent.com/pod-product-compliance
Lightning Source LLC
Chambersburg PA
CBHW050526190726
48284CB00003B/962